YORUBA TRICKSTER TALES

Yoruba Trickster Tales

Oyekan Owomoyela

University of Nebraska Press, Lincoln and London

© 1997
by the University
of Nebraska Press
All rights reserved
Manufactured
in the United States of America ∞ The paper in this book
meets the minimum requirements of
American National Standard for
Information Sciences – Permanence of Paper
for Printed Library Materials, ANSI Z39.48-1984.
Library of Congress Cataloging-in-Publication
Data. Owomoyela, Oyekan. Yoruba trickster
tales / Oyekan Owomoyela.   p.   cm. Includes
bibliographical references. ISBN 0-8032-3563-1
(cloth : alk. paper). ISBN 0-8032-8611-2
(pbk. : alk. paper). I. Yoruba (African
people) – Folklore. 2. Tales – Nigeria.
3. Turtles – Folklore. 4. Trickster – Nigeria. I. Title.
GR351.32.Y56086   1997   398.2'08996333 – MDC21
96-37321
CIP

For Joan

Àkànse lofà ìmàdò

CONTENTS

CONTENTS

INTRODUCTION

Storytelling is a popular form of evening entertainment in traditional African societies, typically taking place after the last meal of the day. Nighttime outdoor activities are rare and after-dark public entertainment occurs only on special occasions, so the members of each compound or household must devise their own means of passing an idle evening. The solving of riddles and the telling of folktales serve this need. A favorite subgenre among folktales, the trickster tale is found in Africa and in many cultures around the world.

Usually embodied in animal form, the trickster is strikingly human in habits, predisposition, and weaknesses. The animal differs from culture to culture: in Africa it could be the spider (like the Asante Ananse, the Zande Ture, and the Hausa Gizo), the hare (like the Kikuyu Wakaboko and, in East and Central Africa, Sungura or Zomo), the jackal (as in southern Africa), or the tortoise—like the Yoruba Àjàpá, the hero of the tales in this collection.

Invariably, folktale tricksters have so impressed their human observers by some exceptional qualities that they have become invested with uncommon mental agility and extraordinary capabilities. The spider, for example, inspires awe because of its seemingly miraculous ability to secrete the thread by which it fashions its web; the tortoise impresses with its ageless look, its deliberate gait (suggesting the sagacity and dignity of a venera-

ix

ble elder), and portable armor. Moreover, tricksters are endowed with a mental nimbleness that more often than not eases their passage through a treacherous and dangerous world, usually in spite of and at the expense of more powerful adversaries. Unburdened by scruples, they often concoct vicious disasters for their would-be tormentors, and as often blithely reward their benefactors' generosity with sometimes deadly betrayals. They dupe friends, acquaintances, and adversaries alike in pursuing their own selfish ends.

ÀJÀPÁ THE TORTOISE

No Yoruba child brought up in a traditional setting escapes exposure to Àjàpá tales, and many children grow up learning a number of them. When European-style schooling was introduced into the Yoruba world in the latter half of the nineteenth century, some of the reading texts were transcriptions of folktales, including Àjàpá tales. While the new social arrangement that came with colonization, and especially with Christianization, was largely responsible for the virtual disappearance of evening storytelling, the new schools paradoxically contributed to the preservation of the tales, with an hour or so reserved each week for storytelling.

Àjàpá reigns as trickster not only among the Yoruba of West Africa, most of whom are in Western Nigeria and the neighboring republic of Bénin, but also among the dispersed Yoruba descendants in the New World, especially in Brazil and Cuba. Beyond the Yoruba world, the tortoise also plays the role of trickster in the folktales of the Kalabari in southeastern Nigeria, where he is named Ikaki, of Cameroon to the east of Nigeria, of the Mpongwe to the southeast along the western coast of Gabon and equatorial Guinea, where his name is Ekaga, and of the Ila of Zambia, where his name is Sulwe.

Whatever his designation—Àjàpá, Ìjàpá, Alájàpá, Ahun, Abaun, or Alábaun—the Yoruba trickster is recognizable as the tortoise. His consort is Yánníbo (or Yánrínbo), but she features only seldomly in tales involving her celebrated mate. So great is Àjàpá's hold on the Yoruba imagination that he is by far the most frequent protagonist of Yoruba folk narratives, appearing in three out of five tales. His popularity rivals that of Ananse, the Asante trickster, who gives his name to Asante folktales, including the ones in which he has no role, *anansesem* (spider stories). As an Asante tale asserts, Nyame (the Sky God) once ceded ownership of the tales to Ananse.

The Yoruba, however, have not granted Àjàpá sole title to their tales, nor have they named the tales after him. They do nonetheless have the hyperbolic proverb "All trouble will not fail to crash on Alábaun's head," which refers to one of the formulaic openings of Yoruba tale-telling whereby the tale sways, snaps, and crashes atop whoever is to be the hero or heroine of the ensuing narrative.

ÀJÀPÁ'S CHARACTER

As his descriptive epithet "Master of Sundry Wiles" denotes, Àjàpá is renowned for his almost inexhaustible supply of mischievous tricks to secure some advantage for himself with little or no expenditure of physical effort or material resource. This endowment compensates for certain grievous inadequacies in his character. For example, Àjàpá is so lazy that he will not work to make a living. Plagued by an inveterate aversion for work, in times of both scarcity and plenty he relies on trickery and the reluctant generosity of some friend or neighbor to obtain food. Matching his shiftlessness is an insatiable appetite so powerful that, as in the story of his instant pregnancy, it gets the better of him even though he had been warned it would be his death.

Aside from being lazy and greedy, Àjàpá is also incomparable in his tightfistedness, his refusal to share with any creature whatever falls into his hands. So remarkable is this trait in him that one of his designations, "Ahun," is colloquial Yoruban for "miser" or "miserliness." A proverb acknowledging this quality says "When Tortoise takes a morsel of food and his child opens its mouth, he asks, Where the hell did you ever get the idea that I would share anything with *you?*" This quality is well illustrated in the story of the Dawn Bird, in which Àjàpá would not spare a bit of his pottage even with the rock that had provided him a place of repose. Gratitude and obligations of friendship have no room in Àjàpá's consciousness. In fact, he thinks nothing of rendering evil for good even to his friends and benefactors, as in the story in which he borrows money from Elédè the Pig and in the one involving Ajá the Dog and the Yams.

Sometimes he engages in his escapades gratuitously (or seemingly so) or in response to some irrepressible instinct, and not to satisfy a real need. The tale involving his friend Ìnàkí the Baboon in particular reveals his seemingly gratuitous contrariness. Small and weak though he is, Àjàpá can and does manipulate much weightier animals, as much because of his own mental agility as because of some flaw in his dupes. His ability in this instance to manipulate the much fiercer and larger Ekùn the Leopard—who is both susceptible to his addiction to sweet foods and gullible—to his own purpose demonstrates the recurring patterns and themes in Àjàpá lore. In many instances mighty Erin (or Àjànàkú) the Elephant also falls victim to Àjàpá's wiles. Erin's mental denseness, vanity, and enslavement to his gullet are the banes that help Àjàpá succeed in playing Erin as the fool, sometimes with fatal consequences for Àjàpá.

Another notable trait in Àjàpá's character is his tendency to persist in dangerous schemes long after more prudent individuals would have desisted. As long as he is ahead, he seems to reason, it would be folly to quit. For instance, he continues his raids on farms even after his accomplices have stopped for fear of discovery. Accordingly, a proverb reports that "On setting out on a journey, Àjàpá is asked when he would return; he says not until after he has disgraced himself."

Knowing his weaknesses, Àjàpá's adversaries sometimes succeed in turning the tables on him. His inability to keep matters to himself—his involuntary tattling—is a characteristic weakness easily discovered, as in the story of the Playful Children. Furthermore, his tricks often recoil on him, and he learns to his shame or cost that the creatures of whose intelligence he is so contemptuous are not as stupid and gullible as he imagined. Thus he discovers that he does not and cannot monopolize the wisdom of the world. Sometimes, an ill-used benefactor outwits him and subjects him to terrible consequences for his perfidy. In the story of Ajá the Dog and the Princess, Àjàpá seeks Ajá's death by falsely and maliciously implicating him in a princess's murder, but his intended victim manages in the end to make the trickster himself suffer the consequences.

One must qualify Àjàpá's reputation as a mischief-maker, though, by noting that he is not always the instigator of trouble, nor is he consistently in the wrong. In some tales he is in fact the aggrieved party who must get even. In the tale of the Bounteous Ladle, for example, Àjàpá is not flawless, but his actions on behalf of the starving creatures are laudable. That he later subjects them to the whip is not excessive or undeserved punishment for their irresponsible destruction of the magic ladle or for their indirectly subjecting him to the whip himself. This tale would appear to undercut the perception of Àjàpá as one incapable of sharing his largesse, although one could argue that he makes the services of the ladle available to the general citizenry because of his vain penchant for wanting to solve every problem.

No discussion of Àjàpá can ignore one of his most remarkable accomplishments: his irresistible musicianship. In many tales his scheme is carried by his singing, which casts a powerful spell on individuals and whole communities, even on other-wordly beings, so that they forget themselves and their present purpose, abandoning themselves to the rhythm of his songs. But perhaps the trickster's most impressive endowments are his indestructibility and immortality, qualities that might justify those instances in which he is elevated to the status of a god. In numerous tales he suffers ignominious death, when the usually reliable spirit of his dead father fails him, only to resurrect himself, wit and armor intact, at the next tale-telling session, nonchalantly resuming his rascally ways.

YORUBA AMBIVALENCE TOWARD ÀJÀPÁ

Àjàpá is undoubtedly related to the tricksters of other cultures, but he does not share all their qualities and characteristics. Assumptions that he does have caused anthropologists to confer such features as supernatural capabilities and phallicity mistakenly on him. Generalized descriptions extrapolated from the known qualities of the tricksters of other cultures, creatures reputed to interact with gods and also to have been ancestors of humankind, are not applicable to Àjàpá.

Despite Àjàpá's popularity, the epithet "Master of Sundry Wiles" signals the ambivalence of the Yoruba attitude toward him, for it is both approbatory and opprobrious. While they find his resourcefulness and resilience admirable, they disapprove of his duplicity and disdain for reciprocity. In the Yoruba scheme, though, nothing—neither action or habit—is good or bad in itself but must be considered in the context in which it occurs. Like the tricksters of other cultures, Àjàpá is a human surrogate, as his anthropomorphic character is meant to attest. As they go through life, humans encounter many and sundry obstacles, and Yoruba culture recognizes the need to devise stratagems to cope with these. It therefore applauds brilliance in this regard, even though brilliance will likely manifest itself in ways exactly contrary to the dictates of convention. Accordingly, what is "good" is what is reasonable, prudent, expedient, or efficacious in any given circumstance, hence the proverb "A grown man who sees a snake and does not run flirts with death." The Yoruba applaud bravery, but the world is full of deadly snakes, and a grown man who lacks an appropriate weapon but nonetheless refuses to run from such a reptile is considered foolish.

The less powerful members of societies have always had an incentive to invent tactics that would enable them to cope with some comfort with the more powerful. Trickster tales attest to the truth that the relation of power between the strong and the weak does not preclude agency, even triumphant agency, on the part of the latter. Moreover, the Yoruba undoubtedly find the trickster appealing because, while providing a ready means by which they can comment on antisocial or otherwise unedifying behaviors, Àjàpá simultaneously enables them to dramatize remarkable qualities that could stand those who possess them in good stead in coping with a difficult world.

AUTHENTICITY AND VARIANCE

The tales in this volume are authentic to the extent that they feature the bona fide Yoruba trickster engaged in characteristic situations and behaving in his accustomed character. But what is true of folktales in general is true of Àjàpá tales and therefore of the ones collected here: they come in virtually unlimited variants.[1] The basic components are "functions," "images," or actions involving the trickster and various other characters. The "functions" that combine to form the particular tale at a particular telling can and do vary widely. For that reason, my telling of the tales will differ slightly—or even significantly—from other versions.

For the most part, I have relied on my recollection of the tales heard in my youth. I have also refreshed my memory with published texts, that is, I was reminded of tales by reading them elsewhere. Certainly, in some cases all I recognized were the basic armatures, the details being very different from the ones familiar to me. I have in such cases used my own variants. In all cases, though, I have attempted to do what the storyteller does in a typical Yoruba setting.

The compound in which I grew up at Osogbo was traditional. My father, a successful building contractor and furniture manufacturer, maintained his large compound as the primary residence for himself and his family of ten wives and numerous children, and for his several apprentices and long- and short-term visitors from our hometown of Ifon (the one close to Owo, not the one near Osogbo). In this setting I was exposed to storytelling sessions from as early as I can remember. We would sit in the evenings on one of the porches overlooking the enclosed open, usually the wives and their children, and sometimes my father and visitors from our hometown, and occasionally the apprentices, to enjoy tales told mostly by the wives, the older children, and perhaps by visitors. I do not remember my father ever once telling a story, even though he might ask someone, usually an older child, to tell a tale. Later, at Otapete Methodist School, my classmates and I were required to tell stories during periods (one afternoon each week) reserved for recreational activities. One of the most popular programs on the Western Nigeria Television Service (WNTV) in the 1960s when I studied at the University of Ibadan was the weekly storytelling broadcast by *apàlópadídùn* (teller of sweet tales) D. O. Alabi and his troupe. Finally, folklore, specifically Yoruba folklore, was a central component of my graduate studies. I occasionally have the opportunity, even now, to bring the delight of Yoruba tales to diverse groups.

I have striven to tell the tales in as entertaining a fashion as I could, drawing on the rhetorical devices the language offers, especially proverbs. My intention has been to both celebrate the irrepressible Àjàpá and to make his delightful career available to a wider community of readers than hitherto had access to it. That preferred community of readers includes all who for one reason or another would be interested in Àjàpá's exploits and is certainly not restricted to those with scholarly interests.

NOTE
1. My favorite Àjàpá tales, which have long been firmly embedded in my memory, and which constitute my standing repertoire (when I am invited to tell tales), are the ones featuring Ajá the Dog and the Princess, Ajá and the Yams, Àjànàkú the Would-Be *Oba*, the Àkàrà Hawker, the Blind Spirits, the Bounteous Ladle, the Dawn Bird, Elédè the Pig, Ìnàkí the Baboon, Jìgbo the Would-Be Hunter, the Playful Children, Àjàpá's Pregnancy, and a few others that are not included in this collection. One or two of the texts listed in the Suggested Readings jogged my memory with regard to the tales that feature Bola the Princess, the Roasted-Peanut Seller, Àdàbà the Turtle Dove, and Òjòlá the Royal Python.

SUGGESTED READINGS
Collections of Tales
Babalola, Adeboye. *Àkójọpọ̀ Àlọ́ Ìjàpá, Apá Kejì* (Collected tales of Ìjàpá, part 2). Ibadan, Nigeria: Oxford University Press, 1973.

———. *Àkójọpọ̀ Àlọ́ Ìjàpá, Apá Kìíní* (Collected tales of Ìjàpá, part 1). Ibadan, Nigeria: Oxford University Press, 1973.

Baumann, Margaret I. *Ajapa the Tortoise: A Book of Nigerian Fairy Tales*. London: A & C Black, 1929.

Cabrera, Lydia. *Ayapa: Cuentos de Jicotea* (Àjàpá: tales from Jicotea). Miami FL: Ediciones Universal, 1971.

Didi (Deoscoredes dos Santos). *Contos de Nago* (Tales of the Nago). Rio de Janeiro: Edições GRD, 1963.

Feldmann, Susan, ed. *African Myths and Tales*. New York: Laurel, 1970.

Odeyemi, Richard T. *Sweet Tales about Tortoise*. Ilorin, Nigeria: Woye Press, 1980.

Ogumefu, M. I. *Yoruba Legends*. London: Sheldon, 1929.

Todd, Loreto. *Tortoise the Trickster and Other Folktales from Cameroon*. New York: Shocken Books, 1979.

Analyses and Discussions

Bascom, William. *Ifa Divination: Communication between Gods and Men in West Africa*. Bloomington: Indiana University Press, 1969.

Ellis, Alfred Burdon. *The Yoruba-Speaking Peoples of the Slave Coast of West Africa*. London: Chapman and Hall, 1894.

Evans-Pritchard, Edward Evan, ed. *The Zande Trickster*. Oxford: Clarendon, 1967.

Fadipe, Nathaniel Akinremi. *The Sociology of the Yoruba*. Ibadan, Nigeria: Ibadan University Press, 1970.

Finnegan, Ruth. *Oral Literature in Africa*. Oxford: Oxford University Press, 1970.

Gbadamosi, Bakare. *Oríkì*. Ibadan, Nigeria: Mbari Publications, 1961.

Greenway, John. *Literature among the Primitives*. Hatboro PA: Folklore Associates, 1964.

Idowu, E. Bolaji. *Olodumare: God in Yoruba Belief*. New York: Praeger, 1963.

LaPin, Deirdre Ann. "Story, Medium and Masque: The Idea and Art of Yorùbá Storytelling." Ph.D. diss., University of Wisconsin 1977.

Lucas, J. Olumide. *The Religion of the Yorubas*. Lagos: C.M.S. Bookshop, 1948.

Owomoyela, Oyekan. "Tortoise Tales and Yoruba Ethos," *Research in African Literatures* 20, no. 2 (summer 1989), 165–80.

———. "The Trickster in Contemporary African Folklore." *The World and I* 5, no. 4 (April 1990), 625–32.

Pelton, Robert D. *The Trickster in West Africa: A Study of Mythic Irony and Sacred Delight.* Berkeley: University of California Press, 1980.

Ricketts, MacLinscott. "The North American Indian Trickster." *History of Religions* 5 (1965), 327–50.

Sekoni, Ropo. *Folk Poetics: A Sociosemiotic Study of Yoruba Trickster Tales.* Westport CT: Greenwood, 1994.

Wescott, Joan. "The Structure and Myths of Eshu-Elegba, the Yoruba Trickster: Definition and Interpretation in Yoruba Iconography." *Africa* 32, no. 4 (October 1962), 336–54.

The Obligations
of Friendship

Àjàpá and Elédè the Pig

A weakling who knows he cannot fight cultivates powerful friends. No creature possesses all things, and no one is without some character deficiency. Deficiencies are then no cause for shame or embarrassment; shame and embarrassment are proper only to those who are blind to their deficiencies or are incapable of compensating for them, or even converting them to assets. Living creatures are up against sundry obstacles in their efforts to make their brief existence on this earth meaningful; it behooves such creatures to be inventive in circumventing or surmounting these obstacles. The stratagems one adopts need not be heroic; indeed, heroism is foolhardy if one's ends are achievable through wile. The elders say "One who has strength but is thoughtless is the father-figure of laziness . . . Wisdom is superior to strength . . . The shiftless person lives by his or her wits, and the blind person will not go to bed hungry." The last is a tribute to blind people, who may shun work because of their affliction but yet find benefactors to satisfy their needs.

Destitute and nearly dying of hunger one day, Àjàpá approached his new friend Elédè the Pig for a loan. Elédè, who had known his friend for only a short while, had not heard of Àjàpá's reputation as a welsher who not only cheated his creditors out of their loans but insulted them as well; as the saying went, he not only scraped their skulls clean but tarred them for good measure. Elédè subscribed wholeheartedly to the sentiment that if the choice is between material wealth and wealth in friends, friends must

3

always win out. He lent Àjàpá the money but took care to extract the promise that it would be returned without fail on a certain day a few weeks hence.

The sages say time is not an endless vista; twenty years hence soon becomes tomorrow. The day appointed for the repayment arrived, and Elédè sat at home expecting Àjàpá to appear with the money. The sun climbed the sky until it was directly overhead, but Àjàpá had not appeared. Elédè waited patiently; it is the person with a thorn embedded in his foot who must limp to the person who has a needle to extract it, not the other way around. He had done a friend a favor, and he should not go to any trouble for his goodness. But the sun continued its journey. Its harsh glare dimmed, and the gloom of the waning day thickened as the sun descended towards night, and yet there was no Àjàpá. In the end, Elédè, put off by the untoward behavior of his friend, swallowed his pride and made his way to Àjàpá's home.

The latter was full of apology and improbable tales.

"The gods will spare you the scourge of robbers!" he prayed for his creditor. "It was my misfortune today to fall victim to a band of vicious robbers! They accosted me on my way to your house," he continued. "How they knew I carried money, only the gods know. Look at me, my friend: but for the vigilance of the spirit of my dead father the report you are hearing now would not be what would be entering your ears. Only the gods insisted that the day of my death has not yet come."

Elédè studied his friend as he spoke, and what he saw would not keep company with what he heard. He thought it wise to keep his disbelief to himself, though, for as the elders say, the name one would give to one's new child was best kept to oneself. He was also quite mindful of the saying that no king can take from you money you don't have. The best he could do was set another date when he would recover his loan without fail. He did not care that Àjàpá was a friend; he would wrest his money from Àjàpá's hands and rinse them with water, as the saying goes.

"The spirit of your dead father has done well," he said politely. "When shall I have the money back?"

4

"If anyone tells you that Àjàpá does not appreciate favors, tell him he lies!" he assured his friend. "Your kindness helped me out of my earlier difficulties and shielded me from disgrace. I gave you my word that I will repay you, and repay you I will!"

"Fine, but when?" Elédè asked again.

"Ever since my misfortune today I have been trying to come up with other money, but unfortunately the gods have not provided it."

"Five days should suffice for the gods to help," Elédè said patiently. "In five days I will expect you to return the money."

Àjàpá readily agreed, swearing that this time he would die before falling victim to robbers. He knew, of course, that he could not, and would not, find the money to repay his debt, so he fell back on the repertoire of tricks for which he was notorious. First he called his wife, Yánníbo.

"Yánníbo, dear wife, our fathers say that when a terrible disease descends on the town, combat it with terrible medicine."

"What terrible disease has descended?" she asked, troubled.

"What disease can be more terrible than a debt one cannot repay, especially when the creditor threatens scandal or, worse, violence?"

Yánníbo could think of none.

"What powerful medicine do we have?" she wondered.

"I have thought of something," Àjàpá assured her. "When Death is not quite ready to make off with someone he brings a powerful healer their way. The gods surely wish us no disgrace, for they have shown me the way out of this plight."

"And what might that be?"

"In five days Elédè will come back for his money," Àjàpá told her. "As soon as you catch a glimpse of him, lay me on my back, place some pepper, . . . no, some melon seeds, on my belly, and grind away at them. Whatever he says and whatever he does, don't stop; just keep grinding."

"How will that repay the debt?" asked Yánníbo, perplexed.

"Do as I tell you, and the gods will do the rest."

On the appointed day, Yánníbo got the melon seeds ready, and she and

Àjàpá fixed their eyes on the approach to their house. In time they saw Elédè ambling toward them, and swiftly, Yánníbo did as she had been instructed. She flipped Àjàpá on his back, placed some melon seeds on his belly, and began grinding. Elédè arrived at the door and greeted her:

"Homage to the owner of the home! Do I have leave to enter?"

Yánníbo ground away as she responded, "Leave granted."

Elédè entered and asked for Àjàpá, and Yánníbo said that her husband was out. To the visitor's question if Àjàpá had forgotten this was the day he was to repay his debt, Yánníbo affected ignorance, and all the while she kept grinding the melon seeds.

Elédè was angry that Àjàpá had apparently skipped out to avoid confronting his creditor, but he became even angrier at Yánníbo's discourtesy in not stopping her chore to attend to him.

"If I were a stranger new to you and not your husband's friend, if I were a wayfarer and not your husband's creditor, would it not yet be proper for you to stop your grinding and at least offer me some water to drink?" he demanded indignantly.

"Forgive me, good friend to my husband," she replied, "but if my husband returns and finds that I have not prepared food for him to eat as a good wife . . ."

Elédè did not wait for the rest; in anger, he grabbed the grindstone from under her hands and flung it out of the door into a muddy patch beside the house. Then he turned on her and vowed he would install himself in the house and await Àjàpá's arrival. Yánníbo cowered in a corner, wailing at Elédè's mistreatment of her in her own home.

In the meantime, Àjàpá had extricated himself from the mud and scrambled to a nearby stream to wash. Clean once again, he hurried to the house. When he entered, he feigned anger at being met by a woman's wailing on his return from a difficult errand. Pretending not to see Elédè, he demanded of Yánníbo:

"What disaster has befallen you that you greet me with wailing?"

Sniveling, and apparently unable to talk, she pointed to Elédè.

6

"Ah, Elédè, good friend!" Àjàpá greeted him cheerfully, pretending to notice his presence for the first time. "I was going to change my clothes quickly before coming to your house with your money. You did not have to make the trip here. You were generous, and you have been patient, and you should have waited at home and not exerted yourself."

"Whether one takes the breast to the child or the child to the breast," Elédè responded, "all that matters is that the child is suckled. I am here, so let's get on with our business."

Yánníbo continued to wail, and Àjàpá turned to her.

"Why won't you cease your bawling! Are you wailing because you think I did not hear your story the first time?" he asked. Then, turning to Elédè, "Women and their antics!"

"No," Yánníbo whimpered. "He threw my grindstone away."

"What?" Àjàpá asked.

"My grindstone," she repeated. "He threw it away, with the melon seeds I was grinding for my stew. . . ."

"I was angry," Elédè said. "She ignored me, and I became angry. I am sorry; I will fetch it."

Àjàpá looked sternly at his wife. "Woman, how were you raised that you don't know how to welcome visitors?"

He then turned to Elédè and apologized.

"But," he added, "the grindstone is precious, because it has been in the family for countless generations. If you will fetch it for us, I will have your money ready when you return."

Elédè scurried out of the door and began looking. He looked and he looked and he looked.

When people say that Elédè the Pig hasn't a clue as to what is becoming, when they say he is afflicted with a morbid attraction to filth, they do him an injustice, compounding the one his devious friend had already done him. As the elders say, it is the hard rain that turned the earth into mud. There is good cause for Elédè rooting in the mud.

Àjàpá and Àdàbà the Turtle Dove

In the first days of creation, Àjàpá and Àdàbà were firm friends. So close was their friendship that they pledged to combine all their efforts and resources in all matters—to farm together, to trade together, and, indeed, to do everything together; and neither considered the day done until he had shared the other's company and bade him goodnight. They in fact thought of living together, but reasoned that even the best of friends should preserve some space between them for privacy and for their families.

The two friends farmed a sizable plot, large enough to feed their two families year round and to permit surpluses they could sell or barter for goods they did not produce themselves. Characteristically, the lazy Àjàpá loathed doing any work on the farm. He always had some good explanation for his abstention from work—some illness, a quick journey he had to make, a divination barring him from work on certain days—but he willingly volunteered the services of his wife and children. Good friend that he was, Àdàbà took Àjàpá as he was, especially since the latter's wife and children made up for his constitutional and other deficiencies. When the harvest was in, the two friends shared it and the proceeds from the sales of any surpluses alike.

Thus matters stood for some time. The sages say that one's true nature is like smoke: one cannot hide it in the folds of one's garment. Eventually, Àjàpá's true nature, which to some extent he had managed to suppress for a time, curled into view like the proverbial telltale smoke. Since he was so much larger than his friend, he reasoned, there was no justification for his settling for an equal share with him of their farm produce or the proceeds from the sale of their surplus. Thus he undertook to correct what he reckoned to be an imbalance. True to his nature, he dismissed the thought of approaching his intimate friend with this "problem" so they could find a solution together; he would resolve matters his own way, one that would satisfy his sense of justice without threatening their friendship. His scheme was simple: when the harvest was ready he would secretly gather some of it, blaming thieves for the mischief, and share the remainder equally with his friend as usual.

At harvesttime Àjàpá put his plan into action. Each night he sneaked to the farm with his wife and their children to gather as much of all variety of crops as they could carry, returning home well before daybreak. When in the light of the following day the two friends met on the farm and saw the evidence of the theft, Àjàpá's fury far surpassed his friend's as he cursed the thief.

"The earth we farm will strike the thief who has no claim to these crops and yet comes to steal them!" he swore.

Still fuming, he vowed that if he found the culprit he would make him wish for death. But despite his impressive show of anger, he would not agree to any of Àdàbà's suggestions about how they might snare whoever might be responsible, not camping out in hiding all night on the farm, not paying someone else to lie in ambush, and not consulting the diviners to expose the criminal.

"The thief might succeed every day for a while," he counseled, "but in time he will slip up. That one occasion is worth waiting for. Why should we assume unnecessary impositions because of him? All things come to the patient."

Àdàbà went along with his friend's reasoning for a while, but patience brought neither the thief's exposure nor an end to the stealing. When it finally appeared to Àdàbà that the rogue would end up with more of the harvest than the owners of the farm, he decided to act on his own without consulting Àjàpá. He approached a well-known hunter and bade him catch whoever was ravaging their harvest. From Àdàbà's description of the annoyance, the hunter could tell that no supernatural agency was involved and that the simplest and most direct plan would suffice. One night the hunter supplied himself with a large number of traps and set them at all the approaches to the farm. Then he went home to await the morning, confident that the traps, which had never failed him, would at the break of day bring an end to the career of the thief.

On that fateful night Àjàpá roused his family as usual and bade them go to work. His wife was by now becoming uneasy about their escapades. She argued that they had enough food in their home to last several weeks, even not counting the legitimate share still due them.

"Thus far we have skirted ridicule and disgrace; but it is wise to know when to stop courting disaster," she argued, but her husband would not listen.

Still, perhaps because she had a strange premonition, she suggested they avoid the paths to the farm and instead cut across the forest. Àjàpá impatiently agreed, but only to shut her up and get on with the business at hand.

They arrived at the farm without mishap, again harvested as much food-stuff as they could carry, and set off for home. This time, though, Àjàpá insisted that they take the direct route home. Impatient with his still recalcitrant wife, he briskly stepped ahead of her, leading the way. He had not gone ten paces when there came a loud snap, followed by an ominous rumbling, and then an earth-shaking crash as a huge pile of rocks collapsed on him.

His wife and children did not stop to see what condition he might be in, but threw off their loads and scrambled home as fast as their legs would carry them.

When the corpse of the head of their household was discovered in the morning, they even earned some sympathy from their neighbors, as well as from their father's friend, Àdàbà. They told themselves that, since the earth had spared them, their only error was to have been deceived by the devious head of their household.

Àjàpá and Àdán the Bat

Àjàpá and Àdán were once intimate friends, so close that their neighbors said they were like the snail and its shell, for wherever the animal went, its shell was bound to follow. Because they wanted to spend as much of each day in each other's company as they could, they chose to live next door to each other. A creature of the air and branches, Àdán naturally lived with his family among the leaves of a large *àràbà* tree, while Àjàpá, a dweller on the earth, made his home with his family at the base of the same tree.

According to the custom of their community, whatever concerned one person, be it good fortune or ill, concerned all. Their strong sense of community derived both from the knowledge that wealth was a matter not of how many material possessions one had but of how many people one knew and from the realization that, although nothing was easier than breaking a single broomstick, breaking a broom made of many individual sticks was quite another matter.

So it was that whenever someone fell on hard times his or her age-mates, friends, and relatives weighed in with succor and solace, and when some occasion called for celebration, they likewise rallied round and contributed presents commensurate with their closeness or esteem for the celebrant, lent a hand in the many chores that had to be done, and generally made the celebration their own. Whoever hopes some day to become a parent, the elders say, must join those who are already blessed with children in their rejoicing.

In their great friendship Àjàpá and Àdán observed this custom meticu-
lously, even though one was a daytime creature and the other nighttime.
But, though Àdán's devotion to his friend brooked no reservation, Àjàpá
rigorously defended the wisdom of the sages, who said that, however much
one loved a friend, one should always make room for quarrels. In the case
of these two friends the caution was appropriate, for they were plagued by
a persistent problem.

It derived from the fact that Àjàpá's inability to climb the great *àràbà*
tree where his friend made his home prevented him from attending Àdán's
ceremonies and thus deprived him of the pleasure of partaking in the feasting. The wise say tears in the eyes do not keep them from seeing; deep
friendship did not blind Àjàpá to inequities of the arrangement whereby,
although he always gave presents to his friend on his frequent festive occasions, he could never attend because of the lofty branches. He had to remain at the base of the tree suffering the irresistible aromas that wafted
down from the branches and the sounds of the animated revelry of those
in attendance at the feasts. Àdán was not particularly helpful when Àjàpá
alerted him to what troubled him.

"Don't think it does not pain me not to have you, the friend of my life,
at these events. But what can we do? The gods have decreed different habitations for us, and we must live by their wishes."

"But," Àjàpá almost whimpered, "to be forever excluded from these
feasts! It is not the eating and drinking," he lied, "but the fellowship of
the friend of my life! To share your joys with you!"

"I would hold my feasts on the ground if I could, or in your home,"
Àdán said, "but what would the world think of that? It would be unheard
of; one's home is where one performs one's important rituals."

Nonetheless, Àjàpá chafed under the imbalance in their friendship. The
gods may have left matters the way they pleased, but one had to take one's
own being in hand and rearrange it as one would. He had never before
been stumped by a problem, and he did not think the present one should

be an exception. He therefore set his mind to work, and soon his cognitive efforts bore fruit.

When Àdán apprised him a short while later of the birth of his first son and announced the impending festivities, Àjàpá activated his plan. From his inner chamber he selected the most valuable garment he had, one sewn from expensive, hand-woven cloth, and gave it to his wife Yánníbo with instructions that she conceal him carefully in it and tie it into a bundle. When Àdán called for his gift, as he was bound to, she was to present the bundle to him, charging him to carry it home with the utmost care, for in it was a most precious but delicate present for the new baby and its mother.

Àdán duly arrived for his gift as expected, and Yánníbo did as she had been told. To questions about her husband's whereabouts, she proffered the lie that an urgent summons had taken him to a nearby town. The richness of the gift, which Àdán could determine by merely looking at the garment wrap, both surprised and impressed him; it was all he could do to restrain himself until he returned home before he unwrapped the bundle to find out what precious gifts it concealed for his wife and son.

Àdán gripped the bundle firmly in his beak and soared into the branches. Once home, he hurried to unwrap the gift, leaving his wife to wonder about his great rush. In no time at all he had the bundle untied, finding, to his surprise and annoyance, that the precious gift was nothing other than his good friend, Àjàpá. Such was Àdán's surprise that he was momentarily speechless. Àjàpá, on the other hand, was full of excitement, quite at his ebullient best.

"The bush path will not close on a man who wields a cutlass," he cheerfully told his friend. "The birth of a first son is no mean matter, and I simply had to find some way to join in the festivities, like a good friend. I even contrived to add to your delight at my solution to our stubborn problem by including this element of surprise."

Àdán was undoubtedly surprised, but he had no other option than to be a good sport and pretend that he was delighted to see his friend.

The feasting suited the occasion, and Àdán earned his reputation as a feast-maker all over again. The eating was hearty, as was the drinking, the dancing, and the general merriment. Excepting Àjàpá, all the visitors were birds, and when the celebration came to a close, each one flew off, leaving Àjàpá, who had no means of returning home. For his part, Àdán was still so put off by his friend's audaciousness that he offered no help. The cutlass that opened the way for him to come to the feast would have to open the way for him to return home, Àdán said.

Curiously, Àjàpá showed no sign of consternation, assuring his friend, rather, that he took care of his return at the same time that he planned his outward trip. He was putting off his departure only because, in true friendship, he had a gift with a difference for Àdán, with which he intended to mollify his host in case he had been discomfited by Àjàpá's unexpected presence at the feast. It might be of only limited benefit for Àdán personally, he said, but it would make all future generations of Àdán among the most admired of forest-dwellers. Although Àdán was still somewhat miffed by his friend's behavior, he was also not one to be indifferent to gifts or to anything that might enhance the social standing of his offspring. He therefore asked to know what Àjàpá had in mind.

"It's all about size," Àjàpá said.

"Size?"

"Yes, size," Àjàpá repeated. "Stature."

He went on to elaborate that he had lately made the acquaintance of the Àùnjònnú-Erin the Medicine Elephant, whose knowledge of herbs and charms was without parallel. He had wondered within the elephant's hearing why certain animals, like elephants, were large, while certain others, like tortoises, were small. He was curious, he said, because for jungle-dwellers, size was a treasured advantage. Àùnjònnú-Erin had told him then of the secret well guarded by the clan of elephants. Every creature was born with a tailbone whose form was unique to the species. In birds, for example, it was in the form of a feather, whereas in other animals it took the form of a tail. This appendage, though diminutive, had an insatiable appetite, and most of the food a creature ate wound up in it. Ever since elephants learned the secret, a long time ago, as soon as a baby elephant was born the first thing its parents did was to clip its tailbone. Rid of that gluttonous appendage, each elephant's body retained all the food fed into it, with the result that elephants were the largest of all land animals.

Àdán's eyes grew larger and larger as he listened to his friend's fluent narration. Anything that promised such a boon to himself and his children and their children he must embrace.

"Your words command reflection," Àdán commented.

"Better action than reflection," Àjàpá replied.

"Let's find my son's tailbone feather and pluck it!" Àdán offered after a brief pause.

Àjàpá told him there was no hurry. First, as parents they should set the example, he said, and remove their own first. After all, there was still time left for them to put on some size and perhaps become better parents and protectors. After removing theirs, they could attend to the child's.

Àjàpá had no difficulty persuading Àdán to submit first to the operation at Àjàpá's hands, after which Àdán would return the favor for his friend. In a thrice, Àjàpá had plucked a feather from Àdán's tail, with some slight discomfort to the latter, who, however, reasoned that the anticipated benefit was well worth the pain. After all, the compliments one receives for the beauty of one's facial scarification more than compensate for the pain the operation entails. It was now Àjàpá's turn to have his tailbone plucked.

He opened the gap at the rear of his shell to expose the appendage, and into that gap Àdán inserted his hand. And no sooner had he done so than Àjàpá's shell clamped on the hand like a vise.

"Áábò!" Àdán screamed in pain. "My hand!"

In response, Àjàpá only increased the pressure on the hand.

"What is this?" Àdán demanded. "You are hurting me. Let go of my hand!"

"Take me home, and I will release your hand," Àjàpá responded, tightening his grip on his friend's hand.

The pain grew more excruciating by the second, so Àdán wasted no more time: he took to the air with Àjàpá to bear him home.

When Àdán swore that was the end of their friendship, Àjàpá's smug response was, "When an expensive concubine tells you the affair is over, you should rejoice, not fret."

ÀJÀPÁ AND ÒJÒLÁ THE ROYAL PYTHON

In days long, long ago, when the earth had only just come into being, all animals lived as one big family. Food was so plentiful that little exertion was necessary to procure it. In the absence of competition for what to eat, or indeed for anything, peace reigned among the animals.

Àjàpá and Òjòlá were close neighbors and cordial acquaintances. Whenever their ways brought them together, each took the time to inquire about the other's health and those of the members of his household. After this practice had continued for a while, Àjàpá thought it was a relationship worth nurturing. Even in those days, the belief was already common that a friendship that remains outdoors is not much of a friendship. Friendship, after all, indicates a sharing of habits and tastes, and how can friends know each other's habits and tastes if not by knowing each other at home? It's too easy to maintain a good reputation at a distance; only those who have seen friends at home can really claim to know them.

Having made the decision to deepen their friendship, Àjàpá hastened to act on it. The sun was high in the sky when he turned his face towards Òjòlá's home to pay him a visit.

"I ask leave of the owner of this home!" Àjàpá called from the entrance to Òjòlá's abode, and after a short but significant period, during which no response came from inside, the latter's somewhat muffled voice responded.

"Leave granted."

Àjàpá entered the home and saw his friend Òjòlá at his midday meal.

17

The food was arranged on the floor, and Òjòlá was coiled in a large circle around it.

"Now I know why on the way here all the rocks in the path insisted on stopping my feet," Àjàpá said cheerily. "My stubbed toes bleed, but now I understand the good omen."

Òjòlá understood the reference to his friend finding him at his meal, and he did what was expected of him.

"You find me in happy circumstances," Òjòlá said by way of invitation to Àjàpá, although there was little in his voice that was inviting.

Àjàpá failed to make that observation, however, since he was intent on sharing his friend's meal. He lived by the principle that one should never refuse an invitation to eat, for no one knows when death might call. Having missed an opportunity to eat while one is alive, one cannot return from death to make up for lost opportunities. Since his host made no move to uncoil himself, Àjàpá walked around him, seeking the easiest point to climb over him into the food circle. The area of Òjòlá's tail suggested itself, and Àjàpá made to climb over his friend at that spot.

"What?" Òjòlá exclaimed. "Àjàpá, what insult is this? I ask you to eat with me, and you trample on my tail! In my own home!"

The reaction from Òjòlá startled Àjàpá and immediately made him wonder about his desire for a closer friendship. Àjàpá was transfixed where he stood when the import of his friend's inhospitable behavior hit him. Àjàpá breathes in and out like other animals, as the saying goes, although his shell disguises that fact. Like other creatures he knows embarrassment, and so great was his present embarrassment that only by exerting supreme effort was he able to move toward the doorway and escape from the scene of his disgrace. He ambled toward the doorway, consoling himself with the saying that only fellow feeling makes one share a friend's cornmeal, for the well-born and well-bred has enough to eat at home.

As Àjàpá nursed the wound to his pride, he contemplated how he could make Òjòlá pay for his behavior. Meanwhile, toward Òjòlá he affected a nonchalant attitude because he did not wish to give him the satisfaction of knowing how much he had wounded him. As he thought of how to avenge himself, the idea came suddenly to mind that he would simply visit Òjòlá with an exact reprise of the python's behavior. That way, no additional words or comments would be necessary to deliver his message. A hint is all one needs to give an adult with any sense; in the adult mind, a hint blossoms into a full statement. But how could he get Òjòlá to walk into his trap? The answer that came to him was that only forgetfulness would make him susceptible. Only after time had made his behavior fade from Òjòlá's mind could he, Àjàpá, repay him in kind. He was willing to wait, though; it might be true that one scrambles to rid oneself of a burning garment, but if one is to eat steaming-hot stew, one must learn patience.

Time passed during which the two friends saw each other as before and Àjàpá acted as though seeing Òjòlá was the most pleasurable event of his day. He betrayed no sign that he still smarted from his injury and gave no inkling to Òjòlá that he held a grudge toward him. After a year of this, Àjàpá finally decided that it was time for revenge. When next he saw Òjòlá, he berated him for not being a good enough friend.

"Òjòlá," he asked, "how long have we been friends?"

"How long?" Òjòlá considered the question for a while before answering. "A long time."

"Indeed!" Àjàpá agreed. "Children born when we became friends now have children of their own."

"True! True!" he agreed.

"And have you in all that time seen the inside of my home?"

"No," Òjòlá responded.

"What sort of friendship is it," Àjàpá asked, "that says it must be kept out-of-doors? Perhaps you fear that my home is filthy?"

"No, no, my friend," Òjòlá protested.

"Or that I might poison you?"

"How could you have such suspicions about me?" Òjòlá responded indignantly.

19

Àjàpá turned to go, feigning anger. When he was a short distance away, he said over his shoulder:

"You know the path to my house. If you are truly my friend, let your actions show it."

His elation was boundless when he heard his friend say:

"Tomorrow! I will visit you tomorrow."

Àjàpá headed directly not to his home but to a part of the forest where bananas grew in abundance. From several trunks he ripped long strips of their bark and labored home with them. All evening he busied himself twisting and forming the strips into a long, thick, and supple trunk that tapered off at one end into a tail. Satisfied, he ate and settled down to rest.

He rose early the next day and, knowing that his friend Òjòlá could not resist the sight and smell of yam pottage, he addressed himself to cooking the most inviting and aromatic yam pottage his skill allowed. When it was done, he set it on the floor and arranged around it the trunk he had formed with the banana strips, and then he sat at the end opposite the tail so that anyone who saw him would see a suddenly elongated Àjàpá sporting a tail.

Òjòlá kept his word: soon after sunrise he set out for his friend's house, and when he drew close his movements involuntarily quickened in response to the irresistible aroma of yam pottage filling the forest. If he had any doubts about how much Àjàpá held him in esteem, or how much he valued their friendship, the aroma and what it promised dispelled them.

He was still some distance from the door when he announced himself:

"I ask leave of the man of the home!"

"Come in, come in, my friend," Àjàpá responded.

Àjàpá gave his visitor no opportunity to take in his new shape or to wonder at it.

"You know well how to time your visit," he said to Òjòlá. "Share this food with me."

Òjòlá did not wait to be asked twice, but immediately made to slide over the trunk and get at the pottage. But as soon as his head rested on the banana trunk Àjàpá exclaimed:

"Ha! What is the meaning of this, my friend? I asked you to share my meal and you step on my tail! And in my own home, too!"

Òjòlá recoiled, stupefied. It had not occurred to him that the thing ringing the food was part of Àjàpá, the friend he knew very well. While he wondered and wandered around the new, elongated Àjàpá trying to find a way to get at the food, the latter consumed all the pottage, noisily grunting his pleasure at its deliciousness.

Disappointment made Òjòlá's eyes red, but his age and self-respect forbade him tears. They were in his voice, though, when he asked his friend:

"Àjàpá, when did you become so long?"

"My good friend," Àjàpá responded, "others teach one to be short, and others teach one to be long."

Àjàpá and the Blind Spirits

In an age long gone, when humans sported eyes on their shins and cracked palm-nuts with their buttocks, a terrible famine descended on the earth. In those days, humans, spirits, and animals consorted freely together and shared their fortunes and misfortunes. So desperate were they all for food that any green leaf they saw in the bush was cherished as a delicacy. Àjàpá was much worse off than the other creatures; the prolonged dearth of food made his shell an almost impossible burden to bear, but it was one he was unable to shed.

In his town there flourished a market where all sorts of creatures came to exchange what little they had. Among the regulars at the market were three spirits whose arrival always attracted a good deal of notice. For one thing, they were always in masquerade, and for another they were blind, and they walked in a single file. The leader found his way with the aid of a stick; the next in line followed with a hand on the leader's shoulder, and the third who brought up the rear had his hand on the shoulder of the spirit in the middle. Their arrival invariably caused Àjàpá, also a regular at the market, to marvel, not because of their attire or their ambulatory style, but because, despite the famine that had reduced all other creatures to skin and bones, these spirits were healthy, sprightly, and—even more extraordinary—they always came with piles of yams to sell. Many market patrons came solely for the opportunity to trade whatever articles they still owned for these yams. Unfortunately for Àjàpá, because of his legendary shiftlessness he had nothing to trade. But he vowed that one way or another he would find the barn where the spirits stashed their abundance of yams.

One day, after the market-goers had dispersed, he followed the spirits as they made their way home. He allowed a prudent distance between himself and the spirits lest any noise he made alert them that they were being followed. Even so he almost gave himself away, for when he rounded one bend that had momentarily concealed them from his view, he found himself almost at their heels. Fortunately for him, no dried twig or dislodged pebble had registered his passage, and the spirits' ears reported no other presence to them. He learned from that experience and was henceforth wary of bends in the pathway and careful to stop each time they halted to listen for any suspicious footsteps. In time the spirits approached a hill in the forest and stopped again. They strained their ears to catch any alien noises. Satisfied that they were alone, they approached a rock resting against the hill and chanted:

Sentry Rock, Sentry Rock,
The wayfarers now are home!
Sentry Rock, Sentry Rock,
Remove yourself and let us in!

Obediently, the rock shook mightily and slid aside to reveal the entrance to a cave. The spirits entered, and before the rock slid back into place Àjàpá scrambled after them as fast and as quietly as his wobbly legs would allow. He had barely made it inside before the rock slammed back into place, only narrowly missing crushing him.

His eyes took some time to adjust to the cave's dim light, and when they finally did he was amazed at what they saw. The cave revealed itself as a veritable warehouse of assorted goods the spirits had taken in trade over the years. Most interesting to Àjàpá, though, was the abundance of foodstuffs stacked in their different ranks about the cave, especially yams and dried meats. The spirits did not dawdle before they embarked on the business of preparing a meal, nothing less than everybody's favorite—pounded yams and *ègúsí* stew, seasoned with dried shrimps and a congestion of dried bush meat. Àjàpá silently thanked the spirit of his dead father for bringing him together with the spirits. Such was the strength of his anticipation of the meal he saw in the offing that he was barely able to control himself, and when he saw a king's portion of steaming pounded-yam and a large dish of stew brimming with meat set on the floor, he almost gave himself away as he scrambled for a space where he could get at the food without bumping against any of his unintentional hosts.

Àjàpá fed like the famished creature he was, one who was not sure there would be another meal coming for days, and the spirits were befuddled as to why the food was eaten more quickly than usual. Finally concluding that they must have made some mistake in their measures, they retired for their customary postprandial nap. Àjàpá welcomed the opportunity to rest his stuffed stomach, and he enjoyed a happy and contented sleep, the likes of which he had not had in a long, long while. Only the commotion of the spirits' after-siesta movements woke him, and when they ventured outside again he followed them as stealthily as before and was soon on his way home.

Following the spirits home uninvited and sharing in their meals undetected became a routine for Àjàpá, almost character traits in fact that would live and die with him, and before long his complexion, his walking gait, and his general demeanor began to reflect his newly found fortune. Whereas before his encounter with the spirits he was practically a rattling sack of bones, now he looked robust and his shell took on a healthy sheen; whereas his movement had previously been a slow drag, now his feet hardly touched the ground as he pranced about; and whereas he had been an ill-humored and morose wretch, now his cheerful greetings to all and sundry were so out of character as to be almost unbearable.

Àjàpá's new condition piqued the curiosity of every observer, but most especially of his good friend Àkùko the Rooster. Like the others, Àkùko was having a rough time coping with the dearth of food, and he reasoned that his friendship with the suddenly prosperous Àjàpá should be turned to good account. He therefore approached Àjàpá and observed that, from all appearances, he must have found the antidote to the raging famine. Àjàpá was evasive.

"The god that cooks the stew has not abandoned the cooking hearth," he responded flippantly.

"That may be," Àkùko said, "but how is it that others waste away with hunger while your cheeks grow more puffy by the day?"

"Well," he replied, "you know our fathers' saying: the Creator who made the mouth horizontal knew how He would feed it."

Àkùko was in no mood for circuitous talk, as he impatiently informed his friend. He knew that Àjàpá had solved the problem of starvation, and he meant to share in the boon. His importunity paid off. Àjàpá was of course loath to reveal his secret to anyone, for the more creatures knew about it the more he would have to share the food with. In the end, his vanity and an almost irresistible desire to win some accolade for his cleverness gained control and compelled him to let Àkùko in on his stratagem. He thought it wise, however, to set some conditions because of Àkùko's involuntary habit of flapping his wings and belting out crows whenever he felt life to be good. It was, he always explained, his way of paying homage to his ancestors, that is, by doing as his fathers did. Àjàpá presented him the options of forswearing the habit during their escapades or continuing to starve, and Àkùko eagerly assured his friend that his crowing was not like his feathers, which he could not discard; crowing he could forego at will. Reassured, Àjàpá arranged for the two to meet during the market on the morrow.

On the following day, Àkùko was the first creature at the market, arriving before sunrise, so that he was already seething with anger induced by impatience by the time Àjàpá finally sauntered along when the market was already at full bustle. Under the circumstances, though, he was in no position to vent his rage. His forbearance was tested further still when his friend told him that their trip would not begin until after the market had folded. He could not understand what Àjàpá was up to when he found himself a seat and coolly watched other market-farers; he could not understand his particular interest in three masquerading characters; and he did not care for the answer his friend gave to his constant needling to do as he promised and lead the way to food.

"Food that comes after long abstinence makes up in deliciousness for the hunger endured," he would repeat as he pressed further patience on Àkùko.

For Àkùko, though, the wait was an eternity, but in time the market wound down, and the spirits set out for home. Àjàpá beckoned to Àkùko and they followed at a discreet distance. When the procession arrived at the cave, the spirits chanted the usual formula and the guarding rock slid aside to admit them. Àjàpá signaled to Àkùko to follow, and they both scrambled into the cave before the rock slid back into place. When the spirits sat down to their meal, Àjàpá and Àkùko did likewise, leaving the spirits wondering again why their plates lately seemed to empty more quickly than usual. Accusations flew back and forth that one or another among them was becoming too greedy and antisocial; they stopped short of an actual quarrel, though, as they would not permit matters of the gullet to interfere with their fellowship.

A few trips was all it took for the evidence of good living to become evident on Àkùko, just as it did on Àjàpá: his plumes regained the gloss they had lost, and the comb which used to droop on his head sat up more jauntily than ever before. So appreciative was he of the boon his friend had brought his way that whenever they visited the cave he made every effort to remember to act according to the promise he had given Àjàpá, that he would not yield to the urge to crow. But who can repress his nature forever? After many uneventful visits Àkùko naturally became more and more relaxed, especially when he had eaten his fill. The urge to relax was reinforced by his perception that the spirits did not seem particularly intelligent. He in fact developed some contempt for them. If he and Àjàpá were inclined to overpower them and take over their cave and its stock, he wondered, what could the three blind creatures do to two who had perfect vision?

Lost in such ruminations one fateful day, Àkùko forgot himself. The food had seemed on this occasion more delicious than anything Àjàpá and Àkùko had tasted there before, and there had been a good deal more of it, their hosts having adjusted the portions they cooked to accommodate what they had resolved was their growing appetite and stomach capacity. When the spirits settled down for their after-dinner nap, Àjàpá too prepared for a short snooze before it was time to depart. Àkùko was also heavy with food, but his heaviness did not induce sleep. He was so overwhelmed by the feeling of well-being that his instincts urged him to remember his fathers and pay homage to them. He resisted the urge for a while, but eventually his will yielded to it and he began to raise his wings. Àjàpá saw what was happening in time to stop his friend with a withering look.

Àkùko settled down, but not for long. The second time he raised his wings Àjàpá had to stop him with a kick, almost giving their presence away by so doing. Àkùko was again quiet for a short while. Finally, however, unable to contain the powerful forces goading him, he raised his wings, flapped them loudly a few times, and let loose with a crow that shook the walls of the cave.

Had the spirits been deaf as well as blind the noise would have awakened them, anyway. They started out of their sleep, unable to believe their ears. A cock in their cave! A dog in a mosque! They tore around the cave, bumping into one another and into objects lying about, in their effort to corner the intruder. Àkùko flew about wildly in his search for safety, but he repeatedly gave himself away with his excited cackling. Àjàpá quickly found himself a relatively safe hiding place, but with Àkùko flying all over the cave he feared that it was only a matter of time before one of the spirits stumbled upon him. When Àkùko came uncomfortably close to where Àjàpá was hiding, self-preservation won over friendship, and he quickly shoved his friend into the arms of his pursuers. Without much ado the angry spirits wrung Àkùko's head from the rest of his body, and shortly thereafter his remains could be found simmering in a pot of stew. The spirits, exhausted by the excitement of the day, set the stew aside and lay down again to resume their interrupted rest.

By now Àjàpá had come to the conclusion that he would be much more comfortable outside the cave, but he thought he owed his departed friend one last duty before making his escape. The stew, whose aroma kept his mouth salivating, called to him to save his friend's remains from the worst of fates, winding up inside the spirits who had taken his life. If their fates had been reversed, he told himself, the least he would have wished from his friend would be that he save his remains from such ignominy. Dutifully, Àjàpá crawled to the stew, slipped off the piece of cloth with which the spirits had covered the pot and tied it around his waist. Then, very quietly, he consumed every bit of the stew and licked the pot clean. Without loitering any longer, he tiptoed to the mouth of the cave and very softly chanted the magic formula to the guard rock. It responded, but the noise of the opening woke the spirits. Before they could ascertain what was happening, Àjàpá was outside the cave, making away as fast as his legs would go.

The realization that Àkùko had not been alone in violating their cave angered the spirits greatly, and they were even angrier when they discovered that the second culprit had consumed their new stew. Their only solace was their failure to locate the cloth they had covered it with. If it was not in the cave, they reasoned, it must be in the possession of the thief. This cloth happened to possess magical qualities, among them the ability to communicate with the spirits and lead them to wherever it might be. They hurried outside the cave in pursuit of the thieving intruder.

Àjàpá was scurrying along as fast his bloated stomach would permit when he heard the pursuing spirits call from afar.

"Magic Rag, where are you?" they called.

To Àjàpá's astonishment some voice responded from the neighborhood of his loins.

"On Àjàpá's loins!"

Àjàpá was momentarily paralyzed with terror. What sort of weird rag was this? he wondered. The approaching sound of the spirits' pounding feet stopped his wondering and redoubled his speed, as he desperately tried to rid himself of the rag at the same time. His natural slowness and the distraction of the talking rag enabled the spirits to gain steadily on him. Fortunately, just as he was about to despair, he saw Àgbò the Ram foraging for food in the bush nearby. He slowed his pace and assumed a nonchalant aspect as he sauntered toward him.

"I saw you from the path," he told Àgbò, "and the great esteem I have for you directed my feet toward you."

Àgbò paused, wondering what Àjàpá had in mind.

"As soon as I saw you," Àjàpá continued, "I was reminded of the saying that a venerable person must look and act accordingly."

"When you speak that kind of garbage, you are up to some mischief," Àgbò commented.

"On the contrary," Àjàpá replied, "I am here to do you a favor. What I saw of you from the path disturbed me. It is not fitting that an elder should allow everything to swing wildly about."

Thus speaking he removed the rag from around his waist and presented it to Àgbò.

"It would be much better," he suggested, "if you would cover what should be covered with this."

Àgbò began to say he was grateful, but Àjàpá had already concealed himself in a brush nearby. The explanation for Àjàpá's uncharacteristic generosity and strange behavior appeared to Àgbò soon enough. He was just returning to his search for food when he heard the sound of running feet and the call from very close by:

"Magic Rag, where are you?"

Àgbò was in turn amazed to hear the rag around his waist answer and announce its location:

"Around Àgbò's waist!"

He whipped the rag off his waist and flung it aside. He had no time for anger at Àjàpá's treachery, though, before the spirits emerged from the forest screen and made for him. Àgbò was not an animal to be bullied or trifled with, however. He lowered his head and charged the spirits. The struggle was brief; after taking a few butts from Àgbò's horns, the spirits conceded the fight to him and hobbled back home.

Àjàpá now came crawling toward Àgbò, pleading for forgiveness.

"One seeks refuge with whomever one has," he pleaded. "Forgive me, I had no one besides you."

Àgbò was inclined to administer some punishment to the rascal, but he remembered the proverb that it is unwise to take a bite from an unripe banana, and equally unwise to beat a naughty child to death. The best course of action, he told himself, was to forget Àjàpá's treachery and leave him to his ways. For his part, Àjàpá promised to leave his benefactor in peace, but first he wished to sit against a nearby tree and recover his breath.

Àgbò went back to his foraging, but he could not keep his mind off Àjàpá, whose eyes burned into him. Experience told him that some other mischief was brewing behind those eyes. Sure enough, after a short while he heard mumbling from Àjàpá's direction. He disregarded it for a while, but it went on unabated until Àgbò was obliged to do something to stop the annoying distraction.

"What is the meaning of your mumbling?" he snapped.

"Oh," Àjàpá said in answer, "I was saying that it surely must have been the spirit of my dead father that brought you this way today. Otherwise, who would have saved me?"

Àgbò grunted and returned to his business. Before long he had to stop again to ask Àjàpá what he was mumbling this time, for it had continued, even gaining in volume.

"I only said," replied Àjàpá, "that creatures like you are rare, with horns that make cripples of spirits, even."

Again Àgbò grunted and went back to his affairs, doing his best to ignore his mischievous companion. It was no use, and when a third time he stopped to ask what Àjàpá was saying, the response he received was far from pleasing to his ears.

"You asked me a question as an adult to an adult," Àjàpá responded cockily, "and I shall answer you as an adult to an adult. When an adult says something, he should not be afraid to repeat it. As I sat here watching you I could not keep my eyes from those pendulous things swinging back and forth between your hind legs. How do you walk with such a burden? Why are yours so big, anyway? Did you think, perhaps, that testicles were things one could cut up for sale?"

If one does a favor and receives no gratitude, one has in effect been robbed. Àgbò felt that his manhood had been questioned by the rascal who had rewarded his favor with insults. In anger he bore down on the impudent and ungrateful Àjàpá, but the latter was too nimble for his assailant and managed to disappear under the carpet of dry leaves on the ground before suffering any damage. Àgbò rooted angrily under the leaves for him, but when he finally got a hold of Àjàpá's foot the latter sneered:

"Ah ha! All you've got is a handful of roots."

Àgbò let go and grabbed a root.

"My foot! My foot!" Àjàpá yelled.

While Àgbò was struggling with the root, Àjàpá sneaked away and scrambled up a nearby tree. Unable to dislodge what he thought was Àjàpá, Àgbò went in search of some embers to smoke the rascal out, and Àjàpá took advantage of his absence to arm himself with a forked branch from his perch.

Soon after returning, Àgbò had a good fire going where he thought Àjàpá was hiding, and he stood back waiting for the smoke to send him scrambling out. From his hiding place the latter watched for a suitable opportunity, and when it came he pushed Àgbò into his own fire with the forked branch and pinned him there. The more he struggled to escape, the harder Àjàpá leaned on the branch, until the hapless Àgbò was dead and thoroughly roasted.

Àjàpá again thanked the spirit of his dead father, who had obviously not forgotten his earthly charge. He had lost his steady supply of free food from the spirits, but his dead father had found for him a substitute to last at least a few days. He bundled up the roasted carcass and managed to lift it unto his back, intending to carry it home where he could consume it free of the danger that some wayfarer might happen by and obligate him to share the bounty. Still, carrying such a conspicuous load all the way home without arousing some curiosity presented a problem, but not one that could stump his fertile brain. His scheme was to scare every wayfarer into taking to the bush on his approach. Accordingly, as he trudged slowly along with his burden he proclaimed at the top of his voice,

"Death approaches on the path! Those eyes that wish to avoid a glimpse of death had better flee!"

The effect of the proclamation on those who heard it was as Àjàpá wished: everyone's thought was, "If you will not run, get out of my way!" Except, that is, for one animal for whom death was no stranger, and who stopped to wonder what sort of death would warn potential victims to flee. Ekùn the Leopard had seen both his father and his mother die and had dispatched numerous victims himself; death was thus a figure with which he was quite familiar. Besides, he thought, a worthy creature dies only once. He would wait and see what nature of death approached on the path.

When Àjàpá came into view with his burden, Ekùn was so angry at his insolence that he knocked the load off Àjàpá's back and gave him a few good swipes of his paws, failing to draw blood only because his victim had the presence of mind to leave no fleshy part of him exposed outside his shell.

"What is the meaning of this impudence?" Ekùn demanded.

"Treat me gently," Àjàpá panted, "and hear my words."

"Speak it so I can hear it!" Ekùn commanded.

Àjàpá assured him that he anticipated that all fainthearted creatures would flee on hearing his words, leaving only the intrepid and worthy ones, like Ekùn. His intention, he assured Ekùn, was to clear the area of the cowardly so that the stalwart alone might enjoy the food he was carrying. Ekùn sniffed at the roasted meat, and his anger yielded to his hunger. Without further delay he settled down to gorge himself on the food providence had brought his way.

Àjàpá seethed with anger as he watched the speedy disappearance of the food he had thought would keep him for several days; worse yet, when he attempted to get some of it for himself, Ekùn's flaming eyes and threatening growls warned him away, and he could do nothing but pretend happiness; if a powerful person hits you, the sages say, you would be wise to respond with a wide grin. But as Ekùn ate, Àjàpá's brain was busy cooking up a stratagem that would both replenish his food stock and afford him a revenge against the bully. Before long he had it.

"Did you know," he asked Ekùn, "that I am the most accomplished braider of hair in these parts?"

"No, I didn't," Ekùn responded without paying much attention; his mind was wholly on the food.

"Oh yes," Àjàpá continued, "I am. Nobody comes close to me where hair-braiding is concerned."

"Hmm," Ekùn grunted, ripping the flesh from a piece of bone.

"You have children, don't you?" Àjàpá asked.

"Yes," he replied, "so what?"

"Seven of them, in fact?" Àjàpá continued.

"So?"

"I thought," said Àjàpá, "that as the proud father everyone knows you to be, you would want to show your children off at their best."

"Who says I wouldn't?" Ekùn responded

"Well," Àjàpá asked, "what would show them off better than beautifully braided hair? Think of it. How many animals do you see walking around with braided hair?"

Ekùn thought for a moment and confessed he saw none.

"And do you know why?" Àjàpá asked.

Ekùn did not.

"It's because there are none. Not one," Àjàpá affirmed. "If I were to braid your children's hair," he continued, "they would be unique in the forest. Your position among animals deserves no less."

Ekùn's vanity was being tempted, and Àjàpá continued his appeal.

33

"It would be such an honor for me to announce to the world that I was your children's hair-braider," he assured Ekùn, "that I will happily do the job for free."

"You would?" Ekùn asked somewhat suspiciously; Àjàpá was, after all, not known for his generosity.

"I cannot think of better advertising for me," he explained.

Ekùn was soon won over by Àjàpá's glibness, and they agreed that the latter would braid the hair of Ekùn's seven children without fee. All Àjàpá required was that Ekùn build a modest enclosure with no doors but only one small opening big enough to peep through. It must not be large enough to admit any animal larger than Ekùn's children. The rituals of the trade, he explained, necessitated his braiding the hair of only one child each day, and, moreover, ensconcing himself in the enclosure with all seven children for the duration. The opening would permit Ekùn to look in and see the progress he was making without exposing the children to any danger from hostile marauders. Ekùn thought the arrangement reasonable and soon had the structure ready. He thereupon delivered his seven children to Àjàpá, who crawled with them into the enclosure.

The next day Ekùn came to have a look at what the celebrated hair-braider had accomplished. Àjàpá brought one of the children to the opening where Ekùn could see it. The truth has never asked not to be spoken. Clearly, Àjàpá's account of his hair-braiding skill was no idle boast. The child's hair was so exquisitely done that Ekùn could hardly recognize his own child. He went away satisfied that in seven days his children would be the talk of the forest. Each day he went on his inspection visit; each day Àjàpá showed him a well-braided child, and his anticipation of the seventh day mounted.

The big day finally arrived, and Ekùn went to receive his newly spruced-up children, but he was in for a bad, bad surprise. He called and called, but there was no Àjàpá, there were no children, and there was no sound from inside the enclosure. Whoever has children can imagine the panic that gripped Ekùn at the thought of losing all seven of his children, and at the hands of a lowly creature like Àjàpá at that. He pranced frantically around the structure, then he clawed at it until he had made an opening large enough to admit him. He squeezed inside, and there before him lay the stripped skeletons of his seven children.

He poked his claws into his eyes, but even tears had deserted him; the disaster that befell him was beyond weeping or lamentation. He hopped wildly about like a thing on fire, and, indeed, he was on fire inside. Eventually he calmed down somewhat and sat down to compose himself. When he finally emerged from the enclosure, it was with an absolute resolve to find Àjàpá and make him pay with his life for his terrible crime.

As for Àjàpá, he had no doubt about what Ekùn's reaction would be on discovering what sort of plaiting job he had done on the children. So when he crawled out of the enclosure during the night he made as fast as he could for the nearby town, which had for several days been in a bustle in preparation for the festival that marked the annual visit of the spirits of the dead ancestors. He initially thought that losing himself among the crowd would be the safest way to avoid Ekùn's ire, but, characteristically, his indefatigable brain came up with an even better idea.

The spirits of departed ancestors materialized annually in masquerades. Their hosts plied them with the best of what they had: the choicest of foods and drinks, and a rich assortment of gifts. Most important to Àjàpá was the consideration that their physical forms were sacrosanct; whoever sought to look beneath their masquerades courted certain death, as did any creature who was so irreverent as to touch them. Àjàpá went home and made himself a shroud that would transform him into a visiting spirit. When the grand day arrived and the whole community had assembled before the palace, with the *oba* resplendent on his throne, Àjàpá assumed a royally slow gait and approached the gathering singing:

Hail your oba'*s father come to earth!*
Worship him!
Your guest from above,
Worship your oba'*s father!*

35

Since his death, the *oba*'s father had not made the trip back to earth, as far as his royal son knew, anyway. The *oba* was therefore understandably overjoyed that he had finally returned. He rose from his throne and half danced, half ran to meet his august visitor. He fell prostrate before the spirit, expressing his happiness and asking for blessings. Àjàpá placed his hand on the royal head and mumbled some blessings on it. The *oba* rose happily to his feet and conducted the spirit to the throne. Thereafter the festivities became virtually a celebration of this one spirit's visit, for when the others arrived they caused as much excitement as anticlimaxes are wont to do.

The *oba* and his subjects could not think of enough presents to offer the heavenly visitor; in a trice foods and assorted gifts formed a small mountain before Àjàpá. To add to Àjàpá's pleasure, as he surveyed the crowd, his eyes alighted on Ekùn, glancing wildly this way and that, obviously in search of the object of his retribution. Àjàpá's instinct for mischief was aroused again; he beckoned the *oba* and said softly that nothing would please him more than to honor Ekùn by asking him to sit at the foot of the throne and serve him. This was completely understandable, since the spirits may not expose any part of their bodies; it was necessary, therefore, for someone else to lift food to his mouth. The *oba* immediately gave the order.

Ekùn's grief was mitigated by this rare honor of being singled out from among all the creatures present to serve the visiting spirit, and he performed his duties conscientiously, despite the visitor's strange habit of each time almost biting off the fingers that introduced the food into his mouth, and occasionally spitting on Ekùn's head as a blessing, and bidding him massage the spit into his skull. When the visitor began talking about Ekùn's children, however, especially about how their recent death was not altogether a loss, he became suspicious. He knew a great deal about Àjàpá and would put nothing past him, not even the impersonation of a spirit. But he had no way of ascertaining the true identity of the spirit of the *oba*'s dead father.

Time does not stretch endlessly into the distance, however, and the time soon came for the festivities to end and for the spirits to depart again for their heavenly abode. But whereas it was customary for the visitors to take their leave burdened only by what they had been able to consume, the spirit of the *oba*'s dead father broke precedence and ordered that the food he had been unable to eat and all the other presents given to him be wrapped in a bundle and given to Ekùn to deliver to a certain location in the bush as a sacrifice. The *oba* assured him that his order would be carried out, and Àjàpá took his leave amidst much fanfare.

Once out of sight of the revelers, Àjàpá quickly rid himself of his shroud and hurried to the place he designated in the bush to await Ekùn's delivery of his booty. Before long he saw his unwitting servant arrived with it. But if he had thought the latter would simply deposit the load and make himself scarce he was mistaken; Ekùn had apparently concocted his own scheme. As Àjàpá watched unseen, he untied the bundle and crawled inside, loosely pulling the mouth shut after himself. Àjàpá immediately realized what the game was and prudently remained where he was, pondering what to do next.

His feet might not make much of an impression in the soil, yet the gods did not begrudge Àjàpá intelligence. As noiselessly as he could, he emerged from his hiding place and approached the bundle from the end opposite the mouth. When he was well positioned, he quickly grabbed the drawstring and secured the opening in such a way that Ekùn could not get out unaided. Too late, Ekùn realized his folly and began to struggle, but Àjàpá held fast. Ekùn struggled mightily, but even the strongest of animals tires in time. His struggling became weaker and weaker, until at last he was motionless. Then, tying the sack even more securely, Àjàpá heaved it onto his back and started for home. When he came to the forge, he asked if the blacksmith would do him the favor of pounding the load a few times on his anvil to make it settle better. The smith kindly obliged. When he arrived at the place where cloth merchants were smoothing their cloths with cudgels on blocks of wood, he asked the same favor, and they also obliged.

When finally he came upon women pounding dried yams in a mortar, he asked if they would deliver a few blows to his load with their pestles. They too obliged. Satisfied that he had nothing any longer to fear from his load, Àjàpá carried it home, knowing that for a few more days at least he would not go hungry.

Once home, he gave thanks to the spirit of his dead father and thought how true the saying was that a cow that lacks a tail can count on the gods to keep pestering flies away from him.

Appetite

Àjàpá and the Àkàrà Hawker

Àjàpá lived in a town whose fame was widespread, for it counted among those who dwelled in it a woman who made her living by frying and selling *àkàrà*. So incomparably delicious were these delicacies that people came from the towns and villages all around to patronize her and to marvel at the wonders she performed with ingredients as ordinary as black-eyed beans and seasoning. For the benefit of those unable to make the trip to her stall she sent her young daughter on a round of the neighboring villages with trayfuls of *àkàrà* to sell. As she made the trip between the towns and villages, and through their streets, the young girl called out loudly to prospective customers:

Here it comes, delicious àkàrà!
Get yours while it's still hot!

All who knew Àjàpá knew also of his unmanageable appetite, but they did not know that even more unmanageable was his craving for *àkàrà*. Another claim he had to fame was his shiftlessness, because of which he rarely had the wherewithal to purchase food or anything else. As far as the legendary *àkàrà* was concerned, therefore, while he could and did avidly devour it with his eyes, his lips had no opportunity to close on even one tiny piece. But Àjàpá would not be Àjàpá if he did not consider himself called upon to think up a means, however devious, of eating as much *àkàrà* as he wished without paying for any of it. Knowing that the young *àkàrà* hawker always made her rounds of the neighboring towns and villages all by herself, Àjàpá was certain that relieving her of her wares would present no great difficulty, and he vowed to do just that.

He set to work piecing dried, dead leaves together and making for himself a body-concealing shroud. He also strung together bells made from snail shells to tie around his legs and those of his wife and children. When all was ready, he took his family to the bush along the path the hawker usually took, and there, after he had thoroughly coached them on what he expected of them, they hid and waited.

In due course the young girl came walking down the path, loudly proclaiming the otherworldly virtues of her *àkàrà*:

> *Here it comes, delicious* àkàrà!
> *Food fit for the gods.*
> *It puts hunger to flight.*
> *Get yours while it's still hot!*

Àjàpá remained in concealment in his strange regalia until the girl was almost abreast, then he jumped suddenly into the path right in front of her and began dancing, with a great deal of foot stamping. His concealed family increased the racket by stamping their feet also, such that the bush came alive with the loud clanking of snail shells and the stamping of many feet. Above the din Àjàpá sang nasally:

> *Yield the path to the lord of leaves!*
> *Palm-oil sellers, stay away,*
> Àkàrà *sellers, do likewise.*
> *The path belongs to the lord of leaves!*

The poor girl had never before seen such a sight, and never in her brief life had she known the bush to produce such sounds as it now did. In her frightened escape from the suddenly weird scene, she paid no mind to what happened to her tray of *àkàrà;* she ran so hard that her heels stamped out a tattoo on the back of her head.

When she arrived home, nearly fainting from lack of breath, she haltingly told her mother of her strange encounter.

"A spirit blocked my path," she panted, "and the forest began to shake!"

The mother was first incredulous, then furious. She wondered if her daughter had learned some wayward tricks, either to get out of her usual chore or perhaps to consume her *àkàrà* with some newfound friends.

"Where did the spirit come from?" she demanded. "What fool put you up to such a frivolous story?"

The poor girl protested that she spoke the truth, but her mother remained unconvinced. Whatever the girl's ruse was, she was determined to wean her daughter from it in no uncertain terms.

"Your talk smells of madness!" she snapped. "And when madness lodges in a child's breast, a good whipping dislodges it."

With that she went for her whip and applied it zestfully to the hapless young girl, who tearfully but vainly tried to convince her mother that she spoke the truth.

"You will go back to sell *àkàrà* again tomorrow," the mother told her after the flogging, "and you would be wise not to see any weird spirit or hear any noise from the forest."

The following day the girl set out on her journey with much trepidation, dreading the possibility of a repeat of the previous day's fright and knowing that if there was a repetition she could not count on comfort and sympathy when she got home. Since it was Àjàpá's nature to exploit every trick repeatedly and relentlessly as long as it worked, he and his family were waiting for the unfortunate girl at the same place, and once again, she discarded her load and fled. Fortunately for her, her mother found it difficult to believe that she would repeat the trick for which she had been so severely flogged only the previous day. There must be something to her story, she concluded. She resolved to see with her own eyes what new thing had lately come to threaten her livelihood.

When the next day broke, the *àkàrà* seller fried a batch, arranged them in a tray, and set it on her daughter's head. Then, girding her waist tightly with her head scarf, as women do when they go into battle, she told her daughter to lead the way, and resolutely followed.

Àjàpá was waiting as usual with his family, and when he judged that his sudden emergence would have the maximum impact on the two wayfarers he leaped from the bush, his concealed family began making their din, and he commenced to stamp his feet and to sing:

Yield the path to the lord of leaves!
Palm-oil sellers, stay away,
Àkàrà sellers, do likewise.
The path belongs to the lord of leaves!

The effect of the sight and the sound on the mother was no different from what it had been on her daughter. In both hearts and souls was the urge, "If you are of a mind to tarry, get out of my way!" Neither stopped until both had gained the safety of their home.

After they had recovered their breath and rested, the mother announced that the new apparition in their town, the strange new thing that was preventing normal commerce with neighboring communities, was something the *oba* must hear about, especially since the welfare of the community was his responsibility. With her daughter in tow, she went to the palace and gave an account of their strange experiences to the *oba* and his chiefs-in-council. The council deliberated for a while, and then the *Basòrun* said what was in most minds.

"Some matters human minds might peer into for long and yet see nothing."

"Indeed!" the others agreed.

"This is one such matter."

"So it is."

"*Kábíyèsí,*" he said, addressing the *oba*, "I say we leave it to the master of mysteries whose eyes see beyond ours."

The *oba* agreed and sent for the *babaláwo*.

On his arrival, the *babaláwo* listened to the woman's account, nodding and smiling knowingly as she spoke. When she was done, he cast the sixteen palm-nuts he had brought with him several times and studied the patterns they formed. Satisfied with the message they conveyed, he announced that the agent the *oba* wanted was the one-legged Òsanyìn, who was well known to be incomparable as far as medicine and charms were concerned, and who among the Òsanyìn alone had the knowledge and the means to solve the problem. The *oba* accordingly sent an urgent summons to the one-legged Òsanyìn.

The creature was soon before the *oba* and his chiefs, and on learning why they had sent for him, the Òsanyìn confidently assured them that he would rid them of the trouble that plagued their town. In three days, when the sun stood directly above the head in the sky, he would dispatch the mysterious nuisance.

On the appointed day, according to the Òsanyìn's instructions the àkàrà woman fried a generous amount of àkàrà, which she arranged on a tray and placed on her daughter's head as usual. They then set out for the forest. The Òsanyìn, armed with a long, sharp-tipped iron spike, trailed them out of sight. Emboldened by the knowledge that the Òsanyìn was nearby the girl lustily advertised her ware, and on cue the apparition jumped out of the bush and began its antics, accompanied as usual by the loud commotion from inside the bush.

Àjàpá was not entirely wrong in his assumption that his trick would work again, for the two women lost heart again and fled, leaving the load of àkàrà behind. In his overconfidence Àjàpá did not bother to ascertain that he and his family alone remained in the area before he discarded his shroud and made for the àkàrà. But as he stretched his neck to sniff at the abandoned food, the lurking Òsanyìn lounged at him and impaled his neck with the sharp spike.

Àjàpá screamed in pain and struggled to get free, but to no avail. Still concealed, the rest of his family saw what was happening and took advantage of the Òsanyìn's preoccupation with their husband and father to make their escape.

"You've got me, you've got me," he pleaded, "but spare my life, please!"

The *Òsanyìn* was, however, in no mood to listen. He held his victim pinned to the earth until he was lifeless. In triumph, he bore the carcass like a trophy through the town and to the palace, where the grateful *oba* decreed that henceforth the sacrifice for invoking an *Òsanyìn* would be a live *àjàpá*.

Thus ended the threat to the *àkàrà* seller's livelihood and the danger that those who lived in the town and nearby would be deprived of the treat to which they had become accustomed.

Àjàpá and the
Roasted-Peanut Seller

There once lived in Àjàpá's town a woman famous for the incredible, mouth-watering roasted peanuts she prepared and sold at the daily market. Each day market people waited expectantly for the breeze to waft the aroma of roasting peanuts to their nostrils, signaling them either to make their way to the woman's stall or to send a child or servant to purchase some of the treat. They simply would not feel right about starting their day until they had satisfied the craving the irresistible aroma unfailingly provoked in them.

There was no more faithful market-goer than Àjàpá, not because he had anything to sell, for he was incurably lazy and incapable of addressing himself to any productive venture, nor because he had anything to buy, for without producing anything he lacked the means to purchase anything. No, he was religiously at the market each day because he could always find some compassionate trader to extend some alms to him. Yet each day at the market was also torture to him, because like everybody else his gullet involuntarily commenced to swallow emptiness whenever the smell of roasted peanuts reached his nose. Unfortunately, that was one commodity no one seemed willing to share with him, and the peanut seller was herself a hard-hearted woman as far as Àjàpá was concerned. Nothing he did, no plea he made softened her to offer him even a taste of her peanuts.

"You made no gash on the palm-tree, nor did you sling a shot to pierce the pate of the wine-producing tree; yet go to its base and expectantly up-

lift your open mouth. Do you think palm-wine flows of its own accord?"
she sneered at him in response to his importunity.

The scolding was salt on Àjàpá's wounded pride, and being who he was,
it was not long before his frustration and anger triggered his propensity for
mischief, and he set about devising a way to get his fill of the delicious
peanuts despite the mean seller. He sought out Òkété the Giant Rat, who
was renowned for his great burrowing prowess, and asked what it would
take to get him to dig a tunnel from the nearby forest to the peanut
woman's stall in the market. Òkété assured Àjàpá that if the latter would
provide him with a sackful of palm-nuts he could consider the job as good
as done. For once Àjàpá submitted himself to the necessity of self-exertion;
he scoured the bases of tens of palm-trees in the forests around, gathering
the nuts scattered thereabouts, and before long he had the sackful to pay
Òkété. The latter lost no time in setting to work as he promised, and in no
more than two days the tunnel was ready, its mouth right by the peanut
seller's seat. Under cover of night Àjàpá sneaked into the market and concealed the opening with dried leaves so expertly that no one could suspect
its presence. That done, he went home to await the propitious time when, as
he told himself, the boil that had long plagued him would at last be lanced.

At daybreak, market-goers flocked to their stalls as usual, and so did the
peanut seller. The day had dawned like any other, offering no hint that it
harbored any surprise for the traders, but Àjàpá had installed himself at
the mouth of the tunnel just below the leaf covering, armed with his drum
and ready to act as soon as his nostrils announced to him the moment. He
could not see any of the above-ground activity from his concealment, but
he could hear it all. From there his keen nose registered the progress of
the peanut roasting, and when he was satisfied that the seller had roasted
a sufficiently large amount, he applied the stick to his drum and launched
into song:

Peanut seller, do lend an ear,
Crackle, crackle, pop!

Peanut seller, please hear my song,
Crackle, crackle, pop!
Shouldn't you be dancing?
Crackle, crackle, pop!
Yield yourself to my music,
Crackle, crackle, pop!
Leave your stall in my care,
Crackle, crackle, pop!
You really should be dancing!
Crackle, crackle, pop!
Peanuts, crackling and popping,
Crackle, crackle, pop!
Peanuts, popping and crackling,
Crackle, crackle, pop!

Had Àjàpá but known it, and had he not been perversely addicted to idleness, he would have acknowledged his true calling and lived gainfully by it. For in truth few creatures were capable of making music as irresistible as his, music that could set the most reluctant feet dancing with abandon in spite of themselves. The effect of his performance on the peanut seller, on her customers, and indeed on everybody in the market was as Àjàpá hoped. All gave way to dance with such vigor that they were soon enveloped in a cloud of dust, and in the time it would take a crab to blink their momentum had carried them almost to the other end of town. It did not matter that the music that got them dancing had long stopped, and they had danced so far from its source anyway that they could not have heard it even if it had not. Befuddled and shamefaced, they returned like suddenly sober drunkards to the market, where they found the peanut seller's roasted nuts completely gone. No other stall had been disturbed.

She raised the alarm, and people quickly established a connection between the new musical phenomenon that had intruded into their midst and the disappearance of the peanuts. They had no option in such cir-

49

cumstances but to report the incident to the *oba,* in whose charge the welfare of the town lay.

Since the market was close to his palace, occupying a large open expanse in front of it, in fact, the *oba* had himself been aware of the unusual commotion, and he was therefore not entirely surprised when his people trooped into his courtyard and asked for an urgent audience. On hearing the peanut seller's story he concluded that the culprit must be a clever rascal, a daytime rogue with a taste for roasted peanuts. He consulted with his chiefs, who advised him to assign the task of apprehending the culprit and preventing a repetition of the visitation to the seasoned hunters of the town, whose task was also to keep thieves and burglars at bay.

Dutifully, then, all the hunters gathered on the market day following, sporting their fearful weapons and festooned with powerful amulets and charms. However intrepid the rascal, he was about to discover the mettle of the town's hunters, they vowed. A huge crowd, much larger than usually found at the market, had gathered to witness the confrontation between hunters and peanut fiend. The hunters kept the crowd back as best they could, positioned themselves around the peanut stall, and asked the seller to commence her usual activities. She obliged and began to roast peanuts, but for a while nothing happened. Then, after she had roasted a sizable heap of nuts, and just as the hunters and some in the crowd were becoming convinced that the phantom singer had allowed good sense to master his wayward appetite, the singing began:

Peanut seller, do lend an ear,
Crackle, crackle, pop!
Peanut seller, please hear my song,
Crackle, crackle, pop!
Shouldn't you be dancing?
Crackle, crackle, pop!
Yield yourself to my music,
Crackle, crackle, pop!

Leave your stall in my care,
Crackle, crackle, pop!
You really should be dancing!
Crackle, crackle, pop!
Peanuts, crackling and popping,
Crackle, crackle, pop!
Peanuts, popping and crackling,
Crackle, crackle, pop!

When some time later the hunters came to their senses and found themselves amidst the market crowd, bereft of their weapons, medicines, and charms, they knew something had gone badly awry. On looking around and recognizing their whereabouts, the end of town farthest from the market, they could not look one another in the face. This time the townspeople had no need to be embarrassed; rather they directed their mirthful ridicule at the hunters, making snide remarks about weapons that were no better than dancing staffs. The whole crowd trooped back to the market to find what they knew they would find: a depleted stock of peanuts.

The hunters' disgrace convinced the *oba* of the severity of the problem on his hands. If his hunters were powerless against the mysterious thief, perhaps he was no mere human after all; perhaps the creature was an *iwin*, a fairy. With that suspicion in mind he sought the intervention of his diviners and medicine men. They gathered at the market on the next market day bristling with their own charms and assorted paraphernalia, all ready to make an end of whatever it was that plagued their town, or at least teach it to give it a wide berth thenceforward. When the singing began, however, not even these masters of mysteries could control themselves. They surrendered to the music just as all the others had done before them.

Once sober again, the town was thrown into a panic, for even though the mysterious musical creature seemed interested only in peanuts, it nevertheless kept everyone from their trading. Moreover, any phenomenon that could humble the trusted hunters and medicine men could also wreak greater havoc on the town if it chose. It had to be stopped. The *oba* could think of nowhere else to turn but to the *Òsanyìn* clan. These were humanlike spirits endowed with great magical powers, and they regularly held commerce with humans as trouble-solvers of last resort, especially when the trouble involved other spirits. In appearance they were very much like humans, differing only with regard to how many legs they had: whereas humans normally had two, an *Òsanyìn* could have as many as ten legs and as few as one, but they could not have two, for a two-legged *Òsanyìn* would hardly be distinguishable from a human. When the *oba* turned to them for help, the ten-legged patriarch *Òsanyìn* assured him that he and his town would be rid of the music-playing, peanut-stealing wonder the next day. He gave instructions for the peanut seller and other marketers to carry out their routine the following day and leave matters to him.

The patriarch assigned the task first to the three-legged *Òsanyìn*, the one-legged one being considered so handicapped that the idea of his confronting the phenomenon was thought ludicrous. The next morning the first creature at the market was the prospective hero of the day, the three-legged *Òsanyìn*. Before anyone else arrived he pronounced fearsome incantations on the peanut seller's stall and its vicinity, incantations designed to confuse and paralyze any wayward spirit that might venture near there. In time the market filled up, this time with the *oba* and his councilors in attendance. They would not miss the confrontation of spirits, nor a sight of the thing that had so disrupted the life of the town these past few days.

When all was ready, the *Òsanyìn* gave the word, and the peanut seller began roasting her peanuts. For a while nothing happened, until she had filled her calabash with a sizable mound of roasted peanuts, and the aroma suffused the air of the whole town. Then the music commenced:

Peanut seller, do lend an ear,
Crackle, crackle, pop!
Peanut seller, please hear my song,
Crackle, crackle, pop!

Shouldn't you be dancing?
Crackle, crackle, pop!
Yield yourself to my music,
Crackle, crackle, pop!
Leave your stall in my care,
Crackle, crackle, pop!
You really should be dancing!
Crackle, crackle, pop!
Peanuts, crackling and popping,
Crackle, crackle, pop!
Peanuts, popping and crackling,
Crackle, crackle, pop!

The Òsanyìn danced so hard that he danced two of his legs off, and the *oba* and his councilors were indistinguishable from the ordinary people when the effects of the music wore off and they found themselves well away from the market.

Unable to bear the disgrace, the Òsanyìn clan went into conclave and vowed to bring the musical spirit to heel or permanently remove themselves from the vicinity of the town. They sent the four-legged Òsanyìn into the fray, but he also proved a failure; *he* lost three legs! The same fate befell the five-legged Òsanyìn and then the six-legged. To make a long story short, all the others, including the most powerful of them all, the ten-legged patriarch Òsanyìn, failed in their confrontation with the musical phenomenon, and they prepared to remove themselves into disgraceful exile.

Now the *oba* himself was in a panic. The chief duty the ancestors entrusted to him was to keep the town and the community secure, and on his departure from this life to hand them in full security to his successor. If in his time the town was laid waste because some unknown creature disrupted its life, what report would he give to those who preceded him when he was reunited with them in afterlife? But just when he felt most hopeless, the *oba* found the one-legged Òsanyìn standing before him.

"The crown will live long on your head, your Majesty," he greeted the *oba*.

"So be it," the latter responded rather listlessly.

"The shoes will stay long on your feet," the Òsanyìn continued.

"So be it," the *oba* responded again, almost showing his impatience at this visit from one of the failed clan of Òsanyìn. He had too much on his mind for pleasantries.

"You have a message for me, perhaps, from the rest of your kin?" he asked.

"No, your Majesty," the visitor responded. "I came on my own."

"Well . . . ?"

"It is about the nuisance that's causing you and your town all this trouble."

"Yes?" the *oba* said questioningly.

"I will catch and deliver him to you," the Òsanyìn said matter-of-factly.

"You?" the *oba* asked, hardly able to keep the incredulity from his voice. There was a glint in his eyes, but one of wonderment. The creature *was* serious, but he was also being ridiculous, the *oba* thought. As the saying went, if an àgó, the smartest of rats, fell victim to the snare, what chance had the olósè, the most sluggish of rodents?

"I know what you are thinking, your Majesty," his visitor said. "The Òsanyìn who had more limbs than I failed at the task, so how can I accomplish it? Remember, though, the needle may be tiny, but it is nothing for a chick to swallow. Let me at the troublesome wretch. If I succeed, you are well rid of the nuisance. If I fail, you would hardly be any worse off than you are now."

The *oba* considered the offer and consulted with the chiefs sitting around him. In the end he agreed with his visitor. Since the town stood to lose nothing from the Òsanyìn's try, he might as well be given an opportunity to prove himself. He needed three days to prepare, he said, after which he would be at the market to take on the musical nuisance.

When the appointed day arrived, the market was so crowded that there was no room for one more foot or one more arm. In the crowd were the Òsanyìn whose earlier efforts had failed, very angry and present only in anticipation of the pleasure of laughing at their overreaching, upstart kin. The one-legged Òsanyìn had come armed with a sharp iron spike and nothing else—nothing, that is, except the cotton he had stuffed into his ears. He stuck his iron spike into the peanut seller's fire until its tip glowed white-hot. Then he instructed the woman to commence roasting peanuts. Soon there was a small mountain of roasted peanuts in the calabash, and as the crowd had expected, the music started:

Peanut seller, do lend an ear,
Crackle, crackle, pop!
Peanut seller, please hear my song,
Crackle, crackle, pop!
Shouldn't you be dancing?
Crackle, crackle, pop!
Yield yourself to my music,
Crackle, crackle, pop!
Leave your stall in my care,
Crackle, crackle, pop!
You really should be dancing!
Crackle, crackle, pop!
Peanuts, crackling and popping,
Crackle, crackle, pop!
Peanuts, popping and crackling,
Crackle, crackle, pop!

As usual, the whole assemblage succumbed to dancing, including even the other Òsanyìn whose restored limbs had not quite healed. Very soon all that could be seen of the dancers was the cloud of dust that trailed them as their gyrating movements carried them farther and farther away. As for the one-legged Òsanyìn, having stuffed his ears with cotton he heard none of the music, and having one leg only, he would not have felt the urge to dance, anyway. He spared only one glance for the disappearing crowd before riveting his eyes again on the stall.

Soon he noticed the ground moving under the peanut seller's abandoned seat. Carefully, he withdrew his iron spike from the fire and held it ready to strike. In a short while Àjàpá had cleared the dry-leaf covering over the hole and was in plain sight. His eyes and mind were so fixed on the peanuts that he paid no attention to whatever or whoever else might be around as he closed in on them—until he felt a powerful, muscle-jerking, burning, piercing sensation in his nose. He writhed in pain, but his adversary was unrelenting. The Òsanyìn's spike went all the way through Àjàpá's nose and impaled him to the ground. He screamed and squirmed painfully, but the Òsanyìn showed no mercy. Àjàpá became weaker and weaker, until, satisfied that there was little fight left in him, the Òsanyìn relaxed his pressure, lifted him up, and carried him to the oba's palace.

There Àjàpá was put on display for the returning crowd to see. No one would believe that Àjàpá could have had such powers on them, but they had the testimony of their eyes, the words of the oba and the Òsanyìn, and the confession of the culprit himself. As for Àjàpá's fate, the oba decreed that it was only fitting that he spend the rest of his life serving the agent who proved powerful enough to apprehend him.

Thus Àjàpá became a servant to the Òsanyìn, and thus it came to be that to this day the sacrifice offered to an Òsanyìn is a tortoise. If anyone ever heard Àjàpá's speech he or she would notice its pronounced nasality, the enduring legacy of the Òsanyìn's spike.

Àjàpá and the Dawn Bird

Although Àjàpá seldom had anything to buy or sell, he religiously attended the market, believing that one never knew when, as the saying went, things might unexpectedly do right by one's mouth. As he strolled among the stalls one day, he was startled to see in the palm-oil area a young woman he had never seen before. What startled him was her appearance: she was the be-all and end-all in terms of beauty, and her comportment spoke of good breeding in a good home. Àjàpá resolved immediately that he would find out where she lived. He found himself a seat from which he could keep his eyes on her, and waited for the close of the market. When toward nightfall the market was over, those who had homes to go to headed for home, those who had paths to follow took to the paths, and the girl set out to return whence she came. Àjàpá too shook the dust from his seat and followed her.

For some distance, traffic was heavy enough along the path for Àjàpá to be inconspicuous. But gradually the wayfarers dropped off as they arrived at their destinations, until only the girl remained, followed, of course, by Àjàpá. She was aware of another presence on the path, which now led to her town and nowhere else, and she became curious about the other person's identity. Perhaps some neighbor of hers had been at the market without her knowing? When she looked back and saw that her companion was Àjàpá, she was puzzled. What business could he have in her town? He had never been there before; if he had she would know, because his reputation made a great deal of noise.

Thinking that the gathering dusk had perhaps played a trick on her vision she stopped to have a better look, and to her greater puzzlement the figure stepped quickly into the roadside bush, but not before she was able to confirm that her companion was indeed Àjàpá. Her puzzlement quickly became apprehension. Why did he jump into the bush? Had his presence on the path anything to do with her? The thought was most unwelcome to her, and she quickened her pace to increase the distance between them.

The faster the girl walked, the faster Àjàpá did, too, frustrating her desire to shake him off. In the end she gave up the effort, determined to confront him and discover what he was about. She would not wait until whatever trouble he represented materialized; if one does not want a twig in one's eye, one looks out for it from a distance. When she rounded a bend and was temporarily out of Àjàpá's view, she quickly stepped off the path and waited. As he came by, she emerged suddenly from hiding, causing the unsuspecting Àjàpá to jump almost out of his shell.

"What sort of game is this?" he demanded, trying to recover his wits.

"It is a game called 'Where are you bound?'" she responded.

Àjàpá quickly regained his composure and set his mind to work.

"Bound?" he queried.

"Where are you going?" she clarified.

"Going? Where else would I be going?"

"This path leads to only one place," she said, "and you could not be on your way there."

"And why not?"

"It is a town that is wary of strangers, especially strangers of a certain stripe," she said. "You will find no welcome there."

"What kind of land is it that rejects visitors?" Àjàpá asked.

"A land whose inhabitants value their peace. Wherever you go, Àjàpá, trouble is never far behind."

Àjàpá made a great show of injury.

"Now, is that a way to talk to someone you have never met?" he whined. "Only kind words should issue from the mouth of beauty. I came this far out of my way because when I saw you in the market I told myself that any eyes that have seen you might as well cease their search for beauty."

Such words from Àjàpá did nothing to win the girl over but merely increased her apprehension. The last thing she wanted was attention from him. She pleaded with him to turn around and go back to his home.

"I invoke my mother's head to beg you to turn back," she pleaded. "When I left home this morning it was to sell my wares; let me not return home with something my arms cannot encircle."

Àjàpá would not be dissuaded. He complained that having come that far he could not very well turn around and go back, since it was almost dark and he would have to travel an unfamiliar road in darkness. If she did not appreciate the compliment he was paying her with his attention, then he would leave her alone and return home in the morning. But he would not travel a strange road alone at night. She must either agree to his accompanying her to her town, he said, or they would both spend the night right where they were.

After much arguing the girl came to appreciate even more the truth of Àjàpá's reputation as a walking disaster. There was nothing to do but give in to his company, but in doing so she warned him that his movements in the town would be strictly restricted: he could stay the night in a room in her home, but she would have to lock him in the room, and at the first light he must start for home. Àjàpá agreed to the conditions, and the two continued to the town.

It was dark when they arrived, and the girl had little difficulty in spiriting her troublesome visitor into her compound (a rather large one, to Àjàpá's surprise) without anyone seeing him. She showed him to the room he would occupy for the night, and before she left she gave him a stern warning.

"'That is our custom' in one town is taboo in another," she said. "Therefore, you must heed what I will now tell you."

Àjàpá assured her that he would.

59

The compound he was in, she informed him, housed the Dawn Bird. "I have nothing to do with birds," Àjàpá replied.

"This is no ordinary bird," she continued. "This bird marks the passing of time; he ushers in the morning when it is due and the night in its own time. He also has one taboo: when he calls, as he does at regular intervals, no one may make a sound."

Àjàpá assured her that he had no intention of conversing with strange birds, and that in any case he was too tired and too sleepy to be interested in birds.

Thus reassured, she locked him securely in the room, promising to return at the break of dawn to let him out.

Àjàpá's escapades had landed him in worse predicaments before; he did not quite like the thought of going to sleep without food, but he reminded himself that the dizziness of hunger will not make a sleeping person fall from a prone position. He arranged himself comfortably and waited for sleep.

The noises of daily living gradually died down outside, and the sounds of the night took over. Frogs croaked, and crickets chirruped, and an occasional bat flapped away in search of food. Sleep was long in coming to Àjàpá, for when hunger fills the stomach it blocks the eyes from sleep. Eventually, though, he felt an agreeable lightness spread though his limbs, all over his body, and into his head as sleep lifted him and began to carry him away. Just then a loud noise startled him from the arms of sleep and brought him crashing down with such force that his head almost exploded. A heavy beating noise was shaking the rafters, and when it stopped there came the shrill announcement:

I am the bird,
I am the bird,
I am the bird that calls to the night.
I am the bird!

Àjàpá was angry that his sleep had been disturbed for such a senseless announcement. He could not imagine that the information was of any use to anyone, especially in the middle of the night. The more one traveled, he thought, the more strange things one encountered.

After grumbling for some time, he settled down again to try to sleep. But before sleep came the same noise repeated itself, and the same announcement rang out from the bird. To his dismay he recalled the girl's words that the bird called at regular intervals, and he knew that his night did not promise to be good—unless he could make it so himself. He tried all in his power to ignore the noise but failed. Trying to sleep eventually became futile, because his anticipation of the noise kept him on edge. Finally, he resolved that whatever might issue from his action would have to be endured; he would make the bird know that under the same roof with him was another creature whose name was Àjàpá.

The night plodded on, and soon it was time again for the bird's announcement. It came, preceded by the loud commotion:

I am the bird,
I am the bird,
I am the bird that calls to the night.
I am the bird!

As soon as it stopped Àjàpá pounded his chest and cried,

I am Àjàpá,
I am Àjàpá,
I am Àjàpá that eats the bird
That cries to the night.
I am Àjàpá.

Since the birth of time no one had been audacious enough to bandy words with the bird; when he heard the noise from Àjàpá, therefore, he thought that a new echo must have crept into the building. To be certain, he flapped his wings again and repeated his call, and when the response came again he knew that there was no echo. The world had become confused; something with no regard for taboos had invaded the compound.

For the bird, only one course of action was possible: he must destroy the miscreant and restore proper order. He reared his head and with his enormous beak struck a blow that knocked down the wall in the direction of the noise. But the room beyond it was empty. He called again, and again the response came, this time a little louder. He knocked down the next wall and repeated his call; this time also the answer came, yet louder than the last time. Three more walls, and the bird knew that now only one separated him from the source of the abomination. He flapped his wings once more and called:

I am the bird,
I am the bird,
I am the bird that calls to the night.
I am the bird!

Before he was quite done the response came as clearly as though its author stood right by the bird:

I am Àjàpá,
I am Àjàpá,
I am Àjàpá that eats the bird
That calls in the night.
I am Àjàpá!

The bird demolished the last wall and came face to face with his adversary. They measured each other with their eyes. When the bird saw Àjàpá, his anger turned to disgust. Why, he thought, the creature was not much more than the sort of thing he might use to adorn his tail plumage.

"Did you not learn," he asked Àjàpá, "that whoever or whatever answers the Dawn Bird pays with his life?"

"Did you not learn," Àjàpá asked in return, "that whoever disturbs Àjàpá's rest answers to him?"

Unaccustomed to such impudence, the bird was momentarily nonplussed; could there be anything else to this wretched and scrawny creature than met the eye? he wondered. Whatever it was, thought the bird, it would perish with the rascal.

"The day a flame stumbles upon water is the day its life ends," he told Àjàpá. "Yours has so stumbled, and your end has come."

With that he spread his wings and made to pounce on his prey, but the latter startled him with a sharp, "Stop!"

"Have you no regard for the innocent people sleeping in the compound?" Àjàpá asked. "Must they lose their sleep because you lack self-control? I will match my strength against yours, but I will not fight here."

The bird considered his words and found some sense in them. Besides, he thought, he could concede to Àjàpá the right to choose his own grave.

"Where, then?" he asked.

"In the marshes," Àjàpá replied.

"The marshes it is," the bird agreed, becoming impatient because the night had not stood still since the disturbance occurred, and his duties awaited him.

He led the way to the marshes on the outskirts of the town. There Àjàpá found himself a spot that suited his strategy and awaited the bird's move. Anxious to put a timely end to the aggravating episode, the bird lifted its wings and charged at his adversary. Àjàpá held his ground. The bird closed on him, lifted his beak high in the air, and brought it down with such force as could crush a rock. Had the blow landed on Àjàpá this tale would have been much different, but the day of his death had not arrived. Just at the last moment he skipped aside, and the bird's beak, instead of striking him, sank deep into the mud, along with his head and half of the neck.

Àjàpá gave him no opportunity to recover. Instantly, he picked up a rock, and whenever the bird tried to extract his neck from the cloying mud, he drove it back in with a blow from the rock. The bird was soon dead.

The excitement of the fight over, Àjàpá remembered that he had been deprived of dinner, and marveled at the unexpected ways the spirit of his dead father supplied his wants. How true the saying that the Creator who made the mouth horizontal knew all the while how he would fill it! He gathered some wood and prepared a fire to roast the bird, then he settled down to a feast that ended only when he had consumed every bit of meat on his victim's bones and sucked the last trace of marrow from them. Then he gathered the feathers and headed back to the inhospitable town. There he went from door to door, placing one feather outside each house. By the time his supply ran out he was so fatigued that he did not much care where he lay himself down and yielded to deathlike slumber.

The town inhabitants knew that something was amiss when even the sleepiest sloth had no more sleep left in his eyes and yet the light of dawn did not brighten the sky. The people of the Dawn Bird's compound slowly realized that they had not heard his call for some time and went to investigate. When they saw the shambles but no bird, they thought he must have gone berserk and escaped. The news spread quickly, and the townspeople gathered to consider what to do. Then came the report from each household of strange feathers outside every door.

There was much debate about the significance of the events. Some suspected the worst, but none was willing to speak it. But when the girl who had let Àjàpá into the compound confessed what she had done, they thought that their worst fears were probably justified. A witch announces its presence one day and a child dies mysteriously the next day; what more evidence does one need to conclude that the death is the doing of the witch? The disappearance of the bird after Àjàpá's arrival in the town could not be a mere coincidence. The order went out that all approaches to the town be sealed and Àjàpá apprehended. In the meantime, the elders consulted the oracle to learn what sacrifices they must offer to induce day to break again.

Àjàpá was still sleeping off dinner when the searchers found him. They took him to the town common, where everybody had gathered to see the sacrilegious criminal and to lend a hand, perhaps, in paying him his due. He was duly arraigned before the assembly and told what the accusation against him was. He of course feigned ignorance and berated the people for falsely accusing him because he was a stranger. Where was their common sense, he asked? Were they so distracted by the disappearance of their bird that they had also lost all ability to think?

"Look at me," he invited, "do I look as though I have the strength to kill your bird?"

It occurred to no one to ask how he knew how much strength would suffice to kill the bird; they merely compared his size to the bird's and began to doubt that they had the real criminal. Taking advantage of the doubt and confusion, those who had secret grudges against others accused them of probably having a hand in the bird's disappearance. The assembly was about to degenerate into pandemonium when the elders decided on a sure-fire means of settling the matter. The ways of the town provided that in circumstances such as the present one, the truth must be determined through an ordeal by boiling oil.

In a trice a large cauldron was placed on a huge fire in the middle of the common, and the oil in it was brought to a rolling boil. All suspects, including Àjàpá, were brought forward and made one at a time to take a cup of oil and drink it down. In turn each drank the cup, and, being innocent, survived.

The crowd fell silent when it was finally Àjàpá's turn. He was the last suspect, and if all the others had survived, must he not therefore be the culprit? He stepped forward, but instead of going to the cauldron he turned to the crowd.

"I know," he declared, "that you all believe that I killed your bird. I know also that even if I survive this ordeal some of you will say that I did, not because I was innocent but because I used a trick. I am all alone in your midst, and who does not know that the snake that travels alone invites attacks with a machete? But I will make it difficult for anyone to accuse me of playing a trick."

Having said that, he stepped to the cauldron and dipped a cup of boiling oil. Again, instead of drinking it he carried it to the assembled people and showed it around, all the while singing,

Look into Àjàpá's cup—
Àjàpá took the full measure.

Slowly he walked completely around the circle, and each person looking into his cup agreed that it was indeed full. By the time he had completed the circuit, his palms told him that the oil was safe to drink, and he
gulped it down.

The assembly waited for him to drop dead, but no such thing happened.
Instead, he flew into a well-practiced rage and ranted all over the common
claiming that his reputation had been ruined, and that the people had un-
justly endangered his life. The whole world would know, he swore, how
the town treated strangers.

The elders broke into another panic. A town's treatment of strangers
said a great deal about it, and if its reputation in that regard was besmirched
the elders bore the blame. They consulted anxiously about what to do, but
no one seemed to have a good idea, until there came a thin cry from a
small boy.

"I know what Àjàpá wants," the youth called over Àjàpá's ranting.

"And what is that?" an elder asked.

"*Èbe, àsáró,* yam pottage," the boy announced triumphantly.

As soon as Àjàpá heard the mention of his favorite food, his rage evap-
orated. He became all smiles and ran to pat the boy on the head.

The townspeople were so relieved to get off so lightly that they very
gladly cooked a sizable pot of *èbe* and delivered it to Àjàpá. They were even
happier when he said that he would not eat it in their town but take it
home. The sooner he left, they thought, the better.

He carried the pot and left the town, thinking of taking his spoil home
and enjoying it at his leisure, but its aroma would not leave his nose in
peace. A short distance from the town and unable to hold off any longer,
he stepped into the bush and sought a rock to sit on. There he set the pot
down and prepared to eat the *èbe.*

In appreciation of the protection the spirit of his dead father had given him, he took some of the food and placed it on the rock, asking the spirit to accept it as a token of gratitude. He considered that the spirit of his dead mother also deserved some gratitude, and for it he placed another bit of *èbe* on the rock. Finally, he thought that the rock that offered him a place to sit deserved something, and he gave it also a bit of *èbe*. That done, he settled down and ate the rest.

Much sooner than he liked, the pot of *èbe* was empty. There was little he did not know about *èbe*, and he would swear that he had never tasted any nearly as delicious as the one he had just eaten. But, he consoled himself, there was nothing one ate that was not eventually finished. He would rest for a while and then resume his journey home.

As he rested his eyes wandered in spite of him to the shares of *èbe* he had left for the spirits of his dead father and mother and for the rock. He did not much like their distracting him from his rest, but he was too full to move to another spot. Soon his glances at the morsels lingered longer and longer, until at last an argument developed in his head.

If I had died in that town from drinking boiling oil, he asked himself, would the spirit of my dead father have died with me? The answer was clearly no; therefore, he took the spirit's share of *èbe* off the rock and ate it. He asked the same about the spirit of his dead mother, and since the answer was the same he ate its share, also. Lastly, because the rock would most certainly not have accompanied him in death he ate its share too. He was finally able to snooze.

When he had rested long enough, he thought it was time he went home and he made to rise from the rock. To his alarm, something held him down. He tried all he could, but he remained glued to the rock. He kicked, and strained, and pushed, but he could not free himself. Finally, in desperation he screamed, calling upon the spirit of his dead father for help. His screams resounded through the forest, and all the animals within hearing distance responded. But, looking at them Àjàpá thought it wise to protect his reputation, and he explained that he had heard the same noise they heard, but on arriving where he thought it came from he found no one. They accepted his explanation and dispersed.

The lie saved Àjàpá's face, but it did not cure his disease; he remained stuck to the rock. His desperation soon returned, and in spite of himself he screamed again, calling on his dead mother's spirit. The animals reassembled, but only to be told the same story. Once more they went their way.

There was, however, one animal for whom Àjàpá's explanation seemed suspicious. Ekùn the Leopard thought to himself, "Àjàpá is not known for his speed. How is it, then, that he always arrives first at the source of the noise?" To find the answer, instead of returning to his haunt he hid in a nearby bush where he could observe Àjàpá without himself being seen.

When all was quiet again, he saw Àjàpá look this way and that, then kick and strain and push, and eventually raise his head to scream for help. The animals responded again and Àjàpá began to repeat his story, but Ekùn stepped forward and stopped him short.

"If what you say is true," he said, "come with us to search the surrounding for the creature in distress."

Àjàpá was unable to respond, of course, so the two of them simply glared at each other. It quickly became clear to the other animals that Àjàpá could not move and that in fact what they had all heard were his screams for help. Because his past behavior had not endeared him to any of them, they felt no remorse at ridiculing him.

While the other animals teased Àjàpá and laughed at him, though, Ekùn set about freeing him. He dug his paws between Àjàpá and the rock and yanked. Àjàpá came unstuck, but some of his skin remained behind. Once free he did not pause to retrieve anything he might have dropped, but quickly scrambled away from his laughing audience. For his part, Ekùn rewarded himself by licking off what was left of Àjàpá on the rock.

He was free, but it was on that day that he came by the scars that caused the roughness of his shell.

Àjàpá's Sudden Baldness

No god matches the gullet in importance—that is what our fathers have established in their infinite wisdom; for what other god insists, and effectively, on receiving multiple propitiations each day? Our fathers' observation both expresses their awe of this particular god and hints at the nature of that awe. A clearer indication emerges from another statement about the gullet, one to the effect that the pathway it constitutes is a gateway to heaven. Our fathers, despite the conclusion one would draw from the logic of their assertion that this life is only a market we as humans temporarily must ply, our real home being heaven, harbored no great impatience for ending their market-faring and returning home. Their conception of heaven was, indeed, of an unfortunate inevitability terminating a not-quite-undesirable exile in this marketplace of a life. Their description of the gullet as a pathway to heaven must be understood, therefore, from the perspective of people for whom the association of heaven with bliss would seem to spring from an addled mind. One escapade of Àjàpá illustrates well the sage's meaning in connecting the gullet with heaven.

The whole world knew of Àjàpá's congenital shiftlessness, a condition that rendered him incapable of procuring his and his family's daily meals by the strength of his arms. His "condition" had prompted the observation that, with Àjàpá, laziness was a disease that worsened daily. He was far more lenient with himself, though. The Creator, Àjàpá told himself, created the fingers to be uneven, and no one quality did He distribute equally among His creatures. Some arms He created stronger than others, and knowing how He had arranged things, He kept a watchful eye out for the weak. The cow that has lost its tail, the saying went, could rely on the Creator to shoo flies away from it.

Much unhappiness and discontentment would disappear from the earth if all creatures only knew their limits and devised means of living well within them, Àjàpá reasoned. He considered himself fortunate to have learned his limits, and he had no qualms about adopting whatever stratagem would minimize the adverse impact of his deficiencies, such as timing his visits to his better-endowed friends to coincide with their mealtimes. Fortunately, the ancestors in their wisdom had established the etiquette obliging hosts — even unwilling ones — to ask visitors who find them at their meal to join in. It was a mere formality, though, and the visitor, according to form, was also expected to decline the invitation graciously, unless the host insisted up to three times. At the fourth invitation, the visitor might help himself to a taste and then retire to await his host's completion of his meal. If the visitor ignores form and jumps at the invitation on the first asking, however, the host must resign himself with good grace to sharing his meal and must betray no displeasure.

It was in keeping with that stratagem that Àjàpá set out one day to visit his friend Ehoro the Rabbit.

On arriving at Ehoro's house, Àjàpá was somewhat surprised to find him alone and contemplating the visage of the world, as the saying goes. Ehoro's wife, who ordinarily would be bustling about either in the final stages of cooking the meal or actually serving her husband, was nowhere in sight. What was emphatically in evidence in the room was the aroma of *èbe*, yam pottage, so overwhelming that it almost caused Àjàpá to faint. *Èbe* was his favorite food, of course.

"My friend," he greeted Ehoro, "I trust all is well with you."

"Look well where you step, my good friend," Ehoro responded amiably. "You find me in peace, thanks to my ancestors."

"Thanks indeed!"

"Sit down," Ehoro urged his visitor, "sit down. Is all well at your home?"

"The spirit of my dead father keeps watch."

Àjàpá sat himself down and looked around discreetly. The question clamoring in his head to be asked was simply too awkward to blurt out, even for a creature as brash as he. Had he missed the meal? Could it be, he worried, that his friend had altered his eating schedule in order to confound him? But, remembering that other creatures were not as given to scheming as he was, he assured himself that there must be an innocuous explanation.

"Your wife . . . ?" he finally ventured tentatively.

"Ah, she remains firm in body."

Àjàpá could not very well tell his host that his wife's health, or body firmness, was far from his mind, and Ehoro did not seem inclined to volunteer information about her whereabouts.

"She will never know weariness," he said in prayer.

"So it will be!"

His imperviousness to the subtler emotions kept him from any embarrassment at the taciturn mood that enveloped his host, but in the silence the quite audible rumbling of the restless worms in his stomach forced him to keep a conversation going, and a conversation, at that, that was germane to his present concerns.

"She is not home?" he queried.

"Who?"

"Your wife."

"Ah, my wife. She stepped outside, but only on one leg; she'll be back sooner than it takes a drop of spittle to dry in the sun."

"The day outside shimmers," Àjàpá observed, "and skull smarts from the scorching fingers of the sun. It must be a weighty matter that drew her out of the cool shelter of her roof."

"Those are true words you have spoken, and what could be weightier than the affairs of one's lineage?"

"Nothing. Indeed, nothing."

"A husband's claim must yield to those of a father and a lineage."

"True!" Àjàpá agreed, nodding gravely.

"And so, when an urgent summons urged her to throw a one-eyed glance in her father's direction, what could I do, even though it was at the cost of delaying my meal?"

"Hmm, hmm!" Àjàpá would not commit himself on that question, since he knew that no father-in-law could possibly come between him and his food. After all, the sages say the stomach is a deity whose worship one would be wise not to slight. But he also knew that Ehoro was all duty, decorum, and good form.

"What was it our fathers used to say?" Ehoro continued, going on to answer his own question. "The man who gives you his daughter as a bride has done you the ultimate in favor."

"Just so! Just so!" Àjàpá agreed.

"*Èbe* simmers on the fire, the food in which she takes the greatest pride; she is not one to let her effort go to ruin."

"That would be such a pity," Àjàpá observed. "And anyway," he added, "she has done her part, the cooking. Your part, the eating, you can do in, er, in her . . ."

He did not complete the sentence because Ehoro's eyes had transfixed him, wide with astonishment. They softened, though, on seeing Àjàpá's discomfiture.

"No," Ehoro said, chuckling. "Certainly not. What you see hanging on me like a garment is age. Certain things accord with age, and certain other things offend it. My stomach can await her return."

Ehoro was not deceived as to the reason for his visitor's solicitousness; he could hear the relay of growls and rumbles issuing from Àjàpá's stomach, which even his covering conversation did not quite drown out. Although a kindly person and not in the least inclined to begrudge Àjàpá some food, he nevertheless enjoyed his game of keeping him in awkward suspense. Eventually, though, his visitor's presence began to weigh on him. He knew that Àjàpá would not leave until he had been fed, and he worried that irritation might soon cause him to do something that would earn him the reputation of a bad host. He therefore became impatient for his wife's return.

"What a pity your wife tarries so long," Àjàpá's voice cut into his thoughts. "It has been a while since I saw her. My feet only infrequently bring me in your direction, and now that I am here, would it not be a pity if I left without setting eyes on her? Without satisfying myself in person about her health?"

With that he rearranged himself more comfortably, giving the impression that he might take a short nap while awaiting Ehoro's wife.

That move propelled Ehoro to action.

"I ask leave of you," he said, making for the doorway. "I must know what keeps her away so long. It is not my desire to leave you, but my return will be swift."

With that he slipped out, leaving Àjàpá to endure the torture of the *èbe* aroma alone.

The Creator might have left Àjàpá deficient in industry, but not in mental agility. Schemes that require considerable coaxing before they form in the minds of lesser creatures, and take even more worrying to develop fully, spring instantly fully formed in Àjàpá's mind when occasion calls for them, sometimes surprising Àjàpá himself. So it was that as soon as Ehoro's figure slipped out of his sight Àjàpá was on his feet, acting on a sudden whim. He stepped briskly to the cooking pot of *èbe* and lifted off the lid, almost swooning from the force and the deliciousness of the aroma that wrapped itself around his head. But it was time for action, not for swooning. He removed the cap from his head, filled it with steaming *èbe* and slapped it on his head.

In his haste he had not considered that the *èbe* was scalding or what it would feel like on his bare head. The sudden realization caused his knees to buckle and his feet to dig into an involuntary dance. Time, he thought, to get out of Ehoro's house and run for a secluded spot where he could save his skull and fill his stomach. He dashed for the doorway, crashing into his returning host. A quick movement of his hand kept the cap and the scalding *èbe* it concealed securely on Àjàpá's head.

The astonished Ehoro was the first to speak.

"Is the house on fire?"

Àjàpá concentrated on ignoring the fire consuming his head, trying to act as normally as he could under the circumstances, but he could not keep his legs from their involuntary dance.

"A sudden ache has gripped my head, a malady that began a short while back. I must rush home. The remedy is at home."

Ehoro was all commiseration.

"Ah, a pity. The ache seems bad."

"It is. I must go!"

"A little rest, perhaps . . ."

"No, I must get home." Àjàpá was becoming frantic.

He inched towards the doorway, but Ehoro blocked his way. He had seen something that alarmed him.

"Ha!" he exclaimed, pointing at Àjàpá's head, down which oil from the stolen *èbe* was dripping. "Your head . . . your head. I say, sit and relax a while. The burning sun won't help your headache."

"The sun is no bother. I must go home," Àjàpá pleaded, inching towards the door.

"If you must," Ehoro said, "and I don't think you should, at least let me accompany you, just in case . . ."

"No!" Àjàpá shouted, causing Ehoro to jump. "No," he repeated, more calmly this time. "Do not trouble. I will make my own way. Permit me."

He was out of the door and tearing down the lane as fast as a tortoise could tear, even before the last words were out of his mouth. Ehoro was left standing there at his door, looking after the disappearing Àjàpá and wondering if he ever thought he would live to see the day when any malady would make Àjàpá forgo a free meal.

Àjàpá hurried home with such speed that his feet hardly made contact with the earth. Those he passed on the way wondered what disaster pursued him, but he had no eyes for them; his whole consciousness was focused on the burning in his head.

He was hardly within his door when he tore the cap off his head, and with the *èbe* came the skin covering his skull, and all the hair attached to it. His wife could find no words to express her astonishment, and one look into her husband's eyes persuaded her that she would be wise to ask no questions. If the person who fouls the air wears a baleful look, she remembered the sages saying, one would be foolish to call attention to the stink.

Like a dutiful wife, she set about nursing the wound on Àjàpá's head. In time it did heal, but his hair would not grow back, his baldness remaining as a lesson, if he were one to learn a lesson, that shiftlessness has its woes.

Àjàpá's Instant Pregnancy

As a song went:

Today at the market one buys clothing,
Tomorrow at the market one buys clothing.
When death comes, clothing avails one nothing.
Should one, then, not prefer children?

Àjàpá and Yánníbo had lived together as husband and wife for many seasons without a sign that Yánníbo would soon kneel on the birthing mat. She was weighed down by the great sadness of her failure to earn the coveted name of "Mother." For his part, Àjàpá did not slacken his efforts to find some means of unlocking her womb, all to no avail.

Not even the richest of beings can find children to buy, and Àjàpá was by no means the richest of beings. In common belief a man's failure to find himself a wife is nothing to endure in silence; it is a matter for public airing, for, who knows who might know how to end the calamity? The same applies to childlessness, perhaps even more so. Thus it was that one day a friend to whom Àjàpá had confided his problem came to him greatly excited, bearing news of a *babaláwo* unmatched in his knowledge of herbs and charms. This *babaláwo* lived in a town not far from theirs, and he was famous, among other things, for his amazing ability to open the most recalcitrant of wombs. Àjàpá needed no great prompting before he readied himself and went in all haste to the medicine man.

At the home of the *babaláwo* Àjàpá pleaded his case with the utmost passion. "The sages say children are the best clothing one can have," he said.

"Indeed they are," agreed the *babaláwo.*

"The only worthwhile profit in this transaction of living."

"Your words are true."

"They are much to be preferred over money."

"True, indeed!"

"In death the ember enfolds itself in ashes," Àjàpá continued, the *babaláwo* nodding his agreement. "When the banana plant dies it yields its place to a sapling. They leave something of themselves behind as testimony that they lived."

Àjàpá paused and looked earnestly at the *babaláwo.*

"When I die," he pleaded, "let me not die completely. Let me leave behind a child to perform funeral rights for me."

The *babaláwo* was not unmoved, but he thought it proper to decline the assignment of supernatural powers to him lest he anger the gods.

"Only the Creator makes children," he said.

"Then," Àjàpá urged him, "plead my case with the Creator. You have his ears, all the world knows. Make my case with him."

In the end the *babaláwo* assured Àjàpá of his help and assured him that his wife Yánníbo would have a baby to dance with in her arms before a year passed, unless the leaves in the forest suddenly forgot their nature. He ordered Àjàpá to procure a white cock, a white pigeon, and a white duck as ingredients for a stew that would unblock Yánníbo's womb.

Àjàpá did as he was told. The *babaláwo* cooked the birds with special barks and herbs, and two days later the stew was ready. Before handing it over to Àjàpá he gave him a stern lecture.

"Àjàpá," he said, "the stew I am handing over to you works without fail just as fire burns without fail. What's more, it does its task without regard to who eats it, man or woman."

Àjàpá could not conceal his impatience to get the stew to his wife, but the *babaláwo* was unrelenting.

"Àjàpá, how many ears have you?" he asked.

"Two," he replied, somewhat put off by the seemingly pointless question.

"And what do you use them for?"

"To hear with, of course," he almost snapped.

"Good," the *babaláwo* said. "As I told you, this stew will not fail to place pregnancy in the stomach of whoever eats it, man or woman. It is for your wife and her alone. In no event must you eat of it, or even touch your tongue to the barest taste of it. If you do—well, you know the consequence."

Àjàpá obliged the *babaláwo* with the necessary assurances, paid his fees, and hurried homeward with the stew.

No one has yet discovered a way to cook the vegetable *ebòlò* and rid it of its strong forest smell. Similarly, no one has learned what manner of admonition can alter Àjàpá's nature. His servitude to his appetite was legendary, as was his intractability. Furthermore, so convinced was he of his own cleverness that he could always find some folly in other people's actions. As he walked home with the stew its irresistible aroma worked on his will. Apparently, apart from knowing all about barks and herbs and their deep mysteries, the *babaláwo* was a cook one could not dismiss lightly. For a while Àjàpá fortified himself against all temptation, but the aroma gradually anesthetized his determination. Soon, true to his nature, he began to question the logic of the *babaláwo*'s injunctions.

"So, whoever eats the stew, man or woman, will inevitably become pregnant?" he wondered aloud. "But, the earth's Creator created this, too, and who ever heard of a man becoming pregnant?"

The more he thought the matter over the more he was certain that the *babaláwo* had taken him for a fool.

"Next," he said, "the man will be telling me chickens have teeth. What a fool he must think I am!"

Such reasoning led by degrees to Àjàpá sneaking a taste of the stew, eating a mouthful, and eventually consuming the whole thing, before he remembered why he had gone to the *babaláwo* in the first place. Remorse descended on him, but he quickly shook it off. There are more white cocks, white pigeons, and white ducks, and the forest remained full of herbs. He would return to the *babaláwo* for another pot of stew. As long as he was willing to pay the necessary fees, Àjàpá reasoned, why should the *babaláwo* not welcome the additional income?

But even as he pondered what to do, Àjàpá began to notice with alarm that something was happening to him. The *babaláwo* had not mentioned to him that the pregnancy the stew induced was instant, but he soon discovered that. To his horror, his stomach began to increase in rotundity even as he watched. Without dallying, he turned around and made as much speed as his legs could manage back to the *babaláwo*'s house. Before the latter had an opportunity to speak, Àjàpá burst into song:

Babaláwo, please heed my plea and relieve me.
The medicine you gave me a short while back,
Warning me to keep my hands off my mouth,
Warning me I must not trip —
Well, a wayward root tripped me,
I slipped, I fell,
My hand touched the earth and touched my mouth.
I looked at my stomach, it looked distended.
Babaláwo, please heed my plea and relieve me!

The *babaláwo* was not fooled.

"Àjàpá," he said, "what treasure I had I gave you when I warned you against tasting the stew. Unfortunately for you, one reason why the medicine works so well is that it has no antidote. You have done what no man has ever done, and you must experience what no man has ever experienced. With your own hand you have sealed your fate."

Thus persuaded that there was nothing anybody could do to remedy his situation, Àjàpá walked despondently into the bush to await the death that was inevitable. To this day it remains true that no male has ever become pregnant and delivered safely.

Resourcefulness

Àjàpá, Ajá the Dog, and the Yams

In an era long gone, Ajá the Dog fell on such hard times as left him with no means of feeding himself and his family. With no farm and no trade, he had to content himself with whatever he could scrounge in the bushes, by the pathways, and on the dunghills. But there was never enough to glean from those sources, never enough for him to fulfill the role of provider for his family; he knew that he must find a better alternative. He thought long and hard about options available to him, mindful that the sages say if one lacks brawn one should make up for it with brains, and also that a lazy person eats what his cunning provides. He reached down deep into his fount of wisdom and was rewarded with an inspiration.

All around his town were large farms, all planted with yams, where if one were careful one could satisfy one's needs without arousing the suspicion of the farm owners. The farms beckoned to him, and for a time his scruples held him back. But his condition worsened and his scruples became increasingly anemic, until eventually expediency became his motivator and he yielded to the appeal of the farms.

He devised a rotation scheme that would take him on a pilfering circuit of different farms, one that allowed a decent interval between two visits to any given quarry. As an added precaution he resolved never to yield to greed when he helped himself to the largess of the farms. Together these voluntary restraints would make his theft strike each farm owner as a minimal nuisance unworthy of any special measures. The scheme was so successful that he was able to feed himself and his family rather well for quite a while, and very rapidly his emaciated brood became the embodiments of health and good living.

The change that came over the family did not escape the notice of Ajá's good friend Àjàpá the Tortoise, who was constitutionally averse to exposing himself to any labor he could avoid, even if its purpose was to sustain life. He was so widely known as a shirker and idler that the whole world scornfully dismissed him with the appellation *Òlédàrùn,* an expression of the common view that his laziness was no longer just a character trait: it was a disease.

Àjàpá was used to trading commiserations with his friend when they both shared the same condition. Indeed, he was drawn to the other because he was gratified to have company in his destitution. When Ajá began to show unmistakable signs of thriving, Àjàpá judged it only fair that he be let in on the secret of his friend's altered circumstances. Whenever he asked the question, though, Ajá put him off with increasingly convoluted stories. But Àjàpá was nothing if not persistent, and he would not be discouraged; Ajá was obviously onto too good a thing to be circumspect about it. Àjàpá would not relent in his pestering, until Ajá was persuaded that his life would be far easier if he revealed his scheme than if he continued to hold out. He therefore agreed in the end to take Àjàpá along on his next expedition.

When the day for the visit dawned, Ajá led the way out of town and to a farm that seemed to be endless in its expanse and that was abundant with mature yams ready for harvesting

"This is it," Ajá told his friend.

Àjàpá was puzzled.

"This is it?"

"Yes," Ajá answered.

"This is your secret?"

"Yes."

Àjàpá looked around and into the distance where yam plants blended

84

into one another to form a solid mass of wilting foliage. He was almost beside himself with wonder.

"What kind of friend keeps such abundance to himself while his friend starves? How many stomachs do you have? Ten mouths could feed from your farm and still leave enough for ten more. Why have you kept it secret from your friend?"

The puzzlement Ajá had felt at the start of his friend's tirade gave way to understanding when the last words came out.

"No, no!" he corrected Àjàpá. "This is not my farm."

"It's not?"

"Of course not."

"Then, whose is it?" Àjàpá asked, his demeanor indicating that he suspected the answer even as he asked the question.

"Does that matter?" Ajá asked in turn. "Do you want the owner, or do you want food?"

"Food, of course," Àjàpá agreed.

"Here, then, is food. This is no time to ask of the owner of the limb before you bite it. Take what the gods bring your way."

Persuading Àjàpá to do just that was not difficult; his questioning came from puzzlement and not out of any scruples, of which he was blissfully free. Now that he knew how matters stood, Ajá told him, he should also know that their mission was not the type that one could dawdle over.

"A masquerader covered with dry straw may venture into a foundry with open flames," he told Àjàpá, "but he had better not tarry. We must be quick about taking what we need and be off."

They commenced digging up yams, and in a short while Ajá had unearthed two sizable ones. He went into the bush to cut some vine to tie them together so he could carry them more easily. Long after he was done he saw that Àjàpá was still busily digging away, despite the small heap he had already assembled.

"Don't you think you have enough already?" he asked Àjàpá, somewhat alarmed.

"A few more and I will be done."

It was quite apparent to him that Àjàpá already had more than enough to keep him and his wife fed for several days. Besides, apart from seemingly ignoring Ajá's admonition about speed, he was jeopardizing the carefully thought-out strategy for denying any farmer the incentive to come after the raider of his crop.

"No time for a few more," Ajá told him, "it is time to stop, now!"

"Patience!" Àjàpá chided his friend.

"Patience?" Ajá asked, anything but patient. "If you cannot tell when to stop you are headed for disgrace; your greed will get us both into trouble."

"The reputation one gets from stealing one yam is no different from that for stealing ten, is it?" Àjàpá asked his friend. "I have risked earning the name, and I must make it worth my while."

"But," his friend argued in return, "a farmer may ignore the theft of two or three yams from his farm, but he is not likely to overlook the loss of ten. And once the farmer is provoked into vigilance, any further visit to his farm becomes a most risky venture. Your behavior will cause today to bar all tomorrows!"

"There are other farms besides this," Àjàpá said, unimpressed by Ajá's reasoning. "When a door closes, another opens. Besides," he continued, "the elders say there is no fat to this life; therefore, whenever only a little comes one's way, one should take only a little, and whenever abundance comes one's way, one should enjoy the abundance; for you can really call your own only what has already found its way into your stomach."

Ajá knew all along that he was not likely to make any impression on Àjàpá with any argument, and he was anxious to be off the farm before the owner chanced upon them. But he tried one more time.

"How do you mean to carry this many yams home?" he asked.

"The way will show itself," Àjàpá replied and returned to his digging.

"In that case," Ajá said in resignation, "I will leave you. If the farmer catches you, you don't know me, and I don't know you."

The sight of Ajá lifting his two-yam load and the specter of an arriving farmer raised second thoughts for Àjàpá.

"All right, all right," he said. "Lest I appear greedy and unreasonable, I will stop."

As if to indicate that whatever Àjàpá did was now immaterial to him, Ajá turned his face toward the path.

"Keep on coming on," he said, giving his friend the customary parting greeting to tardy fellow travelers, and turned his feet in the direction of home.

"Wait!" Àjàpá called in alarm. "Do you mean to leave me here alone?"

"I promised to show you where to find food, and I have done that," Ajá replied. "You have legs, and they know their way home; I did not promise to walk you back home."

Àjàpá now commenced to pleaded with Ajá to wait so they could leave together.

"We came together," he argued, "and it is only right that we leave together."

Ajá was by now eager to get away from the farm, for something told him that disaster approached, and so he paid no attention to Àjàpá's pleas. He walked briskly away, leaving Àjàpá to fumble frantically with tying his yams together, an impossible job. Finally, in a panic he called after Ajá:

Ajá, Ajá, lend me a hand!
Ajá, Ajá, wait for me, please!
If you don't, I'll hail the farmer
And when he comes,
He won't be pleased.
Ajá, Ajá, lend me a hand!

Àjàpá's words stopped Ajá in his tracks. He knew his friend well enough to know that what he threatened was no bluff. If he was caught he would not hesitate for a moment to implicate Ajá. His anger mounting, therefore, he returned to help his greedy friend tie the yams securely together. He also helped to lift it unto Àjàpá's back.

The load proved so heavy that the Àjàpá could hardly walk, but he would not entertain the suggestion that he discard some yams. Again, Ajá had no choice but to let his friend have his way, and he hurried toward home. But he had not gone very far when the forest again echoed with Àjàpá's call:

> *Ajá, Ajá, lend me a hand!*
> *Ajá, Ajá, wait for me, please!*
> *If you don't, I'll hail the farmer*
> *And when he comes,*
> *He won't be pleased.*
> *Ajá, Ajá, lend me a hand!*

The trip had already taken much longer than Ajá liked. He berated himself for his folly in permitting friendship to cloud his better judgment; after all, no one knew better than he what type of creature Àjàpá was. Thinking thus he ignored the call and hurried along, anxious to put as much distance between himself and the farm and as quickly as he could.

Àjàpá was so weighed down by his loot that his progress was painfully slow. Worse yet, with every step he felt as though the load would flatten him. He called and called in desperation to Ajá, but the latter paid him no further heed. That Àjàpá would be caught he was certain; that he would implicate his benefactor Ajá he had no doubt, either. His best course, he thought, was to hurry to the safety of his home. A person who can truthfully say "I was sitting innocently in my home" is not easily proclaimed a public criminal. The more Àjàpá called, the more Ajá urged his legs into his walk, until soon every sound from Àjàpá faded and died away.

As soon as he arrived home, Ajá instructed his wife to hide the yams quickly in the bush nearby, where nobody would see them. That done, he asked her to make a fire in the hearth and bring him two raw eggs. His wife did as she was told, all the while wondering what her husband was up to. She did not question him about his strange instructions, for she was certain that he had good reasons. When the fire was going, Ajá rubbed himself thoroughly with oil and lay in front of the hearth. He told his wife to cover him up, and to tell anyone who might come visiting or asking about him that he had taken ill, that he had been laid up for a few days and had been unable to go outside. He then placed one egg in each cheek and waited for whatever would happen.

In the meantime, Àjàpá's greed had indeed caught up with him. Unable to make any real progress under his oppressive load and unwilling to let go of any part of it, he inevitably attracted the suspicion of those who came upon him on the road. So well known was he in the surrounding communities that there was only one explanation for his sudden access to so many yams. Every farmer who had suffered some theft on his farm in recent times claimed that the habitual thief was finally cornered. Following custom, people gathered and taunted him with derisive chants:

Behold the face of a thief,
THIEF!
Behold the face of a thief,
THIEF!

Children trooped after him, echoing and clapping to the chant, and occasionally pelting him with stones. By the time he was delivered before the *oba* in the palace, the procession after him had swelled to more than half the town's population.

"Àjàpá," the *oba* said, "if I told you I was surprised to see you here in these circumstances, I would be lying. You, *Òlédàrùn*. You are so lazy you would sooner call down a deluge than do gainful work. Now we see where your laziness has brought you—to stealing."

In response, Àjàpá wished the king a long life.

"*Kábíyèsí*, your Majesty, seeing me in these circumstances, who would doubt the wisdom of your words? But, please bend your ears downwards and you will learn the truth."

"The truth? What truth is there to learn besides what we can all see?" the *oba* responded. "This matter is one for the eyes to see, not something for the nose to sniff out."

"Your breath will be long," Àjàpá persisted. "You say I am lazy, and I will not bandy words with you. But, did I become lazy only yesterday? No! Yet, did anyone accuse me of stealing yesterday? No! How then . . . ?"

"As our fathers said," the *oba* interrupted him, "the thief may range freely for a great many days, but the owner's one day, that day when the thief is caught, is all that counts."

"Your words are wise, your Majesty," Àjàpá responded, "but I am innocent. I am no thief."

"Are these yams from your farm, then?" the *oba* asked, indicating the yams that had been placed as evidence before him.

"No."

"Did you perhaps buy them?"

"No, your Majesty."

"Ah, some kind farmer gave them to you?"

"Your Majesty," he replied, "that is the truth."

Those words provoked some scattered titters, and the skeptical *oba* asked who his benefactor was.

"Your ancestors will not visit you with evil," Àjàpá responded. "Your Majesty, the first person I saw when I woke up this morning, must have been wearing ill-luck like a garment, and must have infected me with it. Otherwise, would I have found myself in the company of Ajá, a friend who told me that he owned a farm he planted with yams? He said he was short-handed, and offered me some yams if I would help him dig some and bring them home."

Correctly reading the incredulity on the *oba*'s face, Àjàpá pressed on quickly.

"I know," he continued, "that I should have remembered the ancient wisdom of you our elder that a lamb that keeps company with Ajá will come to savor shit, but I fell victim to my own good nature. May your ancestors not make your good nature bring you grief."

He continued, claiming that he had no idea that the farm was not Ajá's until others accused him of stealing as he struggled home with his wages for helping Ajá. Only then did he realize why Ajá had acted so strangely, sneaking off the farm, with the story that he was taking a few yams to the barn and would be back shortly.

Since Àjàpá was accusing Ajá of stealing, of inducement to steal, and of deception, the *oba* ordered that Ajá be brought to confront his accuser; one does not judge a case after hearing only one side, he said.

When the *oba*'s messengers arrived at Ajá's house, his wife asked why they had come.

"The *oba* asks that Ajá briefly show his eyes at the palace," they said.

"How terrible!" she exclaimed. "One may not refuse an *oba*'s summons, but certain things make honoring it a problem."

What sort of thing might keep anyone from shaking himself loose from whatever he was doing to run to answer an *oba*'s call? the messengers wanted to know. Was Ajá dead, perhaps? No, she replied, but he was ill and had been laid up for several days.

"That is not what we heard," they said. "If he has been laid up, how was he able to go to a farm to steal yams?"

At that, Ajá's wife exclaimed in convincing disbelief, saying some evil person had lied about her husband. She invited them into the house to see for themselves. The messengers entered, and there they saw Ajá, completely covered and shivering before the fire and looking every bit the invalid at death's door. The messengers looked hard at him and were convinced that he was indeed ill.

"How does the body feel, Ajá?" one of them asked in sympathy.

Ajá rolled his eyes toward the questioner and made as though he would respond. But instead he gave a heave, and the contents of one of his cheeks spurted out. The messengers leaped out of the way, now thoroughly convinced that the creature was in very poor shape indeed.

They commiserated with his wife and consulted among themselves as to what best to do. Their order was to bring Ajá, and whatever the *oba* ordered they must carry out. They explained the situation to his wife and persuaded her that the best evidence of her husband's condition, anyway, was the sight he looked. Her display of anguish was convincing as she helped them wrap Ajá in a warm cloth before they bore him away.

The *oba* and the people assembled at the court were puzzled when the messengers arrived bearing what seemed a corpse instead of marching a supposedly hardened criminal. Had they been heavy-handed in their mission? some wondered. Àjàpá was as puzzled as the rest.

"Your majesty," the spokesman for the messengers reported to the *oba*, "we did as you ordered, but we found Ajá in death's courtyard."

The *oba* looked at him and saw a creature laboring for breath.

"Is this the same Ajá you accused of stealing yams on a farm?" he asked Àjàpá.

Àjàpá moved closer and looked at Ajá, who was now groaning ever so weakly. Àjàpá knew, of course, that he was faking, and he so informed the *oba*.

"This is a trick, your Majesty," he cried. "He's faking! He's a thief, a fakir, and worse things besides."

In his agitation he got hold of Ajá's wrap intending to pull it off, while the messengers rushed to restrain him. Just then Ajá released the contents of the remaining egg in his mouth. Àjàpá caught most of it in his face, and was both halted and silenced.

The *oba*'s conviction that Ajá was really ill and that Àjàpá had made up his stories was aided by a properly queasy stomach that could not endure the sight of vomit. He ordered Ajá returned to his home and pronounced sentence on Àjàpá.

Whoever cannot live as the inhabitants of a town live does not belong in that town. Since Àjàpá would not work but preferred to steal, the *oba* said, his presence in the town was a threat to its harmony. Àjàpá belonged not in the community but in the company of thieves. Accordingly, he ordered Àjàpá from the town, on pain of being shackled and killed if ever he showed his face again therein. Since then Àjàpá has wandered the forest, while Ajá remains welcome in town.

Thus did Àjàpá pay for his greed and his ingratitude to his friend.

Àjàpá and Bola the Mute Princess

The prickly grass does not know or care that the one who trods on it is royalty; the torrential rain does not know or care that the wayfarer is venerable and should be spared a drenching. If that sounds like a proverb, in it is the wisdom of our fathers and mothers who have gone before.

Bola was the daughter of the *oba,* but misfortune did not for that reason leave her untouched. If we were to speak of beauty, we would certainly say she had no equal in the whole community. Whoever says differently engages in willful detraction, the sort of detraction that says honey is sour but cannot make it any less sweet than it really is. Most apt was the description that she was so slender that she swayed in the breeze, that her eyes were snares for whoever looked into them, that her teeth were whiter than cowrie shells, and that, all in all, she was as beautiful among humans as the Kob antelope was among animals.

That meeting in her of beauty and nearness to the throne would normally attract enough suitors to make selecting a mate difficult for her parents, but for the truth of what the wisdom of the sages long revealed—and that was vindicated by her example—that no one comes to this earth unattended by a blemish. For Bola, the blemish was that although she made promising sounds as a baby, she did not ever develop the ability to speak. She was as mute as a pile of cotton that fails to make a sound when struck with a stick.

Bola bore her affliction with consummate grace and a cheerful disposition, never betraying any sign of being aware of any handicap, but her father lived under a pall of sadness. He was convinced that his daughter's show of happiness was indeed only a show and that it concealed a sadness that was the more potentially debilitating for being unexpressed. He therefore wished above all things to find her some relief, if relief was to be found anywhere on earth. One's most pressing problem unfailingly dominates one's thought and discussions. So it was that no matter what the occasion, no matter what issue needing deliberation and resolution caused him to assemble his chiefs, he never failed to bring up the painful subject of Bola's muteness.

"*Kábíyèsí,* you will live long on your father's throne," *Basòrun* his closest adviser told him one day after the *oba* had again brought the matter of his grief before his chiefs. "Our fathers have long maintained that whatever assails the eyes does not leave the nose untouched. How have I spoken?" he turned to ask the rest of the chiefs.

"You have spoken well!" they assured him.

"So," he continued, "a plague that chooses the home of the chief priest for its attack does not spare the devotees behind him. This matter that pains you so has not left us unaffected. Just as you do, we wish Bola to speak."

"You speak well!" the chiefs assured him.

"We wish her to open her mouth and call you 'father.'"

"Indeed!"

"The earth beneath you will protect you," the *oba* said. "I did not doubt your sympathy."

"*Kábíyèsí,*" *Basòrun* responded, "one does not thank oneself. Thanking us, you thank yourself. What matters is how to release Bola's tongue."

"In truth!" the chiefs agreed.

"And since none of us here knows the means, the path to take is obvious. A matter that yields to no ready solution asks to be delivered to the world at large. Make a proclamation inviting whoever has the means to do the task, and we shall see who or what comes forth. It matters not what the required reward might be; nothing that falls from the heavens can prove too heavy a load for the earth to bear."

The crier carried the proclamation to town, village, and farm, and even though it produced responses after the first day, the *oba* ordered it repeated for seven consecutive days in order to ensure that few ears would miss hearing it.

Medicine men came from near and far, loaded down with charms and potions to try on Bola, but none could put speech in her mouth. Incantations and invocations of the gods similarly failed to effect a cure for Bola's muteness. That was how matters stood when Àjàpá began boasting that none but himself could work the miracle of loosening the bond around her tongue.

When the gods deprive a man of head hair they usually console him with a luxuriant beard. The gods did not give Àjàpá much by way of strength, but they compensated him abundantly in other ways: they endowed him with a restless imagination and an uncontrollable mouth. He had no knowledge of medicine or charms and no qualification whatsoever that would enable him to treat even a headache, let alone restore the power of speech to a mute.

Whether he intended his boast to reach the *oba*'s ears or not only Àjàpá knows. But it did, and when the *oba* summoned Àjàpá to his presence his nature was such that he would not deny the boast. Not for him the sages' admonition that if one insults the *oba* in his absence all one has to do is deny doing so when summoned to his presence, for one thus demonstrates one's awe of the *oba*. Instead, he lived by the rule that no one who has any self-respect speaks and then eats his words. One stands by the words that escape from one's mouth, and one endures the consequences.

"*Kábíyèsí*," he told the *oba*, "what you heard is true. I did vow to release your daughter's voice."

"And do you still maintain that boast?"

Àjàpá said he did. He vowed to match and surpass the exertions of the medicine men who preceded him, saying that he could in any case achieve no worse result than theirs.

The *oba* knew, as the rest of the world knew, that Àjàpá was an incurable prankster, and that it was not beyond him to see the occasion as an opportunity for amusing himself. But so desperate was he for any remedy that he accepted Àjàpá's offer, for there was no knowing which would prove successful. But then he did not wish to refuse any offer of help. He warned Àjàpá, however, that severe repercussions awaited him if he failed, for unlike the medicine men who before him tried and failed he lacked the credentials that qualified them to offer their remedy. It would not do to encourage frivolous adventures at the *oba*'s expense.

Àjàpá accepted the terms and went home, trusting the spirit of his dead father to show him a way to make good his vow. After all, the sages say whatever makes one blind also teaches one to find one's way. The gods who gave him his mouth would surely get him out of whatever scrapes it got him into.

When a sudden idea abruptly roused him out of sleep during the night, an idea that promised what at the time seemed an infallible cure for Bola's muteness, he knew that the spirit of his dead father had not gone to sleep but remained watchful over him. He was so excited that he could not return to sleep, and it took all the self-restraint he could muster to wait for the dawn before hurrying to the palace to put the idea into practice.

"*Kábíyèsí*," he excitedly told the *oba*, "the ancestors have heard our pleas! Bola's silence is as good as broken."

Although skeptical, the *oba* could not remain completely unaffected by Àjàpá's obvious excitement.

"And when will it be broken?" he asked.

"Soon, *Kábíyèsí*, soon," Àjàpá responded. "All I ask is that you send Bola to live in my home for seven days. If she does not speak at the end of those seven days, then my father did not sire me, and I will accept your punishment."

The *oba* considered the request only briefly before acceding to it.

"It shall be done. She will prepare as necessary and come to your home, shall we say, in two days?"

"*Kábíyèsí,* why in two days? Why not today? If a task does not force delay on one, one should not force delay on it."

"Tomorrow then," the *oba* said. "There is no reason to rush her out of her own home. She has lived with silence all these years; she can bear to do so one more day."

On leaving the palace Àjàpá sought out Òkété the Giant Rat, whose reputation for burrowing was unrivaled. Àjàpá promised him three large sacks of palm-nuts if he would immediately burrow an underground trench from the nearby forest to a room in his home. The promise of palm-nuts was precisely the sort of inducement to secure Òkété's services, and he set about the task vowing to have it done by the next morning. Àjàpá last stop before he went home to await the completion of Òkété's task was the market; there he purchased a full pot of honey and took it home.

Òkété did as he promised; the trench was ready before dawn broke the next day. As soon as he had conveyed the palm-nuts as payment to Òkété and sent him on his way, Àjàpá set about rearranging the room so as to conceal the opening to the trench. That done, he sat down to await the arrival of his guest.

She arrived suitably attended when the glare of the sun had relented somewhat. As soon as the company departed, Àjàpá showed her the room with the concealed trench opening. He apologized for the clutter in the room, which he said was the only space he had in the whole house for the storage of his most valued possessions. He specifically pointed out the pot of honey that sat close to the concealed trench opening. He would have that at least out of her way the next day, he said. It was to be a gift to a friend who had done him some favor.

Bola settled into her new room and waited, wondering what Àjàpá's course of treatment would be. Her curiosity was neither relieved nor rewarded when at the end of the day her host simply wished her a good night's rest and himself retired. Perhaps the next day would bring enlightenment.

Àjàpá waited until the night was black and he was certain that Bola was sleeping soundly. He sneaked from the house with an empty pot and made his way to the forest where the far opening lay to the trench Òkété had dug. He entered and crept through it to the room where Bola slept. Very quietly he took the pot of honey and poured half of its contents into the pot he had brought. He replaced the half-empty pot and left the room as stealthily as he had entered.

The following morning Àjàpá was a most genial and hospitable host.

"Did you sleep well?" he asked. "Did you wake well?" To both questions Bola nodded in answer.

Àjàpá fussed over her and her breakfast, after which, he said, he would run a small errand, to deliver the honey to his friend. When he returned, he said, he would address himself to the task of making her talk.

With that, he went to the pot of honey and lifted it. The food Bola was lifting to her mouth was halfway to its destination when Àjàpá's loud alarm made her jump, dropping the food in her lap.

"What abomination is this?" he cried. He approached Bola with the pot and fixed his eyes on her.

"Bola," he said, "how did a full pot of honey become half-empty during the night?"

Bola's eyes became wide with indignation.

"You drank half of the honey in the night!"

Bola shook her head angrily and furiously.

"Did a visitor visit you in the night?" Àjàpá demanded, and again Bola shook her head.

"Honey has no legs on which to walk away," Àjàpá shouted at her. "I see no hole in the pot through which it could have leaked, nor do I see any spilled honey on the floor! If you and I are the only two people who have been in this house since last night, and honey disappears, one of us must be responsible. It wasn't me! Who do you think it is?"

Bola continued to shake her head vigorously and to gesture that she did not know what happened to the honey.

"My eyes will not be the only ones to see this," Àjàpá said heading out of the house. "Today the whole town will know your true name. 'Thief'!"

On hearing that, Bola collapsed in tears. She could hear Àjàpá broadcasting her disgrace to the world:

"Bola stole and ate my honey! Bola is a thief!"

The alarm that a thief has been spotted in the community, usually a stranger from somewhere else, unfailingly draws a crowd that would ensure that the thief does not escape, and that he is subjected to severe beating while being led to the *oba*, who would pronounce judgment on him. But in this case, although Àjàpá's alarm drew a crowd around his home, no one knew quite what to do. Indeed, when some in the crowd became certain of the identity of the proclaimed thief, they quickly slunk away.

Bola was the *oba*'s daughter; whatever anyone said about her, the person said indirectly about the *oba*, for, if one pulls at the vine the vine pulls at the bush to which it is attached. Àjàpá might be foolhardy enough to proclaim the princess a thief, but they did not wish to find out what the *oba*'s reaction might be to the dirt thrown thus in his direction. After all, whoever calls the daughter a thief calls the father the father of a thief. And as the saying went, whoever is foolish enough to see the mucus dripping from the *oba*'s nose is the one who will wipe it.

Àjàpá kept up his alarm as the crowd swelled. Satisfied with his audience, he went inside the house and dragged the wailing Bola into the open.

"Look well on the face of a thief," he called to the crowd. "And a brazen thief it is, too! I offered help to her and she rewards me by stealing my honey!"

"Ha!" someone in the crowd exclaimed. "What is this you have done?"

"To come from the palace to steal honey in Àjàpá's home!" another exclaimed. "What an abomination!"

"Dipping from the pot to pour into the well!" yet another amplified.

During all of this Bola was vigorously shaking her head as tears streamed down her face. Unintelligible sounds forced themselves out of her mouth, and her hands and arms flew wildly, wringing and gesticulating. Àjàpá redoubled his accusations.

"Here is the pot of honey," he said, pointing to the pot on the ground. "It was full when we went to sleep last night. This morning it is half-empty. And only you shared a room with it. Bola, you stole and ate my honey!"

Let this matter not be unduly prolonged. In time, Àjàpá's efforts had the effect he hoped for. After much straining Bola's tongue loosened to redeem her good name. The words were hardly intelligible at first, but grief soon lent them clarity. She sang:

> *Bola stole no honey!*
> *Bola ate no honey!*
> *The mother that gave me birth*
> *Has never known me to steal.*
> *The father that raised me*
> *Has never called me "Thief."*
> *The misfortune of silence*
> *Brought me to Àjàpá's home,*
> *And gave me the name "Thief."*
> *But Bola stole no honey!*
> *Bola ate no honey!*

The crowd did not immediately grasp what it was witnessing. For some the drama was whether Bola was guilty or innocent, but the more alert ones realized that something far more important had happened. Bola could speak!

In the meantime, the news had reached the palace that Àjàpá had accused Bola of stealing, and the *oba* had sent his messengers to apprehend Àjàpá and bring him to court to answer for his unheard-of temerity. The messengers arrived in the midst of the commotion Bola's new power of speech had caused. They heard Àjàpá insist on his accusations, and they heard Bola's song of refutation. They sent one among them to run back to the palace to announce the good news.

Within the time that elapses between a crab's two blinks, the *oba* was on the scene, and with his own ears he heard his daughter's song:

Bola stole no honey!
Bola ate no honey!
The mother that gave me birth
Never knew me to steal.
The father that raised me
Has never called me "Thief."
The misfortune of silence
Brought me to Àjàpá's home,
And gave me the name "Thief."
But Bola stole no honey!
Bola ate no honey!

He needed no explanation from Àjàpá, who, on seeing the *oba*'s arrival, had stopped his accusations, and was in fact dancing to Bola's song. Bola herself had finally realized the momentousness of what had happened to her, and the tears streaming down her face were no longer tears of grief. She kept up her song, in a voice that now soared with joy.

"Àjàpá," the *oba* said to his benefactor, "you said you would do it, and you did as you said. Truly, your father sired you. You will find that an *oba*'s gratitude is worthy of him."

As the festive crowd accompanied the *oba*'s retinue to the palace to continue the celebration, Àjàpá looked skyward and thanked the spirit of his dead father who had apparently not forgotten himself in sleep.

Àjàpá and Kìnìún
the Tyrannical King Lion

Alákàn the Crab says he thanks his creator for not giving him a head, for that oversight saved him from the curse of headaches.

An *oba* is to a community as a head is to a body. It has its uses, but it comes with some inconveniences. So the animal community found out a long time ago when they decided to name one among them their *oba*, and in time Kìnìún assumed the position. When first the Owner of the earth created it and all the animals, each creature wandered the land or swam the waters in search of food and shelter, none getting in the way of the other or paying it any mind. With food and space so plentiful, no one knew competition; all was peace and contentment. In such ideal conditions, animals mated happily, producing more animals, until at last foragers bumped into foragers and grazers found themselves in contention for the same spaces. Fights ensued and chaos replaced the earlier tranquillity, until in the end all the animals agreed on a council to end the disorder.

The animals duly assembled and after some deliberation agreed that, since disputes and quarrels had entered into their midst, the wise thing to do was to provide a mechanism for resolving them and also for preventing or minimizing them. Further deliberation resulted in the decision that, because the success of such a mechanism depended on everyone's agreeing to respect the operations of the mechanism, or on the ability of the mechanism to enforce respect for it, logic indicated that the mechanism must center around the most powerful among them.

From just looking around, most of the animals thought the choice was obvious, for who among them could stand up to towering Erin the Elephant? Àgùnfon the Ostrich thought so, too, and he took it upon himself to speak for the company.

"Venerable elder," he addressed Erin, "it seems the mantle of leadership has fallen on you. The welfare of the animal community lies now in your hands."

Erin was readying himself to reply when a sudden commotion disrupted the proceedings. All eyes turned in the direction of the disturbance, and just as they did Kìnìún reared up and released a roar that sent the weaker among them for cover and made even the stout-hearted quiver. Having won their attention, Kìnìún addressed them in the haughtiest of tones.

"Far be it from me to throw water on the discussion, but when the talk comes around to submitting to the "power" of a leaf and vegetable eater, this flesh eater must remove himself."

With that he swaggered off, followed after some hesitation by Ekùn the Leopard, Ìkokò the Hyena, and other carnivorous animals who felt compelled to follow their leader—even Ológbò the Cat joined his kin. This last provoked the silent fury of many in the remaining party by his insolence to Erin's face: he turned his back to the latter, stretched his two front paws as far as they could reach, so that his shoulders were almost to the ground while his rump reared in the air toward Erin's face, and yawned luxuriantly before sauntering after the other carnivores. When a great misfortune floors you, some animals thought, opportunistic irritants assail you.

"Leave if you must," Àgùnfon called after them. "Whoever thinks that without him the company is incomplete deceives himself. See if we do not do very well without you!"

Kìnìún acknowledged the taunt by pausing and fixing Àgùnfon with a glare that made him regret his words. After the pause, Kìnìún continued on his way, leaving Àgùnfon wondering if he had not stuck his foot in his mouth.

"Not wise, not wise," remarked Àdán, who had been watching the proceedings suspended upside down from a tree branch. "It is not wise to dare a powerful bully to do his worst."

After the disturbance, the remaining animals confirmed their choice of Erin as the leader. Whenever a dispute arose among the animals, they would turn the matter over to him and would accept whatever he decided.

"Why only disputes?" Àgùnfon asked. "Why not go to him whenever we have any problem? Like, like . . . if some danger threatened, for instance?"

The rest of the animals agreed that the suggestion was good, entrusting their peace and safety to Erin and then dispersing.

The animals did not wait long to find out how Kìnìún meant to retaliate. Barely two days after the momentous assembly, Àgùnfon was out foraging at high noon when Kìnìún suddenly sprang upon him from the cover of the brush. The other animals about saw what was happening and fled in alarm. When Erin arrived at the spot after hearing of the incident, only Àgùnfon's bones remained.

From then on, Kìnìún became a regular terror with which the other animals had to contend. Almost daily Kìnìún made a meal of one of their number, and none knew who would be next. Hunger in the safety of their several hiding places became more welcome than seeking food in the open. Their despair deepened when, despite their insistent appeals to Erin to do something, he shunned a confrontation with the predator.

So desperate were they that they saw solace in a strange offer Kìnìún eventually made to them. Having surprised a group of them who had sought safety in numbers, he instead of attacking gave them a message for their leader Erin: he Kìnìún would spare them his surprise attacks and the new uncertainty in their lives, provided they would each day select from among themselves who would be his next meal.

At the assembly summoned to discuss the matter, the larger animals found the offer to be fair; the disease that threatened to kill them had suddenly brought a powerful medicine man their way, they thought. But the smaller ones thought it a foul idea. They saw no relief in the new development, for they knew who would be volunteered for Kìnìún's meals.

Suddenly, Àjàpá spoke up and said there would be no need to send any animal to Kìnìún.

"Was there a new message that I missed?" Erin asked.

"No," Àjàpá replied. "No new message. Only that Kìnìún's arrogance compares to that of the dried-mud idol that vows it will frolic in the downpour. Both ask to be humiliated."

"And who will do the humiliating?" Ìnàkí the Baboon asked.

"I mean to teach him humility, vegetable eater though I am. If I know Kìnìún as well as I think I do, we will be rid of the murderous bully by tomorrow; if not, we will be no worse off than we are now, but I will have lost face."

Some sniggered and some tittered at what they thought was drivel, and some were angered by Àjàpá's apparent levity in making jokes on such a grave occasion.

"Talk sense or put your mouth back in its sheath!" Ìnàkí snapped.

Less inclined to be dismissive, Erin asked if Àjàpá was actually offering to confront Kìnìún and somehow vanquish him. This was indeed what Àjàpá intended.

"Why waste time on Àjàpá?" Ìnàkí insisted impatiently. "Does one take an eagle seriously when he vows to swoop down and snatch a snail? He'll only worsen our problems. Kìnìún will quickly send him to his ancestors and then turn on the rest of us with renewed fury. We have no option but to do as Kìnìún says. Protest the fate meted out to you before you have the means to end it, and by so doing you invite a worse fate."

"If Ìnàkí wants to volunteer himself as the next meal for Kìnìún, let us applaud him," Àjàpá replied, unruffled. "To the rest of us, I say Kìnìún's strength has gone to his head, and it is time to teach him that strength without thought is the worst possible weakness."

Few of the animals felt inclined to strain themselves dissuading him. He was right, after all, that his failure would leave them in no worse predicament than they were in already, and if he succeeded, they would be much better off, indeed. The demand he then made of them did not alter that conclusion: they should secure a log and place it across the nearby stream, then rise early the following day to conceal themselves in the bush, emerging only upon his signal. He undertook not to give it unless he knew they would be safe. Secretly they vowed they would not emerge from hiding unless *they* saw that doing so would not endanger them.

Erin, humbled because, having accepted the honorific title of eagle, he had failed in the task of snatching a chicken, saw in the requests an opportunity to redeem himself. Finding and placing a log across the stream was a chicken he could snatch; he therefore volunteered to do the task himself.

Some of the animals thought there was little to choose between Àjàpá and Kìnìún, for were both not subject to the same disease of arrogance? Others, though, reasoned that an animal who swallows coconuts whole must have faith in his bum; if Àjàpá did not have faith in something, they knew not what, he certainly would not have volunteered for the task. They all dispersed from the meeting and anxiously awaited what news the morrow would bring.

The sun was hardly up next morning when Àjàpá made his way to Kìnìún's lair, where the latter was still snoozing. From some distance away Àjàpá hailed him and bade him a good morning.

Kìnìún awakened, stretched, and yawned, and then directed his eyes in the direction of the greeting. He could not immediately decipher what the clumsy creature wanted in his vicinity so early in the day, then it dawned on him that he must be the day's meal the animals had sent to him. An instant later, anger roused him further.

"You!" he roared. "*You?* What do you foolish animals take me for? Not a cow, not a pig, not even a goat. Am I to be contented with your measly shell and bones?"

"Noble, fearsome Kìnìún," Àjàpá responded, "the animals would not think of insulting you so. No, I am not your meal of the day."

"You aren't?" His voice showed distinct relief. "Who, then? Where is it?"

"That is why I am here, noble one. We have a problem."

"What problem? Do you not think whatever it is, it will be nothing compared to the problem you will all have if I do not get my meal?"

"Pardon me," Àjàpá explained patiently. "We were leading your food to you—a hefty cow, in fact—when a creature mightier than you stopped us and ordered us henceforth to send the food to him instead."

Kìnìún could barely restrain himself long enough to hear Àjàpá out.

"A creature mightier than I, indeed!" He was already on all fours, his tail stiffening for a fight. "What is this creature mightier than I?"

"A lion, just like you," Àjàpá responded. "We had not known of his existence because he lives underwater in a brook nearby. But from the looks of him he is a flame that can consume even the green bush."

"A flame, is he"? Kìnìún sneered. "Where is this flame?"

"His home is not far from here."

"Lead me to him," Kìnìún demanded. "This is the day this flame meets the water that will douse it.

Àjàpá led the way to the brook where he had ordered a log laid across the water according to his instruction.

As they approached the bank of the brook, Àjàpá began to feign great fear, quaking in his shell and proclaiming he dared go no farther. Kìnìún was even more insulted that the creature had shown no such fear in approaching him or in his company. He gradually worked himself into a rage that fairly blinded him and rendered him incapable of reason.

"Where is this flame?" He roared.

"He is . . . he is . . . right in the middle," Àjàpá stammered. In the middle of the of the water."

Kìnìún waited no longer, but charged onto the log bridging the brook. Halfway across he stopped and looked down, and, sure enough, there was a lion glaring up at him. He growled angrily, and the other did the same. He roared, and the other replied in kind.

Without further ado he plunged after his adversary, and the animals who had kept in hiding rushed to the edge of the brook to thwart any effort he might make to return to land. Their vigilance proved to be unnecessary, for Kìnìún found his death in the deep without any help from them.

Àjàpá and Àáyá Oníру̀-Méje
the Seven-Tailed Colobus Monkey

On a certain day in long-forgotten times, the *oba* consulted the oracle as he did each year in order to determine what the gods asked in return for another year of peace and prosperity for himself and his subjects. The ending year had brought no war, famine, or pestilence; instead, the rains came in their season and the sun in its turn shone to ripen the harvest. The spirit in the entire community was high, and the *oba* anticipated a festive season of sacrificing and feasting. When the *babaláwo* read Ifá's message, though, his face grew long and his lower jaw slackened. The *oba* noticed the inauspicious sign and asked what the oracle said.

"*Kábíyèsí*," the *babaláwo* replied, "Ifá says you will live long and last long; but what it asks further is beyond my understanding."

"How can that be?" the *oba* asked. "The pathfinder does not say he does not know the way nor the interpreter that he lacks knowledge of the language. If you cannot read the message of Ifá, how are we to find our way into the future?"

Begging the *oba*'s indulgence, the *babaláwo* explained that the difficulty he had with the message was not a result of its darkness but of its strangeness. He would cast his *òpèlè* again he said, to be certain his eyes had not deceived him the first time. Having done so again, though, he announced that Ifá's message remained the same, and troublesome. Impatient, the *oba* demanded to know what the message was. What was dropping from the sky that the earth could not support, he wanted to know.

At that the *babaláwo* looked the *oba* right in the eye and said, "*Kábíyèsí*, live long, last long on your father's throne. What Ifá asks is that this year you sacrifice a seven-tailed Colobus monkey to your father's head. The sacrifice will ward off all evil from you and your people; it will also bring children and riches cascading to your land."

"Did you say 'seven-tailed Colobus monkey'?" the *oba* asked in astonishment.

"So says Ifá, *Kábíyèsí*," replied the diviner.

The *oba* and the chiefs in attendance were dumbfounded. No one had ever seen or heard of Colobus monkeys with seven tails, nor indeed of any animal that had more than one tail. The assembly consulted was thrown into consternation, for the repercussions for not offering the prescribed sacrifice were the very well-being of the *oba* and his community. In the end, the *Basòrun*, the most senior of the chiefs and a venerable sage, spoke up.

"*Kábíyèsí*," he said, "did our fathers not say if the elephant forages all day long and its stomach remains empty, the disgrace is not the elephant's but the forest's?"

There was general agreement that he spoke the truth.

"We feed and worship the gods so that they might put honey in our lives, do we not?"

His audience asserted the truth in his question.

"We asked Ifá to tell us what the gods desired, and they named it. Having named it, they now must help us find it."

The murmur of agreement was less certain, but the *Basòrun*'s logic had some appeal to it.

"Ifá says the gods asked for a seven-tailed monkey, did he not?"

The chiefs agreed that indeed he did.

"Would they ask for something they knew did not exist?"

Of course not, they said, and the *Basòrun* concluded his argument that since Ifá specified the sacrifice, Ifá would help in its procurement. All the *oba* had to do was set the guild of hunters the task, and leave the rest to the gods.

III

The *oba* was relieved, and he accordingly ordered the crier to proclaim throughout the land a summons for all the hunters to report to the palace in three days for an important assignment. By the time the day dawned, the palace was teeming with the whole fraternity of hunters, hunters fearful in their cowrie-bedecked tunics hung with gourdlets of charms, and bearing their assorted weapons of choice. The *oba* had arranged for them to be fed breakfast, and that concluded, he went with his chiefs to the porch overlooking the courtyard and took his seat on the throne. The hunters lifted and shook their weapons in the air in greetings, proclaiming at the same time, "*Sáàkì,* hail the *oba!*"

The *oba* acknowledged their greetings with a wave of the horse-tail switch he carried in his right hand, and then he greeted them.

"Brave hunters, sturdy posts that hold up the fence, I greet you," he said. The hunters hailed him again, and he continued. "You are the pillars without which the roof will collapse. Without you our community is nothing. I greet you."

The hunters reveled in his praises, wondering what was afoot. They did not have long to wonder, for very soon the *oba* told them of their assignment. Masters of the animal and spirit worlds that they were, they were to take to the forest and find the lair of the seven-tailed Colobus monkey and deliver it alive to the *oba* to be sacrificed for the well-being of the community. He concluded by reminding them, "As you know, our fathers say a dutiful woman never fails to find the ingredients she needs for her stew. Let it not be said that you failed to find the means by which the gods will make life for us as clear as dawn water drawn from a stream undisturbed by wading feet."

A palpable silence enveloped the courtyard after the *oba* finished. The hunters looked at one another, wondering if they had heard right. Finally, one of them spoke up.

"*Kábíyèsí,*" he said, "live long on your father's throne. Please do not say I spoke out of turn, but, did you say 'seven-tailed Colobus monkey'?"

Yes, the hunter had heard correctly what the *oba* had said. The gods had specified a seven-tailed Colobus monkey, according to Ifá, so a seven-tailed Colobus monkey was the hunters' quarry. The hunters consulted among themselves for a long while, and in the end they assured the *oba* that they accepted the assignment. If such an animal existed in the forest, they said, they would capture it and deliver it to the *oba*. It was evident from the subdued manner of their departure, though, that they were not the least bit excited about the task the *oba* had set them.

They took to the forest half-heartedly, knowing before they started that their search would be futile, and after a few days they returned to the palace to report their failure to the *oba*. Was it not time, one of them suggested to the *oba,* to heed the words of the sages who said if the oracle calls for a bat and one cannot find a bat, one should substitute a sparrow? But the *babaláwo* was quick to put a stop to such nonsense. A seven-tailed Colobus monkey the sacrifice must be. The *oba* thanked the crestfallen hunters, and they dispersed.

The *oba* and the chiefs were at a loss what to do next, and after some consultation among themselves the *Basòrun* had an idea.

"Our fathers have a saying," he said, and the *oba* encouraged him to re-mind the chiefs of it.

"They say, when one loses something in a strange way, one must search for it in a strange way."

"A sound proverb," one of the chiefs remarked. "You will live long and use more."

"Because the matter called for a monkey," the *Basòrun* said, "our thoughts went immediately to hunters, and so they should have."

The *oba* and the other chiefs nodded and grunted their agreement, not at all sure where the talk was leading.

"But," he asked, "what hunter has ever seen or killed a seven-tailed Colobus monkey?"

No one knew.

"Perhaps what we want is not a hunter after all. But what or who we want, we do not know."

There was general agreement.

"What I say, therefore, *Kábíyèsí*," he continued, "is that you put the matter to the entire community. Who knows who out there will prove to be the one to find the weird creature the gods want?"

The suggestion won the applause of the *oba* and the other chiefs, and he accordingly ordered the crier to make the following proclamation: whoever can deliver alive to the *oba* within seven days a seven-tailed Colobus monkey will never again know want. The *oba* will divide into two all the property in his home and even in his pathways and present one half to the person.

In response, the able-bodied men all took to the forest in search of the strange animal. Those among them versed in medicine and charms invoked them to bring a seven-tailed Colobus monkey their way, but to no avail. As the days passed, more and more of the men despaired of winning instant wealth and returned home. As the seventh day approached, the *oba* himself began to despair of being able to make the sacrifice necessary to ensure the well-being of his people. What would he do if in his time the salt in his community lost its sweetening power? The prospect was unacceptable, and he forced his mind away from it.

The *oba* was deep in mournful depression in his audience chamber when a palace guard informed him that Àjàpá requested an urgent audience with him. The *oba* could hardly believe that he would be disturbed at a time like this by a prankster like Àjàpá, but the guard pleaded for his indulgence.

"*Kábíyèsí*, the words in his mouth brought me to you. Who does not know what he is? But then, who are we to make decisions that affect the fate of the land? None but you is wise enough to weigh his words and see what sense they carry."

At that, the *oba* ordered that Àjàpá be admitted to his presence. He was no sooner within the door than he commenced making the most exaggerated obeisance, almost touching his head to the floor as he slowly advanced, and repeating "*Kábíyèsí*, your illustrious life will be long."

"So be it, so be it," the *oba* said with ill-concealed impatience. "What brought the nocturnal field rat into the open at high noon?"

"*Kábíyèsí*," Àjàpá replied, "forgive me for presuming to cite a proverb in your presence, but would one remove one's loin cloth if one were not called upon to dance, or one's tunic if one were not about to wrestle? What brought me here is the matter of the seven-tailed Colobus monkey."

The *oba*, concealing his irritation at what he was sure was the prelude to another of Àjàpá's pranks, asked his visitor to explain his words.

"As you know, *Kábíyèsí*," he responded, "one sends only a wily dog to go after a leopard. Your efforts to catch the seven-tailed monkey failed because those you sent were the wrong people."

"And who might the right people be?" the *oba* asked.

"*Kábíyèsí*," he said, "the only messenger who can deliver the animal to you stands before you now."

The *oba* looked at him for some time, his inclination to laugh warring with the desire to give vent to anger at being trifled with. But he restrained himself and asked why Àjàpá had come to the palace empty-handed when he could have acted on the general proclamation which, after all, included him. His explanation was that he waited for all who thought they could accomplish the feat to try their hands, which he knew would prove inadequate. The real champion shows his hands only at the last, he said, and he wished to ensure that his success would elicit the acclaim and awe it would surely deserve.

After studying him for a while and wondering further about his temerity the *oba* asked of him, "You know, perhaps, what the reward for success in this venture is?"

"Certainly, *Kábíyèsí*," Àjàpá replied, "no less than half your entire property."

"And what would you suggest the punishment should be were you to fail to carry out your vow?"

"*Kábíyèsí*," he responded, "when a snail fastens itself to a tree trunk, it does not fail to climb it. Whatever task I make my own is as good as done. But, since *Kábíyèsí* asked the question I will answer it. I say if I fail, let me know when you draw your sword, but not when you sheathe it again."

Even the *oba* was impressed by Àjàpá's boldness—or foolhardiness—and he accepted his offer, giving him seven full days to make good on his vow. Immediately upon returning from the palace Àjàpá summoned his clan, saying he had great news for them. When they were all assembled he told them he had discovered the means by which all of them would enter into riches and greatness in their community.

"It sounds like work," grumbled an elderly member of the group, greatly offending Àjàpá.

"You might as well proclaim that my last meal was a mixture of corn bran and madness," he retorted. "Would I go searching for work with a torch, even when it has gone into hiding?"

Other members of the assembly reprimanded the offender for anticipating the song the would-be singer had in mind even though all he had done was open his mouth. Moreover, they said, he had unfairly questioned Àjàpá's integrity. He apologized, and Àjàpá presented his plan.

"All I want you to do," he informed the gathering, "is go to the forest with me and hide until you hear me call."

Then what? he was asked.

"Then rush to where I am and grab the creature I have my arms around."

"Did I say it, or did I not say it?" the earlier complainer exclaimed in vindication. "It is work!"

Before the others fell in line behind the troublemaker, Àjàpá quickly challenged, "Who of you does not lift food to your mouth with your own hands? What I ask is no more work than that! And what awaits you in return is more than full stomachs, but also riches, wealth, and renown in the town!"

His argument swayed the others. After they secured Àjàpá's assurance that the adventure entailed no physical danger, they agreed to do as he asked. He thereupon sent them home, bidding them assemble in front of his home at first light on the morrow.

At first light, Àjàpá's relatives gathered before his house, most bleary-eyed and many harboring second thoughts about the enterprise they were about to embark upon. Àjàpá himself was the very figure of jauntiness when he emerged from the house, laden with a huge sack whose contents he disclosed to no one. Ungainly though his burden made him, he nonetheless cheerfully led the way, and the others straggled after him into the forest. He took the path that led to the stream so far from their town that they regarded it as lying at the edge of their world. They walked until the dew was dry on the leaves, and they could faintly hear the sound of the stream. There Àjàpá stopped them. There they were to hide and await his summons. After thus instructing them, he continued alone and was soon hidden from their sight beyond the bend in the path.

He walked to the stream and followed it some distance to a spot he knew from earlier forest wanderings as the location where the forest's monkeys came to drink. From his vantage point in the undergrowth he had watched as monkeys with assorted deformities came to slake their thirst, splash in the water, and sometimes bask in the sun. He had seen monkeys with no tails and monkeys with two tails; where there were two tails, he reasoned, there surely could be seven tails. And, believer in the gods that he was, he knew that they would not have demanded that a seven-tailed Colobus monkey be sacrificed if there were no such creature. Besides, he had never been more certain that the spirit of his dead father had arranged the whole affair as a means of permanently ridding him of concern.

He set down his sack and untied it to release the contents: a bow and several arrows, a cutlass, and a bundle of mashed and fermented melon seeds whose powerful stink immediately drew a cloud of flies. He scattered the weapons at random on the ground and rubbed the smelly paste all over himself; then he lay down among the weapons in a way that would convince whoever saw him that he was dead. Thus he lay until the sun went down and darkness began to envelop the forest. His ears soon caught the approaching chatter of monkeys as they jumped excitedly from tree branch to tree branch. When they were close to the stream, they left the branches for the ground and approached their drinking hole. The leader of the pack saw Àjàpá first and stopped, also halting the others. Seeing the weapons scattered about Àjàpá and taking him for a hunter, they retreated some distance. Their leader then inched toward the still figure, and for the first time his nose registered the powerful stink. A corpse, he decided, and he was emboldened.

Carefully, he walked right up to the figure on the ground, gave it a tentative kick, and sprang back as a precaution. Seeing no movement from the figure, he advanced again and this time took his time prodding it and inspecting it from all angles. He then announced to the others that death had claimed the death-dealing hunter. One less wretch to worry about. The other monkeys approached Àjàpá, kicked at him, and danced on him and around him in jubilation.

The leader permitted the celebration to go on some time before reminding the others that, as the custom was, any extraordinary event must not be kept from the elders and dignitaries. Accordingly, he said, he would summon the lowest ranking of them, and he cautioned those around him to be on their best behavior in the presence of the elders. He then raised his voice and sang:

> *Two-tailed elder, behold a sight,*
> *A hunter sprawled out by the stream!*
> *His weapons lie harmlessly about.*
> *I see no breath,*
> *He smells of death,*
> *But, caution, still,*
> *Lest a lifeless hand come to life*
> *And grab you firmly by the heel!*

He only had to repeat the song twice before a rustling noise signaled the approach of the dignitary it summoned. Soon a two-tailed Colobus monkey came into view, accompanied by a handful of attendants. He sniffed at the figure on the ground and prodded it with his feet. Satisfied that before him was indeed a corpse, he in turn summoned the next-senior elder, the three-tailed Colobus monkey. He sang:

Three-tailed elder, behold a sight,
A hunter sprawled out by the stream!
His weapons lie harmlessly about.
I see no breath,
He smells of death,
But, caution, still,
Lest a lifeless hand come to life
And grab you firmly by the heel!

The three-tailed elder arrived and made his inspection, and he in turn summoned *his* next-senior elder, the four-tailed Colobus monkey. So the process continued up the line, while Àjàpá's excitement grew almost out of control. So elated was he that his mouth began to water as though in anticipation of a delicious feast.

A day that was twenty years away soon becomes the morrow; so also at last the six-tailed Colobus monkey, satisfied with his inspection of the corpse by the stream took up the song and aimed it in the direction of the seven-tailed patriarch of Colobus monkeys:

Seven-tailed patriarch behold this sight,
A hunter sprawled out by the stream!
His weapons lie harmlessly about.
I see no breath,
He smells of death,
But, caution, still,
Lest a lifeless hand come to life
And grab you firmly by the heel!

As the strain of the singing ended, the leaves overhead nearby filled with activity and soon the patriarch's attendants arrived at the gathering, urging those already there to give way. The patriarch himself then lumbered into view, his seven tails sweeping the ground after him. He peered at the seemingly lifeless hunter, and then he looked again. He was known not to be given to excited gesticulations or any significant display of emotion, but those watching him still thought there was something odd about his reaction. He took another closer look, and then genuine alarm registered on his face. Those among the monkeys that were not already panicking did so when, as the patriarch swung around and made to flee, the dead hunter came to life and grabbed as many of the seven tails as he could enfold and called out to his clan.

When war is only a subject of talk there is much bravery in every chest and every mouth; when it does in fact break out, most wise people trade valor for discretion. For the assembled monkeys, even if they had just purchased pounded yams they were not about to wait for the stew to eat with them. They fled in all directions, their terror multiplying when they saw a host of other hunters coming at them. The patriarch frantically tried to detach Àjàpá from his tails, swinging him about and dashing him against trees, but nothing helped. As for Àjàpá himself, though his shell was cracked and his muscles ached, he clung to the tails with all his strength, reminding himself like the coward who inadvertently found himself in a fight that even the longest day must end. Fortunately, help arrived before his prize could escape. They joined Àjàpá in subduing the captive seven-tailed Colobus monkey, and together they bore him in triumph back from the edge of the world to the town.

In due time the *oba* performed the sacrifice that would ensure peace, harmony, wealth, and fertility for his town and people for another year; and in gratitude to Àjàpá, he fulfilled his promise by dividing all his property in two and presenting one half to him. Asked how he managed the feat that had thwarted the town's best hunters, Àjàpá smiled and said, "There is nothing quite like expertise in one's calling. Why, you should see me walk through a peanut farm—my jaws cannot rest, for somehow my mouth constantly fills with peanuts!"

His listeners looked at one another, shrugged, and agreed that his words were unanswerable.

Àjàpá and Àjànàkú
the Would-Be *Oba*

Outstretched hands pluck a gigantic tale, which comes crashing down and brings Àjàpá scurrying from his lair into the midst of the unrest gripping his town.

It had been two years since the last rain clouds darkened the sky, and much longer since scattered rain drops teased the baking earth, which hissed at them, vaporized them, and sent them reeling skyward. Planted seedlings withered in the earth, or if they germinated the affronted sun in no time scorched the shoots that ventured above the soil, so that by the end of the day if one rubbed them between one's palms they were reduced to dust. Trees and shrubs were bare of leaves, their branches pointing nakedly at the cloudless sky, and the haggard tree trunks wore a brown coat of the dust that occasional hot breezes lifted off the bare earth and sent swirling across the land.

Men gave up trying to work farms no one could coax into fertility in the absence of moisture, conserving the little energy their increasingly impoverished diet afforded them. Women were daily challenged to perform the minor miracle of filling food bowls with something the eye could tolerate, the mouth could accept, and the stomach could retain. Success in accomplishing that feat became their solace, because lack of stamina made them relinquish their roles as mothers. Besides, more children meant more mouths to feed.

The *oba* had long since become a voluntary prisoner in his palace, for wasn't the welfare of his community his responsibility? The ancestors provided no alternative by which an *oba* could evade it and pass the blame for the troubles of his time to the earth or the sun, the gods or the ancestors. Whoever sat on the throne bore the duty, whenever the life of the community was scrambled, of finding out what power had been slighted or otherwise offended, and of appeasing it in order to restore order to life. It was not that he had been remiss in that duty, for one passed the desiccated remains of sacrifices everywhere: at this crossroads, chicken bones sticking out of feathers matted with palm oil; at the base of that *ìrókò* tree, snail shells bleached chalk-white by the sun—the creatures that once called them home had long ago shriveled to nothing; and by that river bank, cowrie shells surrounding the random bones and grinning skull of a he-goat. The *oba* saw in these testimonies to his propitiatory efforts the mockery of the gods, and he did not want to see mockery also reflected in the eyes of his people. So he kept to his palace until such time as the ancestors looked again with kindly eyes upon him and upon his people. He knew they would when the time was ripe, for if the community is destroyed, would the ancestors themselves not perish?

Such was the plight of the people when Olú Awo, the chief of the *babaláwo* who alone can speak to the Ifá oracle and divine its messages, informed the *oba* that Ifá had at long last spoken to the troubles and shown how to end the people's suffering. Even as Olú Awo spoke, the *oba* sent messengers to summon his chiefs so all could hear the welcome news and so that they would lose no time in arranging for whatever sacrifice Ifá would prescribe. But when the *oba* and the chiefs heard Olú Awo's message, their hopeful excitement became considerably tempered.

"Ifá demands the sacrifice of an elephant at the big market outside the palace," he said.

If he had any expectation that his words would stun his audience, the bland expression Olú Awo returned to the wide-eyed and speechless *oba* and chiefs gave no indication of it.

The *oba* finally found his voice. "An elephant?" he asked.

"Yes, *Kábíyèsí,* an elephant."

The *oba* sat back in his chair and looked from one chief to the other. They in turn looked at one another, at the *oba,* and at Olú Awo. Finally, the *Basòrun* spoke.

"*Kábíyèsí,*" he said, "this thing Olú Awo has dropped in our midst is heavy indeed, but not too heavy for the ancestors to lift. It calls for the resourcefulness of our hunters. Olúóde will no doubt rally his men and find us an elephant to sacrifice."

"*Kábíyèsí,*" Olúóde, chief of the hunters' guild, responded, "as long as there are elephants in the forest, the task is not difficult. Within our ranks are numerous men who have scaled the summit of our ranking and earned the title, elephant-killer; we will kill an elephant, and no doubt bringing it to the market afterward is not a task the arms of our people cannot encompass."

Olú Awo shook his head.

"Olúóde, pardon me; don't say I killed the words flowing from your mouth." He now addressed the *oba.* "*Kábíyèsí,* what Olúóde has said is wise, but it is not what Ifá directs. Ifá told us to sacrifice an elephant at the market; Ifá did not ask for the meat and bones of a dead elephant."

The short silence that ensued was ended by Olúóde's soft laughter. The look he directed at the priest was empty of flattery.

"Forgive me," he said with sarcasm, "if my words sound like those of an ignorant child, but, you are not saying . . ."

Olú Awo knew the direction of Olúóde's words.

"I am saying that Ifá asks for a *live* elephant and wants it sacrificed at the market."

Whatever initial hope the assembly had that the end of the community's troubles was near quickly dissipated. Unspoken, the elders' pertinent sayings about the elephant ran through several minds: "The king that will catch and tether an elephant has not yet been crowned . . . The rope maker who will fashion a rope to hold an elephant is yet unborn . . . An elephant is not an animal one awaits in an ambush . . . The liana that attempts to stop an elephant in its tracks will find itself accompanying the elephant on its way."

"*Kábíyèsí*, the errand Ifá gave me is what I have delivered," Olú Awo said somewhat defensively and apologetically.

The *oba* thanked him. Turning to Olúóde, he said, "since the matter concerns an elephant, we will leave it to you and your men. The forest and its animals fall in your domain; if the peace of our land calls for an animal, the duty falls on you to provide it. When a duty falls on a father he does not shift it to his son. The eyes of all our dead hunters will keep watch for you."

The story does not bear undue prolonging. Olúóde failed to persuade his men to set traps to catch an animal; they were not afraid, they said, but they were not imbeciles either. Those among them in the elephant-killer class reminded him that they were elephant killers, not elephant catchers. They were not inclined to test the truth of the saying that whoever attempts what no one before had ever attempted will endure what no one before had endured. In the end Olúóde shamefacedly reported his failure to the *oba*.

After further consultations, the *oba* and his chiefs concluded that the matter must be published. Since they found no path in the direction they now faced, perhaps someone as yet unknown to them might know in which direction to look. The *oba* therefore ordered the town crier to proclaim the news. He would richly reward whoever succeeded in bringing an elephant to the market for sacrificing.

When an elephant dies, all sorts of knives materialize to carve it up. The unusual announcement brought many offers from men for whom the promised reward eclipsed all thought and caution. As long as the volunteer was a man old enough to wash his own face, the *oba* accepted his offer. Singly and in companies they went after elephants; some tried elephant-size nooses as their weapons, some tried loud noises to stampede the animal in the direction of the market, and others tried charms to stupefy the elephant and cause him to obey their directions. All failed, the less fortunate losing their lives in their foolish efforts, and the more fortunate being terrified and chastened for life.

Finally, Àjàpá presented himself at the palace and sought an audience with the *oba* and his chiefs. His wish granted, he grandly announced that he was the one they had been seeking.

"You?" the incredulous *oba* asked.

"None other," he responded. "Me, three stalwarts rolled into one."

Olúóde did not conceal the ridicule in his laughter.

"When a father invites suitors with substantial support behind them to come wooing his daughter, he does not have humpbacks in mind."

"Look," *Basòrun* cautioned him, "our best hunters and medicine men have failed at the task. You no doubt have heard the saying that it is the stranger who knows his place and his limit that enters a community and leaves without incurring disgrace. Go home and cease courting disgrace."

Àjàpá ignored them and addressed the *oba* instead.

"*Kábíyèsí,*" he said "you will long wear the crown on your head and the shoes on your feet."

"So it will be!" the *oba* and his chiefs responded.

"I did not come here to amuse you or myself when weighty problems need solving. I am not here, either, because too much palm-wine has clouded my eyes and thought. I am no child that vows he will do what he cannot do. You want a live elephant in the marketplace, I offer to deliver a live elephant at the marketplace. Is that not an end of the matter?"

The *oba* considered him for a moment before answering.

"Tell me," he said, "you have no arrows, or, if you did, no arms to use them. And you lack the medicine, the charms, and the incantations to work your will on whoever and whatever you please. Those who do have failed in this task. How would you do it?"

"*Kábíyèsí,*" he responded, "it is the finger that is proper for the nose that one sticks into the nose to clean it. There are tasks for which arrows are proper and tasks for which they are not; there are tasks for which incantations are proper and tasks for which they are not. Those who failed before me chose the wrong tools for their task. Now I offer my effort, just as the champion enters the arena only at the last."

The *oba* still looked skeptical.

"*Kábíyèsí,*" Àjàpá urged, "Do I ask that you judge the quality of my stew from afar or from report? I ask you to judge it on your tongue, by its taste! Shall we sit by a river and argue about whether a piece of soap will foam or will not foam? Whether I can do as I say or not is easily proved: if a live elephant arrives at the market I have succeeded; if not, I have failed. Then you may do with me as you please!"

His argument was persuasive, and the *oba* and his chiefs had no option but to give him leave to prove himself. Before he left, though, Àjàpá said that when his plan was ready to be implemented he would need assistance from the people of the town, nothing that was too strenuous or that might endanger them, and he received the assurance of all the help he might need.

Àjàpá's boast that he would deliver an elephant was not idle. Erin the Elephant was no stranger to him: the small, slow, and vulnerable Àjàpá had devoted considerable time to studying the fearful, formidable, and mountainous adversary, for he reasoned that his survival in the same environment with such a creature depended on how well he could read his habits and anticipate his actions. Erin, he knew, was a slave to his appetite for sweet foods, especially any food flavored with honey. As soon as he left the palace, therefore, he procured some honey—and black-eyed beans, palm-oil, an onion, and some salt, ingredients for making *àkàrà*, fried bean fritters that he knew Erin also craved.

He spent the rest of the day preparing the ingredients and frying the *àkàrà*, which he then left to soak overnight in the honey. When the sun had cleared the skeletal branches of the dried-up forest trees, Àjàpá bundled the honey-soaked *àkàrà* and went in search of Erin. He was not difficult to find, the foliage that would have concealed him having burned off in the prolonged drought. Àjàpá was still a long way from his resting quarry when he commanded the other's attention with loud praises, which he accompanied with gestures of worshipful obeisance as he crawled forward.

126

"*Kábíyèsí,* owner of this land!" he declaimed. "Illustrious *oba,* next in stature to the gods."

Erin looked about, wondering how an *oba* came to be in his vicinity without his noticing, but Àjàpá's next words told him he was the object of this strange salute:

Àjànàkú!
All the digits on one's paws do not suffice
To point at you.
With only one trunk you uproot palm-trees;
If you had two you would reduce the sky to tatters.
Àjànàkú!
Majestic one,
Singly you cause tremors in the forest;
One pass through the bush
And you clear a path;
Two passes
And the bush becomes an open space.
Àjànàkú!
You swallow palm-fruits whole
In their bunches, spikes and all.
The hunter boasts at home
That he is an elephant killer;
He sees you in the forest and flees,
Giving his arrows to the swamps;
If I live, he says,
There will be a tomorrow to make more arrows.
Àjànàkú! . . .

His crawling had by now brought him close to the befuddled elephant, and he would have continued his declamation had Erin not stopped him.

"Enough!" he snapped, lifting himself slightly. Àjàpá complied but maintained his respectful pose.

"Are you talking in your sleep, or have you been eating fermented corn?"

"Neither, *Kábíyèsí* . . ."

"Neither!" Erin interrupted. "If neither, what is the meaning of your '*Kábíyèsí*' in the open forest?"

"Great news," Àjàpá assured him. "Hear me out, and you will understand my greeting."

"What news?"

"The humans have chosen you for their king!"

Erin reared up, eyes ablaze, in anger at being thus trifled with by the puny creature, but Àjàpá had anticipated his anger. Erin was just commencing his charge when Àjàpá threw one large ball of *àkàrà* in his direction.

Erin was not so angry that he did not recognize a delicacy. He checked his movement, sniffed at the *àkàrà*, and sat back down to eat it. Àjàpá threw another ball toward him before continuing.

"They sent these as a token of their esteem and sincerity." With that he inched forward and placed the rest of the *àkàrà* before Erin. He sat back and watched Erin eat, listening with satisfaction to the involuntary grunts of delight rumbling from the elephant's throat. Àjàpá could almost see him in the marketplace already.

Erin did not look up until he had swallowed the last of the *àkàrà* and picked up every crumb from the ground. Only then did he recall Àjàpá's presence. Now he fixed the bearer of the curious message and the irresistible delicacies with quizzical eyes.

"Humans want me, elephant, to be their king?" he asked dubiously.

"*Kábíyèsí*," Àjàpá replied, "I know it is strange, unheard of, in fact. But you know the saying that a woman is not named 'Kúmólú' without a good reason. If an ironsmith's dross repeatedly lands on the same spot on the rod, one knows there must be a mark there. There is a reason for their decision. Ifá ordered them to offer you their crown and their throne."

"And what was Ifá thinking . . . ?"

Àjàpá was eager to explain. "It is on account of the great drought that will not end. Ifá says only by crowning you will the disaster end."

Erin took his time in considering Àjàpá's words. The humans' condition was indeed desperate, he knew, and it would not be unusual for Ifá to prescribe desperate remedies. Àjàpá's words interrupted his ruminations.

"If you accept the throne and the crown," he said, "they promise you a daily feast of *àkàrà*, just as the ones they sent you today."

Erin was beginning to feel the crown on his head and to see himself on a throne in the palace. Then a thought occurred to him.

"What becomes of their present *oba*?"

Àjàpá did not hesitate before responding.

"Ah! Did the news not reach you? Ha! The *oba* climbed up into the rafters to join his ancestors a while ago. Only the difficult times prevented the usual grand funeral ceremonies. The throne has been empty awhile. With your consent, they mean to have you occupy it in seven days."

"Seven days?" Erin asked.

"They mean to lose no more time before tasting the happiness of having a new *oba* and seeing the end of their woes."

After another brief consideration, Erin said, "Tell them I will be their king."

"*Kábíyèsí!*" Àjàpá shouted. "Owner of this land. I would dance, I would rejoice, I would roll in the dust to worship you, but that I must not delay to give the good news to those who sent me. I must hurry. But make yourself ready, *Kábíyèsí*, for in seven days I will be back here, with a royal delegation, to conduct you in a fitting manner to your throne."

His elation as he returned home was such that his paws seemed not to tough the earth.

The people of the town, on instruction from the *oba*, spent the intervening days before Erin's arrival carrying out Àjàpá's wishes. The women prepared large amounts of *àkàrà* and soaked them in honey, and the men dug a large pit on the sacrificial spot in the market. This they would cover with rich velvet cloth on the appointed date. At the far end of the pit, the end opposite the approach Erin and his company would take, a richly decorated, elephant-sized throne was to be positioned.

Look well into a drawn-out tale and you will find it is all lies. To cut this one short, the day Àjàpá set for Erin's enthronement arrived. He put on his richest ceremonial attire, and so did the members of the delegation the *oba* had appointed to accompany him on his errand. They set off for the forest on horseback, attended by the royal bugler and drummers, festive dancers and, of course, porters bearing baskets full of honey-dripping *àkàrà*. The drummers played, the bugler blew, and dancers danced as they sang:

We'll make Erin our oba,
Oh, what a joyous day!
Our troubles are over,
Oh, what a joyous day!

It had been years since the town saw any festivity at all, and the scale of the one they now witnessed persuaded them that their woes were indeed at an end.

The entire town had turned out for the occasion on the *oba*'s orders and lined the approaches to the market just as they would if a new *oba* were arriving to take his throne. They watched the cloud of dust the delegation kicked up as it went for Erin, until it disappeared and the sound of drumming and singing died off in the distance. Then they waited.

Erin saw the approaching dust cloud, and then he heard the drumming, and his heart raced. He had groomed himself for the occasion, and he did look royal as he rose to his fullest height and craned his neck, impatient to see the delegation. The bridegroom awaiting the procession bringing his new bride strains to see her from afar, as though her destination were not his chamber.

Soon he could hear the singing and decipher the words, and his excitement mounted. If he harbored any doubts about the life that awaited him on the throne, they vanished when he saw the size of the crowd and their rich attire. Àjàpá urged his horse ahead of the company and summoned the *àkàrà* bearers to follow.

Close to Erin he quickly dismounted and prostrated himself and offered his homage:

Kábíyèsí, *our* oba!
Owner of the forest,
Owner of the town also.
Scion of peerless stalwarts
Who bequeath prosperity to their offspring.
Fathers pray
That their children's achievement
Surpass their own.
Yours compared to your fathers'
Is like a palm-tree
Compared to the earth-hugging creeper.
Kábíyèsí, *your throne awaits you.*

He rose now, and invited Erin to eat the delicacies that his new subjects had sent to fortify him for the journey ahead. "Eat your fill," he urged.

The bearers of the *àkàrà* deposited their loads before Erin, who did not dally before consuming them. That done the delegation headed back into town with drumming, and singing, and dancing, and Erin himself even affecting the dignified, slow movement that his new status required.

The waiting crowd welcomed the returning procession with a roar, and as it passed the people closed behind it, swelling the multitude that approached the marketplace. As was proper, all the chiefs were ranged on both sides of the throne, on the far side of the velvet spread. They welcomed the approaching procession by dancing to its music, and Erin was immensely moved by the esteem the people displayed towards him.

As they approached the throne, Àjàpá halted and addressed Erin.

"There is your throne, *Kábíyèsí.* Claim it, and await your crown!"

With that he stepped aside, and Erin, with as much dignity as an elephant can muster in such a position, stepped forward to walk across the velvet spread to his throne.

131

After he landed in the pit, some moments elapsed before Erin realized that he had been duped. It was too late.

In his agony, he could see Àjàpá looking down on him from above, an evil grin on his face, and he could also hear Àjàpá's shout, "Whoever eats the sweet must not be averse to savoring the sour!"

Olú Awo had already commenced the rites of the sacrifice by the pit, and at the proper moment the waiting hunters lent their services in dispatching the victim.

As Ifá promised, the drought soon ended. Peace, ease, and happiness returned to the community. The *oba* did not renege on his promise to Àjàpá, either. He went away with riches and the admiration of the people.

ÀJÀPÁ HUMBLES ERIN THE ELEPHANT

Our fathers in their wisdom caution against writing anybody off, or concluding from the person's current lowly station or misfortune that he or she will never see better days. "The world turns like a rolling coconut . . . No one season exhausts time . . . Yesterday a king, today a homeless vagrant." And just as they warn that one must not reduce others or their possibilities to nothing, so they point out the folly of making too much of oneself, for the lofty horse one's pride has placed under one might turn out to be nothing but a cockroach. Thus our fathers unstintingly dispense wisdom, but not many heed them. The bean fritters seller, they say, seldom knows how to read the signs until she must reduce her asking price to a tenth.

The animals of the forest lived in awe of Erin the Elephant, so mighty that he could wrap his trunk around a mature tree and pull it from the ground, roots and all, or if the tree's girth was such that his trunk could not encompass it, he nevertheless could fell it by bringing his weight to bear against it. His might, and no doubt his resounding footfall, caused his fellow animals to celebrate him as the lone stalwart that causes the forest to tremble and quake. Unfortunately for him, his self-pride matched and even exceeded his size; indeed, those animals unfavorably disposed toward him had a different word for it—arrogance. They resented his haughty habit of filling the forest with his trumpeting, his way of reminding other forest-dwellers of his overlordship. Further, whenever the animals assembled to discuss affairs of common interest, he not only forced his preferences upon the assembly but also smothered speech in the mouths of lesser animals, causing whoever was the unfortunate object of his rebuke to curl into an insignificant ball.

The armor-plate shell that encases Àjàpá as his outer skin protects him from physical dangers, but in the view of the other animals in the forest it also renders him impervious to insults, ridicule, shame, or any of those inconvenient sentiments that make one do for form's sake what one would not otherwise do. The general consensus was that nothing ever makes an impression on him, but he would prove them wrong.

The animals of the forest had assembled to hear a complaint from Kòlòkòlò the Fox that Kìnìún the Lion had twice in as many days chased him off the prey he had killed and consumed it, thus unfairly causing him to go hungry.

The proceedings had started off awkwardly because Kìnìún had insisted on presiding.

"As the titular king of this forest," he had announced, "it is my prerogative to preside over all momentous matters."

"Even, er, even when you are a party to the dispute?" Ehoro the Rabbit asked uncertainly, nose twitching.

"Especially when I am a party to the dispute," Kìnìún roared.

He glared now at his accuser, who, too late, remembered the admonition that, if someone mightier than one sends one reeling with an unprovoked and undeserved blow, one would do well to cover one's retreat with a broad grin.

"Because some of us are weaker than others of us," he asked lamely, "must we starve even when we labor for our food?"

Kìnìún sat licking his paws for a while, as though the matter under discussion had nothing to do with him, and waited to see if anyone would take up his accuser's cause. No one did. Now he got up, stretched, yawned luxuriantly, and sauntered off. The other animals looked at one another, not knowing what to say. It was Erin who finally broke the silence.

"This is a matter between carcass-eaters," he said. "Let them settle it between themselves. In fact," he added, turning to Kòlòkòlò, "I smell some folly in your talk. Do you not consider yourself fortunate to be able to bring your complaint to this assembly? Do you not know that even you are food for Kìnìún?"

Kòlòkòlò was speechless, and the assembled animals were stunned, not because Erin's words were false, but because they were lacking in delicacy and tact. Wishing to take advantage of the embarrassed silence that enveloped the gathering to ingratiate himself with Erin, Àjàpá spoke up.

"As one plant-eater to another, I place my words next to yours in support. This complaint lacks wisdom or merit."

The murmur that arose from the group could have been of approval or disapproval—not even Kòlòkòlò could tell as he looked, perplexed, around the circle. The look on Erin's face was unmistakable, however. It was one of utter contempt.

"Was that barking I heard?" he asked looking at Ajá the Dog. "My eyes did not see Ajá open his mouth, but I believe I heard a sound like barking." With that he turned meaningfully towards Àjàpá.

"Whoever cannot make the earth take notice of his footfall should sheath his mouth," he sneered.

The other animals quickly shook off their unease at Erin's earlier indecorum and embraced the new opportunity he gave them for mirth at Àjàpá's expense. Their laughter found a gap in his armor like a porcupine's quill, shaming him, and characteristically, sending a rush of blood to his head, lightening it as he thought furiously of a fitting response to Erin's ridicule.

Erin was about to get up when Àjàpá found his voice.

"If I did not know that your brain is smothered every time you sit down, I would be offended by your foolish utterance."

The listening animals gasped. Not one had ever dared to talk back to Erin, let alone insult him to his face! Erin was equally shocked, and also furious. He lumbered up, his ears flaring.

"This is the day your mouth brings you death," he snapped, making for

Àjàpá who, fortunately, was in the midst of other animals. They panicked at the threat of being crushed by the infuriated mass of flesh and bones, and Àjàpá took advantage of their fright.

"Control yourself!" he commanded. "If your age has taught you neither shame nor caution, at least show some regard for this assembly."

Inexplicably, perhaps because he had never faced such a situation before, Erin was checked by Àjàpá's words, and Àjàpá quickly continued.

"Your quarrel is with me, not with these innocent animals your lumbering mass threatens to crush. Name the day and I will meet you in a fair fight. Then I will teach you that there is another life besides this one. I'll beat the crap out of you, exposing your puny brain, and I'll scratch you until you bleed like a pig."

Erin reared in fury, raised his trunk, and trumpeted his outrage to the whole forest.

"Name the day!" Àjàpá shouted back, "and in the presence of all forest-dwellers you will learn to tame your arrogance."

Erin began an involuntary dance as he lurched now this way and now that, sputtering and fuming. The other animals now trained their eyes on him, wondering why he did not take up the challenge Àjàpá had thrown at him. Was he perhaps afraid, unsure of himself? Their eyes bore through Erin's hide, and he realized his revenge could not be now.

"Tomorrow!" he trumpeted. "Tomorrow it is. Tomorrow I kill you!" With that he lumbered off.

"Meet me here tomorrow, at sunrise," Àjàpá called after him, "and I will send you back home a much battered but much wiser animal."

The assembled animals relished the spectacle. They had chafed under Erin's constant overbearing and abusive oafishness, and they were all too happy to watch him discomfited. They cared very little that Àjàpá had this time virtually ensured his own untimely demise, for most of them had one time or another fallen victim to his crooked and treacherous antics. It was in fact with some excitement that they dispersed in chattering groups, commenting on the confrontation between the unlikely pair and having quite forgotten the reason for the assembly in the first place. They gleefully anticipated the morning and its promised entertainment, for if they knew Àjàpá, the knowing ones among them said, he would simply crawl into his shell to await Erin's flattening step; he would perform a feat or two and then embrace death still screaming his defiance.

For his part, Àjàpá had not the slightest intention of embracing death, either meekly or even defiantly. He hurled his challenge at Erin because he could not accept Erin's public ridicule of him. Now that he had achieved his immediate desire of deflating Erin's pride, he set his brain to work to devise some means of getting the better of his almighty foe and protecting his life at the same time. His brain seldom failed to come up with schemes even in seemingly impossible situations, and this time the challenge urged it to unprecedented imagination.

As soon as the last of the loitering animals had departed the gathering place, Àjàpá hurried to the market and bought three gourds and some dried camwood resin. These he took to a stream whose bed contained a generous supply of lime. First he filled one of the gourds with water and dumped the camwood resin into it, and then, covering it with his hands, he shook it vigorously until all of the resin had dissolved in the water. Then he filled another gourd almost full with lime and added a little water to it. He shook the mixture only briefly, making sure that the lime whitened the liquid but remained in clumps. After putting only a bit of water in the third gourd, he carried all three back to the gathering place and hid in the bush the two containing the mixtures. The third he took with him in search of dung, which was, fortunately, plentiful in the vicinity, thanks to the recent gathering. In very little time he had filled it and had thoroughly agitated it to achieve a satisfactory consistency.

That done, he securely stopped the mouths of all three gourds with bundled leaves, and one by one, he carried them to tree branches overhanging the arena where the fight would take place in the morning, and hid them on these. Satisfied with his preparations, he went home, ate a good supper, and slept as though the forest and all that dwelt therein belonged to him.

He woke early and refreshed on the fateful morning. Other creatures in his situation would feel some apprehension about the ordeal ahead, but not Àjàpá. He was satisfied that he had done all in his power to prepare himself, and he was sure Erin's conceit would result in the defeat of the elephant. The only concession he made to the chance of failure was to eat a hearty breakfast. If it turned out that he was sent prematurely to join his ancestors, he did not wish to go before the spirit of his dead father with a growling stomach.

He was not at all surprised that he was not the first to arrive at the arena. Indeed, although the sun had not roused itself from where it passed the night, when Àjàpá arrived at the scene the place already teemed with eager spectators. Nor was he surprised that Kìnìún had appointed himself the master of the occasion, as he ceremoniously informed Àjàpá.

"It is my prerogative as titular king of this forest to preside over all momentous matters."

He looked around as though expecting some comment. None was forthcoming.

"Especially when I am not a party to the dispute."

Àjàpá did not object.

The crowd continued to swell as sunrise approached, until every forest-dweller was present at the scene. Then, just as the sun peeped from behind the distant hills, Erin stumped into view, ears flared and eyes blazing.

"Where is that insect?" he demanded as he charged into the arena, but Kìnìún's growl attracted his attention.

"Patience, Erin," he called. "Your challenger awaits you, but as titular king of this forest I have taken charge of this occasion. My purpose is to ensure a clean and orderly contest. Your tussle is with Àjàpá; do what you will with him, but take care that you endanger no other animal in this gathering. I have no such fear of Àjàpá, of course."

Erin had no time to take offense at what those words implied, so impatient was he to find Àjàpá and crush the life out of his miserable body.

"Where is he?"

"Behind you, you bloated mass of blubber!"

On hearing Àjàpá's reply, Erin laboriously swiveled around intending to grind the wretch into the earth with his massive fore stump. But while he was thus maneuvering himself, Àjàpá had skipped nimbly to position himself directly underneath Erin, carefully watching all four huge stumps and maintaining a constant dance to stay out of their way and yet remain invisible under Erin as the latter tried ever more frantically, and furiously, to locate his adversary.

The forest roared with the laughter of the assembled audience. Nothing seemed more comical than an arrogant giant of an animal reduced to an idiot dancer to no music at all. The more the watchers laughed, the more animated Erin's gyrations became and the more comical he seemed.

In his frantic antics Erin kicked up such a cloud of dust that visibility within the arena became severely limited. Àjàpá took advantage of the situation to slip out from under Erin, scramble up a trees whose branches hung over the arena, and at an opportune moment, drop onto Erin's back.

The dust and the watchers' uncontrolled laughter prevented them from seeing how Àjàpá got Erin to become his bearer, but the new turn of events only increased their delight at the entertainment to which they were being treated. Pointing at the pair, they dissolved in tearful, howling laughter.

Erin was going mad, unaccustomed as he was to such ridicule. His demented lumbering soon brought him to the branch on which Àjàpá had hidden the gourd containing the mixed dung. Still taking advantage of the cloud of dust and the inattention of the crowd, Àjàpá snatched the gourd and smashed it against Erin's rump.

The sight and smell of splattering dung caused a brief, astonished silence as the other animals took in the situation. Then astonished comments shot out from different quarters.

"Erin has soiled himself!"

"I smell excrement, do you?"

"Smell it? I *see* it!"

"Keep him away from here!"

Erin could not account for the moistness he felt on his rump, but he could hear what the crowd was saying. He realized he had to make a quick end of the impossible Àjàpá, and he redoubled his efforts to get at him by reaching behind with his trunk. But the effort failed.

Meanwhile, he had ventured beneath the gourd containing the camwood mixture. As before, Àjàpá reached up, grabbed the gourd, and smashed it across Erin's back, spilling the blood-red liquid all over him.

The crowd was beside itself with amazement on seeing what it took to be blood cascading down Erin's sides.

"That is not blood I see, is it?" a voice cried over the commotion.

"No!" another responded, obviously jeering. "Erin does not bleed."

"Of course not," another joined in. "The animal that can make him bleed has not even been conceived yet."

The forest resounded with the crowd's derisive laughter and cries of encouragement to their newly discovered giant-killer.

Erin's exertions were taking their toll on him. His movements began to slow as a crushing weariness of body and spirit pressed down on him. Yet he staggered about the arena until his nemesis was directly under the gourd containing the lime mixture. Àjàpá grabbed it and broke it atop Erin's head, globs of white substance spreading over Erin's head and dripping to the ground. The crowd reacted to what it thought was brain matter oozing from Erin's cracked skull and plopping into the dust, yelling even more loudly.

"Now Erin is truly dead!" a voice rang out.

"Àjàpá has killed him!" another voice exclaimed.

At that, as if on cue, Erin stopped his drunken staggering, swayed for a few moments, and finally crashed heavily in the center of the clearing.

Àjàpá, who had wisely hopped clear of the collapsing Erin, now hopped back atop his fallen victim, proudly acknowledging the acclaim of the crowd now on its feet and pressing forward to reach him.

They paid no heed to the exhausted and expiring colossus; some even clambered on him to reach their hero, whom they eventually lifted above the lifeless mass beneath them and bore triumphantly away. To hear them, one would think all the animals in the forest had always harbored a secret admiration for Àjàpá.

"Haven't I always said that only modesty kept Àjàpá from proving his worth all this time?" one addressed the crowd.

"Small though the needle is," another threw in, "it is certainly nothing for a chicken to swallow."

"Indeed, one errs to write any creature off prematurely," yet another exclaimed.

If Àjàpá's faith in the protective vigilance of the spirit of his dead father had ever flagged, it was now fully restored. And as he relished the adulation of the admiring crowd he told himself that a person whose footstep could not make an impression in the sand might yet perform wonders if he could make his brain serve him, and, of course, if the spirit of his dead father watched over him.

Mischievousness

Àjàpá and the Playful Children

This tale hovers, and hovers, as though it would not land, but it comes down at last on Àjàpá, the idler, a creature who has hands but will not lift them gainfully, a creature who, instead of finding some useful way to occupy his time, wanders the earth with a lighted taper the better to ferret out mischief even in the darkest nooks.

One cheerful and sunny afternoon the air filled with the twitters of birds and a gentle breeze caressed the ocean, pushing the waves lightly on to the beach and causing them to whisper agreeably as they ebbed and flowed. Three young boys frolicked freely in the open, with not a care in the world, for they had eaten a full meal and it was the lazy season when no work awaited them on the farm or at home. They competed with one another running back and forth on the bank of a huge lagoon lying next to their town, vying to see who could throw pebbles farthest over the water, or who could leap highest. They were blissfully absorbed in their game when Àjàpá crawled by, stopping to watch.

The children played on, unaware of their audience; had they been aware they would have taken greater care about what they said. In what they supposed was their private world for the moment they relaxed their tongues, for in their community it was taboo for anyone, young or old, to claim abilities he or she could not demonstrate. But as they engaged in their playful competitions, each boasted about what great feats he could perform.

"I'm such a great tree climber that I can climb right to the top of a palm-tree and not even use a climbing-rope," the first child boasted.

"That is no feat to boast about compared to what I can do," the second rejoined.

"What can you do to top that?" the first demanded.

"You've never seen anyone who can swim as far as I can. I can swim clear across the lagoon without stopping!"

The third child would not be outdone.

"Neither of you can match what I can do," he declared. "I am so strong that I can shoot an arrow that will fly so high it pierces the sky!"

Thus they bantered back and forth as they played, oblivious of Àjàpá's presence, and unaware that their innocent game would cause them much grief. For having heard those boasts, Àjàpá stole away from the scene and scrambled to the palace. There he sought an audience with the *oba*, claiming to have an urgent report for his ears.

"Long live your Majesty," he greeted the *oba*. "I bring you news about three extraordinary citizens of your kingdom."

Àjàpá's reputation was such that the *oba* felt obliged to warn him.

"Àjàpá," he said, "a day does not become night until you have had a turn at mischief. If what brought you to my presence turns out to be mischief, the earth now beneath your feet will be taller than you when I am done with you."

"If you find my report mischievous, your Majesty," he responded, "do with me as you choose."

The *oba* bade him give his news.

"*Kábíyèsí,*" he said. "Your majesty, I was strolling by the sea, when what did I see, and what did I hear?"

"Tell us," urged the *oba*.

"Three boys boasting about what they can do. One boasts he can climb a palm-tree to the top, without a climbing-rope."

The *oba* and his chiefs said not a word, but their astonishment was clear on their faces.

"Did you hear right?" the *oba* asked after a brief silence.

Àjàpá swore by the spirit of his dead father that he heard correctly and spoke the truth. But he heard more.

"That is nothing compared to what the others vowed they would do," he continued. "One would swim the lagoon without stop," he said, and was greeted with even more incredulous exclamation. "And," he continued triumphantly, "the last vowed to shoot an arrow that would pierce the sky!"

Such boasts were audacious assaults on the good order of the community, unless the boasters could make good on them.

"And where are these extraordinary boys?" the *oba* asked.

"By the lagoon, *Kábíyèsí.*"

The *oba* gave the command, and several orderlies rushed off to bring the boastful boys before the court.

When the three arrived, shivering with fright, and were told what Àjàpá had reported, all they could do was wail; but as they did not deny their boasts, the *oba* set the day when they must perform the feats they boasted or suffer the consequences prescribed for violating the taboo—the separation of their heads from the rest of their bodies.

The tearful pleas of the boys' parents that the *oba* spare them this time were in vain.

"They are mere children," they implored the *oba*. "If for this offense you pull their ears they will remember to speak with care in the future." But the *oba* would not be swayed.

"I did not invent the taboo," he countered. "It has been among us since the Owner of this earth created it. I must do as my fathers before me have done and preserve our ways."

The parents enlisted the intervention of friends, relatives, and well-wishers, but to no avail. In the end, they resigned themselves to the certain death of their children.

The day dawned when the boys were to perform their feats or lose their heads, and the bank of the lagoon was not spacious enough for the feet that crowded it or for the arms that accompanied them. The mood was somber, for everybody in the crowd was related in one way or another—as parents, as siblings or extended siblings—to children just like the ones now in danger of losing their lives. After all, they had only acted as children would. The only being in the crowd in a cheerful mood was Àjàpá, who pranced about with self-importance. After all, was he not responsible for creating the grand occasion?

In due time the *oba* arrived with his court, and after they had taken their seats he ordered the three children to come forward and prove themselves.

The first to make his attempt at carrying out his boast was the would-be palm-tree climber. He walked to a nearby palm-tree and stood at the base and sang:

Three young children at play,
Just a game, just a carefree game;
One vowed to scale a palm-tree,
Just a game, just a carefree game;
Another vowed to swim the lagoon,
Just a game, just a carefree game;
The third's arrow would pierce the sky,
Just a game, just a carefree game;
A climber, a swimmer, a shooter,
Just a game, just a carefree game;
A shooter, a swimmer, a climber,
Just a game, just a carefree game.

Then he walked resolutely to the tree, wrapped his arms around it as far as they would go, and began shinning his way up. He had only reached about the height of a grown man when his progress stopped and he slid down. A sorrowful wail swept through the crowd, for everyone envisioned the approaching end of the boy's life. But the *oba* announced that in trials like these each person had three chances. That was little comfort for the crowd, for they expected the climber's remaining chances to end like the first.

After resting for a short while, the boy turned to the tree again and sang:

Three young children at play,
Just a game, just a carefree game;
One vowed to scale a palm-tree,
Just a game, just a carefree game;
Another vowed to swim the lagoon,
Just a game, just a carefree game;
The third's arrow would pierce the sky,
Just a game, just a carefree game;
A climber, a swimmer, a shooter,
Just a game, just a carefree game;
A shooter, a swimmer, a climber,
Just a game, just a carefree game.

Then he began climbing again. This time, to the amazement of the crowd he was halfway up, exceeding the height of a house, before he slipped down again. This time the crowd's anxiety was tinged with some hope; perhaps he could do it!

When after another rest the boy began his third attempt, therefore, the crowd did not remain dolorously silent but shouted encouragement. Up and up the boy went, past the height of a grown man, higher than the tallest house in town. He kept inching upward, and the crowd kept up its encouraging shout, including the *oba* and his chiefs. And the ovation was thunderous when the boy's hands clasped the neck of the palm-tree just below the palm-fruits, as high as any climber could go.

There was jubilation as he slid down to be wrapped in the embrace of his family and well-wishers. The *oba* and his chiefs were among the celebrants of the boy's victory. The jubilation subsided somewhat, though, when the people remembered that two other lives remained at risk. But their mood was somewhat hopeful when the *oba* invited the successful climber to sit by him while the other two boys attempted their feats.

The next to step forward was the swimmer. At the *oba*'s order a boat was launched, full of the *oba*'s agents who would accompany the swimmer and bring him back to his fate if he failed to fulfill his boast. Already positioned at the other end of the lagoon was a crowd, almost as large as the one at the starting point, to ascertain the boy's success should he make it across. He stepped to the water's edge and sang:

> *Three young children at play,*
> *Just a game, just a carefree game;*
> *One vowed to scale a palm-tree,*
> *Just a game, just a carefree game;*
> *Another vowed to swim the lagoon,*
> *Just a game, just a carefree game;*
> *The third's arrow would pierce the sky,*
> *Just a game, just a carefree game;*
> *A climber, a swimmer, a shooter,*
> *Just a game, just a carefree game;*
> *A shooter, a swimmer, a climber,*
> *Just a game, just a carefree game.*

His song concluded, he stepped into the water and looked into the distance. The crowd was hushed. After some moments of silent contemplation he crouched and lowered his trunk into the water. He swam some distance, the boat in attendance, but he did not get very far. The crowd groaned as it saw him clutch at the side of the boat and lift himself inside. The rowers brought him back to land, where he sat at the water's edge, panting. The *oba* announced that he had two more tries, and his parents went to him to offer encouragement.

On the second attempt he went a good bit farther than on the first, but this time again he had to turn back. After a short rest, the boy repeated his song, and this time he ran purposefully into the lagoon and began to swim, accompanied by the boatload of agents. The crowd that had been under a pall of sorrowful silence gradually became animated when boy and boat became little specks in the lagoon and continued to recede until they disappeared. The people walked to the very edge of the water as though they would follow the swimmer, straining to catch a glimpse of the boy and failing.

Soon, from the distant shore of the lagoon, borne on the gentle breeze, came sounds of excitement, faint at first, then increasing in volume, and the expectant crowd knew without being told that the swimmer was close to making good on his boast. A sustained crescendo of shouting from the far shore told the crowd on the near shore that the feat was accomplished. The people had reason to rejoice anew, and a short while later they were confirmed in their jubilation when the boatload of festive attendants returned bearing the swimmer, who was beaming in triumph.

But, as the saying goes, a weeping person can still see through his or her tears. The people's rejoicing did not keep them from remembering that while climbing a palm-tree and swimming the lagoon might be within human endurance, however extraordinary the endurance had to be, hitting the sky with an arrow was something no human had attempted or accomplished before. Accordingly, when the celebration of the swimmer's success died down and the shooter stepped forward, the silence of the crowd was one of foreboding.

Undaunted, the boy, emboldened by the success of his playmates, faced the crowd and sang:

Three young children at play,
Just a game, just a carefree game;
One vowed to scale a palm-tree,
Just a game, just a carefree game;
Another vowed to swim the lagoon,
Just a game, just a carefree game;
The third's arrow would pierce the sky,

151

Just a game, just a carefree game;
A climber, a swimmer, a shooter,
Just a game, just a carefree game;
A shooter, a swimmer, a climber,
Just a game, just a carefree game.

His voice trailed off at the end of the song, and the crowd's silence deepened. He picked up one of the three arrows he had laid on the ground and put it to his bow's string. The crowd watched as he pulled at the string, the youthful muscle of his arm straining. Then he let the arrow fly. It rose into the sky with some initial agility, but then it slowed, arced, and fell back to earth. Many in the crowd sighed in lamentation for the unfortunate boy, but his look of determination remained constant.

After a short rest, the boy placed a second arrow in his bow and aimed it at the sky. He strained mightily as he pulled at the string, and when he released the arrow it flew so fast and so high that involuntary exclamations escaped from many in the crowd, and some of the seated dignitaries shot out of their seats the better to follow the soaring arrow. It flew and flew, but just as it seemed as though it would pass beyond sight the crowd saw its point rotating downwards. There was a general groan of disappointment. Those who cared to comment reminded others that it was folly to expect an arrow shot from the earth to reach the sky. Whose father had ever told him or her that he had seen it done before?

Down to his last arrow, and his last chance to save his life, the boy fixed his gaze at the sky and sang soulfully:

Three young children at play,
Just a game, just a carefree game;
One vowed to scale a palm-tree,
Just a game, just a carefree game;
Another vowed to swim the lagoon,
Just a game, just a carefree game;
The third's arrow would pierce the sky,

Just a game, just a carefree game;
A climber, a swimmer, a shooter,
Just a game, just a carefree game;
A shooter, a swimmer, a climber,
Just a game, just a carefree game.

His song done, he picked up the last arrow and put it to the bow. Then he pulled with all his might and let it go. It shot off the bow so fast that many eyes in the crowd missed its exit and were unable to follow its course. The crowd gasped as it flew, and roared as it became tinier and tinier, until it disappeared from sight. They waited with eyes strained at the sky, but no arrow appeared in descent. Finally, all eyes turned to the *oba*. Since the arrow had not returned to earth, would he assume that it had reached and pierced the sky? But the *oba* and the crowd, and indeed the *oba* and his counselors, looked searchingly at each other, for no one knew how to solve this riddle.

But there was another *oba* the like of which cannot be found among men, and he is the *oba* in the sky, to whom a solution for earthlings' dilemmas posed no difficulty. The crowd was still waffling in confusion when suddenly the sky that had been bathed in sunlight and free of clouds darkened with swirling and rumbling thunderclouds, which as suddenly cascaded down in a drenching deluge. *Oba* and crowd hastily dispersed to reassemble a short while later at the palace.

The mood among the throng at the palace was far different from the one that prevailed at the beginning of the day. The parents of the three vindicated youths had lost no time in securing the services of drummers to enhance their celebration. All they awaited before returning home for feasting and rejoicing was the word from the *oba*'s lips that the young men had done as they vowed and were free to return home.

It was some time before the *oba* emerged from his council room and took his seat on his throne, flanked by his chiefs. When the noise that had prevailed in the room subsided, he addressed his subjects.

"My people," he said, "the noise of your celebration reached us as we brought our heads together to ponder the events of this day. It has been a day like none other before it, a day in which our ancestors made known to us their constant watchfulness over us. Such days will never end among us."

"So it will be!," the crowd shouted in response.

"These three children," he said, indicating the new heroes, "are no longer mere children. Just as the uplifted hand towers above the head, so they tower above even those who have more years on their heads than they do."

The chiefs nodded in agreement.

"They also are messengers from our ancestors," he continued, "although they did not know it. They brought us the message that when the staff of the *èbìtì* snare is sprung it whips forward, always. We must always strive, they say, to surpass our forebears."

Again there was nodding and the murmur of agreement.

"From this day," the *oba* declared, "our town shall no longer prohibit people from extraordinary boasts, for from such boasts may come extraordinary achievements."

The jubilant crowd cheered and the drummers pressed their sticks to the skins of their drums to welcome the decree.

"Finally," said the *oba*, "we must not forget Àjàpá, the one most responsible for bringing us all together this way."

At the mention of the name a murmur of disapproval rose from the crowd. They had quite forgotten him in all their jubilation, and they would have preferred not to be reminded of him. Least of all would they wish to see the *oba* reward him in any fashion, as he seemed about to do. For his part, Àjàpá stepped forward nimbly, thinking that he did deserve some recognition for starting the events of the momentous day in train.

"Thanks to him," the *oba* said, "we know that we have among us worthy youths whose hands will be sufficient in time for the task of safeguarding the welfare of our community. But who can doubt that when he brought his report to us the end we anticipated was far different from what it turned out to be?"

The assembly agreed, but was still uncertain about the *oba*'s intentions.

"What he sought was the children's death!" the *oba* concluded.

Now the crowd roared in approbation, shouting "Quite so!" "Words of wisdom!"

Àjàpá suddenly became worried about the drift of the *oba*'s words. And what followed did not reassure him.

"Had his wishes been fulfilled, we would be telling a very different story now. For that reason, he will suffer the fate that would have been the youths' had they failed in their attempts."

The roar of approval from the people was deafening. The *oba* let it continue for a while before stopping it with his raised right hand.

"For the rest," he said then, "let the rejoicing continue!"

The crowd resumed its celebration with redoubled vigor, while several stalwarts seized Àjàpá and bore him to the outskirts of the town, where he saw the sword emerge from its sheath, but did not live to see its return.

Àjàpá and Jìgbo
the Would-Be Hunter

In the days of the first arrivals there came to be an illustrious man named Olúwo. A prosperous farmer, he was blessed with three sons. As was the custom, he took them to his farm as soon as they were old enough to help, and he in turn taught them all the secrets of coaxing the richest abundance from the earth. Thus he raised them in preparation for the day they would be ready to strike out on their own. When he judged the season to be right, Olúwo summoned his sons, saying it was time for them to make what might be the most important decisions of their lives.

"You are no longer children," he told them. "You have each come to the age when, on rising in the morning, you know without urging to wash the night from your faces; you never err in telling which is your right hand and which your left; and I am already boasting to my age-mates that you have it in your power now to make any woman fruitful in nine months. Now is the time, then, for each of you to choose a career. I am a farmer, and I have brought you up to be farmers. Our fathers say the scion of a fish takes after a fish; the scion of a leopard takes after a leopard; and the scion of a Fulbe man, whose trade is rope-making, takes after his father. But your lives are your own, and your choices must be yours alone."

The oldest son thanked Olúwo for the opportunity to choose freely any career, and then he opted for farming. The choice delighted his father, who undertook to provide the son with choice land and all other necessities to pursue his chosen occupation. The second son similarly thanked his father and then expressed his own desire to remain a farmer. Olúwo gave him the same assurances and gifts that he had given his oldest son.

The youngest son, Jìgbo, was the favorite of his parents, and nothing would have pleased Olúwo more than if Jìgbo also adopted his father's trade, but when he spoke, his father was stunned.

"Father," he said, "all these years I have watched you tend the farm and helped as I could. I have come to believe that few callings are as noble as farming. Certainly there is no farmer worthier than you, anywhere. My brothers have told you they will take to the farm after you, so that when you have gone where the elders go, there will be ready hands to keep the tradition of our household alive. I am saying all of this because, I dare not to lie to you, the farm does not appeal to me. The calling that most appeals to me, if I am to speak the truth, is hunting. I wish to become a hunter."

The little speech silenced Olúwo for for a long while. He had expected that Jìgbo would take up farming—and if not farming, perhaps some other trade, weaving, perhaps. But hunting!

"A hunter?" he asked, finally.

"Yes, a hunter."

There was another long, uneasy pause.

"The Olúwo lineage has never bred a hunter," Olúwo argued when he could speak again. "Hunting is not a career to contemplate lightly; it is not something you do without special preparations."

"Father, I know," Jìgbo replied. "But it is what I want to do."

"A hunter breaches the realm of the spirits, their forest home. He confronts the animals of the wild in their home and kills them. Such daring requires not just fortitude, but also the protection of powerful charms, powerful enough to stand up to the spirits of his animal victims and ward off the anger of the affronted forest spirits!"

"Pardon me, father, if I presume," Jìgbo said, "but I must ask your leave to repeat what you elders yourselves say. Is it not true, as you say, that a brave heart serves better than the most powerful charm or medicine?"

Olúwo could see that his Jìgbo's mind was set, and, try as he might, he was unable to persuade his favorite son to reconsider; adamancy was one of Jìgbo's best qualities, and he would not be dissuaded.

Having failed to shake his son's resolve, Olúwo consulted with Jìgbo's mother, who suggested that, under the circumstances, they should do their best to prepare him for his chosen career. They would find ways of honing in him the one skill no hunter could do without: good marksmanship. Accordingly, they purchased a gun for him, and also a goat, which they tethered to a tree in their front yard. They asked Jìgbo to stand back from the goat and use it for target practice. But Jìgbo would have none of that. What sort of reputation as a hunter would he be saddled with, he asked, if he were seen shooting at a tethered goat? Again he won his argument against his parents. He vowed that he would do his hunting in the forest, with elephants, lions, and leopards, not in his father's front yard with a tethered goat. In the end, his parents gave in and gave him their blessing.

Garbed in the usual regalia of a hunter, Jìgbo was an impressive sight. His vest was tight and adorned with a few cowrie-shell charms his father had procured for him as protection, and his trousers were smart. Atop his head sat a flap-eared cap, and from his left shoulder dangled a hunter's knapsack. An impressively long-barreled gun—a gun that never before had been fired at a target—completed his equipage.

He entered the forest full of excitement and anticipation, for in his mind hunting was the simple task of ambushing or stalking animals and picking them off at appropriate opportunities determined at the hunter's convenience. But after he had walked about for a long while, during which he caught not one glimpse of an animal but suffered lacerations on his exposed skin from thorns and plants that lashed at him as he passed, he wondered if there was in fact some secret to hunting that he did not know. To top off his first hunting expedition, before he saw his first animal the skies clouded above him and a terrific deluge began.

Jìgbo looked for shelter from the punishing strands of rain that seemed to raise welts on his exposed skin, but the best he could do was cower under the leaky canopy of a large tree. Before long his enthusiasm for hunting began to waver, for the relentless downpour not only soaked him from above, but also began tugging at his feet from below: the waters from the skies had collected into a raging flood that crept relentlessly up his ankles, his calf, and very soon his thighs. The trunk of the tree that gave him indifferent shelter offered no secure handhold, so he hung on to a smaller tree nearby.

The first item he lost was his cap, soon to be followed by his knapsack, and finally his gun. He had no time to lament his losses, for he was soon engaged in a desperate struggle to keep from being swept away himself in the torrent. The charms on his tunic failed him, and in the end he lost his battle and joined the flotsam crashing downstream on the sudden, muddy river. Mercifully, Jìgbo did not struggle long before the peace of unconsciousness enveloped him.

When he came to and the events of his last moments of consciousness drifted back into his mind, he expected to find himself in the presence of his ancestors, but instead his eyes focused on the figure of Àjàpá. His mind made a quick appraisal of his situation and concluded that he had arrived in an afterlife over which Àjàpá presided. He hastened to exonerate himself.

"I assure you that I never in my life killed an animal. True, I thought of hunting, but no animal ever suffered death at my hands. I would not even kill a helpless goat given me to kill."

Àjàpá heard him out but remained silent, regarding him and thinking of how best to use to his advantage this creature he had dragged out of the mud. One thing that struck him as Jìgbo spoke was the sonorous quality of his voice, a captivating lilt that told him that song lurked somewhere not far back in the recesses of his throat. True to form, Àjàpá's brain was quick in concocting a lucrative scheme.

"You do sing?" Àjàpá asked his involuntary guest.

Jìgbo's mind was nowhere near singing at the time, and his reply was slow in forming.

"No matter," Àjàpá continued, "I will drum and you will sing, and thus we will make a living without harm to any creature."

Àjàpá devoted the following few days to making himself a capacious drum big enough to accommodate Jìgbo, and perforated so that he could see into the interior. Before placing the skin over the drum he ordered Jìgbo inside, instructing him to break into song whenever he gave his signal, a rhythm played on the skin. The quality of his singing, Àjàpá warned him, would determine the quality of his feeding.

To test the appeal of his act, Àjàpá lugged his drum to the market at its busiest hour and, selecting a strategic spot, tapped a rhythm on the skin of his drum. As one would imagine, Jìgbo was by now lamenting the misfortune that led to his imprisonment in a drum. The voice that issued forth from the instrument was therefore full of pathos, a quality that enhanced rather than diminished its mellifluousness. Jìgbo sang:

> *I am Jìgbo, Jìgbo son of Olúwo.*
>   *Àgbámùréré!*
> *Jìgbo, Jìgbo son of Olúwo.*
>   *Àgbámùréré!*
> *Mother found me a goat*
> *That I might learn to hunt.*
>   *Àgbámùréré!*
> *Father tethered a goat*
> *That I might learn to shoot.*
>   *Àgbámùréré!*
> *But I vowed, off to the forest—*
> *The forest teeming with leopards,*
> *The forest crawling with elephants.*
>   *Àgbámùréré!*
> *It was a sudden flood that caught my legs*
> *And made me Àjàpá's slave.*
>   *Àgbámùréré!*

I am Jìgbo, Jìgbo son of Olúwo.
  Àgbámùréré!

At that point Àjàpá played a virtuoso tattoo on the drum, drowning out any further sounds from inside it.

As soon as the music had begun, hawkers had stopped hawking and hagglers had ceased haggling, captivated as they were by the music. Now they were kicking up a veritable crowd of dust in their dancing to the irresistible music. They were so enthralled by the rhythm and song that none of the words coming from the drum registered in anybody's mind, and no one even stopped to wonder how a drum could sing. When Àjàpá said he was done playing for the day, the crowd only reluctantly permitted his departure, but not before pressing upon him assorted foods and gifts of considerable value and securing his promise to return on the morrow.

But, why stretch the tale out like an open field or a mat? In very little time Àjàpá's reputation had covered the whole earth, such that no festive occasion was deemed complete without a performance by Àjàpá and his incomparable drum. He grew in riches as he grew in fame. As for Jìgbo, his melancholy deepened, but, curiously, the more pitiable he sounded the more his song appealed to his listeners.

But, as the saying goes, when a disease does not mean to kill the person it afflicts, it arranges to bring a skilled medicine man the person's way. The gods that arranged Jìgbo's woes also arranged an invitation for Àjàpá to play at a festival in the town where Jìgbo's family still lived. The grand occasion drew the entire community together and even brought home those who had traveled far in pursuit of their trade. Olúwo, too, was at the gathering with his entire family. When Àjàpá began his performance, they heard the soulful song that issued from the drum:

I am Jìgbo, Jìgbo son of Olúwo.
  Àgbámùréré!
Jìgbo, Jìgbo son of Olúwo.
  Àgbámùréré!

Mother found me a goat
That I might learn to hunt.
  Àgbámùréré!
Father tethered a goat
That I might learn to shoot.
  Àgbámùréré!
But I vowed, off to the forest—
The forest teeming with leopards,
The forest crawling with elephants.
  Àgbámùréré!
It was a sudden flood that caught my legs
And made me Àjàpá's slave.
  Àgbámùréré!
I am Jìgbo, Jìgbo son of Olúwo.
  Àgbámùréré!

The crowd in Jìgbo's hometown reacted just as the crowds elsewhere had, with the exception Olúwo and his wife, Jìgbo's mother, and the rest of his family. The parents in particular had been so prostrated by their favorite son's disappearance that they had become strangers to dancing, so even the enchanting rhythm was not enough to lure them. Besides, who could hear his own name and not pay attention? It was indeed hearing his own name in the song that alerted Olúwo, who then listened more closely and picked out Jìgbo's name. Listening still more closely he was able to piece together the gist of the song's message.

Besotted by his excitement, Olúwo ran to the *oba* and implored him to stop the dancing. After he had managed to explain to the astonished *oba*, the latter complied and the dancing stopped. The *oba* further obliged Olúwo by ordering total silence and stillness while Àjàpá regaled the crowd with his music. Not suspecting anything unusual, Àjàpá recommenced his playing, and Jìgbo resumed his singing. For the first time the listeners paid attention to the words, and since everyone present knew the illustrious Olúwo and his family well and also knew of Jìgbo's disappearance, when the crowd reacted to the song they were hearing it took the *oba*'s forceful and authoritative intervention to save Àjàpá from instant dismemberment.

With his own hands Olúwo tore apart the extraordinary drum and exposed his son Jìgbo, who looked more dead than alive. His emaciation brought tears to his mother's eyes and to those of other mothers. Jìgbo's family happily took him home to love and tend to him.

As for Àjàpá, he went before the *oba*'s justice conclave, which pronounced a fitting sentence on him: he would witness the sword's emergence from its scabbard, but not its return therein.

Àjàpá, Ìyá-Olódò
the Undersea Mother,
Òní the Crocodile,
and Kìnìún the Lion

This tale hovers, looks here and there, and settles on Àjàpá, around whose town a terrible famine raged. So devastating was the drought that the earth was a network of cracks and only dust and rocks sat on its surface. It made men whose arms were strong indistinguishable from shiftless persons, and it sent mature men and toddling children alike to unexpected graves. People were reduced to mere bones bound by wrinkled skin; so thin were they that they gave thanks to their Creator for outfitting them with shoulders, without which they would have had no hope of keeping on their garments.

The one creature unaffected by the famine was Àtíòro the Hornbill. Despite the drought and the scarcity of food he remained plump, even seeming to put on weight each day, and his feathers shone as though he regularly rubbed himself down with oil. For a long time Àjàpá resisted the urge to seek the help of the bird, regarding such a recourse as an injury to his dignity. In the end, though, hunger and the specter of death humbled him, and he sold his shame to the first comer. He sought out Àtíòro and reminded the bird of their long acquaintance, if not friendship.

"Friends help friends," he said. "I have come to you for help; help me in the drought and I will help you in the deluge. This raging famine threatens to wipe out my family."

"Not yours alone," Àtíòro responded; "the famine is like the sky falling; it is a threat to all."

"But you show no effects of famine, of hunger," Àjàpá observed. "The rest of the world wastes away, but you prosper. How do you manage to fare so well? Surely you must have a secret source of food, for your plumpness cannot come from your opening your mouth to the wind."

"I long ago placed myself in the hands of the gods. You know what the elders say: when it seems most certain that the ward of the river goddess will die from the drought, a sudden torrential rain will fall."

"Show me the way," Àjàpá pleaded, "and I too will place myself in the gods' hands."

"The world is a huge place, and my wings are strong," Àtíòro replied. He was in especially good humor that day, and the good cheer was evident in his voice. "Fly far enough and the gods will not fail to place some food in your mouth. You know the saying: if all the food available will fit in one small leaf and all the stew will fit in a peanut shell, then whichever stomach is destined to be full will be full."

"But, my friend," Àjàpá reminded him, not sharing in the good humor, "the problem I speak about is not too little food, but none at all. Show me where there is *any* food, even so small that it fits in a small leaf, and I will thank you."

Àtíòro regarded him for a while before responding.

"My friend Àjàpá, you no doubt know the saying: the gods in their wisdom took care to leave the partridge ignorant of where the egret washes itself white. Have you ever wondered why they did?"

Àjàpá was having difficulty containing his irritation at being subjected to clever sayings when he was in the throes of hunger. Once hunger has established itself inside a person, it leaves no room for any other matter. He could not be bothered to speculate on the reasons for the gods' actions concerning the cleansing habits of egrets. Apparently, though, Àtíòro really expected no answer from him, for he provided his own explanation.

"It was so that the partridge would not muddy the water and thus tarnish the egret's whiteness!"

Àtíòro was so impressed with his own wit that he flapped his wings and laughed heartily. Àjàpá was indignant.

"Hunger that kills is nothing to laugh about," he said, "just as a snake's young is nothing to toy with. I am starving, and my children are dying. I come seeking help from you; when eyes look into eyes, eyes take pity on eyes. Take pity on me!"

For all his tendency for flippancy, Àtíòro was a kindly creature, and persuading him to be compassionate was not difficult. But Àjàpá's reputation for deviousness, irresponsibility, and general unpredictability was difficult for Àtíòro to overlook.

"Àjàpá," he said, "your reputation makes doing you a favor a very difficult thing."

"Ha!" Àjàpá exclaimed, "whatever do you mean?"

"How? I have eyes, and what I do not see I have ears to hear about. Whoever does you a favor asks for cudgel blows for thanks."

"Àtíòro, my friend," Àjàpá pleaded, "you must be thinking of someone else."

"None other!" Àtíòro insisted. "I think and speak of you, Àjàpá, husband to Yánníbo. Is there another bird in the bush named Àkùko the Rooster?"

"Hear me out, my good friend," Àjàpá protested. "Indeed I am Àjàpá, husband to Yánníbo, but the Àjàpá before you now is not the same Àjàpá you knew in the past. I am now older and wiser, and you know the saying: an elder does not perform his rituals like a youth. This adult before you has given up childish pranks. Help me, help my wife and my children; show us where we might find food."

Finally, Àtíòro said even if he wanted to help Àjàpá an obstacle stood in the way of his doing so. Àjàpá could not imagine an obstacle that could stop him once he had set his mind on a goal.

"Whatever the obstacle might be, we will surmount it!" Àjàpá swore.

"I can fly, but you cannot; nor can you swim."

Àjàpá was working on the implications of those words, but Àtíòro elaborated.

"My source of food lies a great distance away, across a wide sea. You have no way of crossing it."

Àjàpá considered his words for a while, but not for long, for the obvious solution swiftly occurred to him.

"Àtíòro," he said, putting on a most ingratiating demeanor, "you are a great creature, and as long as great ones like you are around, great disasters cannot defeat the rest of us. Feathers you have in abundance; spare me some, and I will fly the sea."

The suggestion was so unusual that Àtíòro laughed again.

"You? Fly?"

"And why not?" Àjàpá responded. "You can fly because you have wings. Make me a pair of wings, and watch me fly."

The idea was so outrageous, and so intriguing, that Àtíòro began to see possibilities in it. He did indeed have enough feathers to fashion wings for Àjàpá, and he knew where to find the wax to attach them. Àjàpá in flight! The idea galvanized him to action.

"Meet me by the river in the morning, after the third cock crow," Àtíòro said, "and we will see if you can indeed learn to fly."

The excitement and the anticipation kept Àjàpá sleepless all night, and he had heard only one cock crow in the distance when he readied himself and made as much speed as he could muster to his rendezvous with Àtíòro. The latter bided his time and did not arrive until full daylight.

"I see you are here already," Àtíòro greeted him.

"One does not dawdle and leave pressing tasks unattended," Àjàpá responded, his impatience lending a tinge of irritation to his words. But it went unnoticed.

Àtíòro set to work, and before long Àjàpá had two wings fashioned from Àtíòro's cast-off feathers and affixed to Àjàpá's forelimbs with wax.

"Now you have wings," Àtíòro told him. "Let me see you fly."

It took some time before Àjàpá could even lift himself off the ground, but in the end he succeeded in becoming airborne. Àtíòro took off after him and led the way towards the sea. Àjàpá had never in his life seen so much water, but thoughts of what lay at the far side of it lent his forelimbs strength and his heart bravery. When they finally arrived at their destination he could hardly believe the lushness of the vegetation and the size of the farm planted with yams that was Àtíòro's secret.

"Now, listen to me," Àtíòro told him. "Eat your fill of yams, and on the way home we will each take one with us."

Àjàpá was so eager to fill his stomach that he paid little attention to Àtíòro. He got busy, and very soon had dug up a small heap of yams. Soon after that he had a good fire going. He roasted the yams and consumed them with the eagerness of one who had seen no food for many moons. Àtíòro had also fed well, and both agreed on a good doze while their food settled, and before returning home.

The sun had climbed only a little when Àtíòro suggested that they begin the journey home. If they left then, he said, they would complete the journey before the sun was at its zenith; even if there was a good breeze, flying when the sun was hottest did not appeal to him. He quickly dug up the one yam he would carry home and, expecting that Àjàpá had done the same, asked him to lift off first. But to his dismay Àjàpá said he was not yet ready. He had dug up several yams, but he was still busily digging.

"Àjàpá," Àtíòro admonished, "do not think of repaying the farmer by harvesting his yams for him. How do you know he would welcome your help?"

"I am helping no farmer," Àjàpá responded. "I must carry enough home to feed my family."

"Ha!" his benefactor exclaimed. "Àjàpá, your greed will surely provoke the farmer into action. Take only one today. Another day will dawn tomorrow, and you can return for more!"

"Pardon me, Àtíòro," he responded, "any creature who speaks of tomorrow as a certainty lies. We know only of today. I will take as much as I can now that I have the opportunity."

Àtíòro felt the anger welling in him.

"I knew I should not have helped you. I knew I should not have believed the story about your change of nature. But tomorrow reveals as folly the act that seems wise today. If tomorrow I believe anything you say you may . . ."

"Àtíòro," Àjàpá cut him short, "I hate to interrupt you. But I am not a child to be whipped with words. If you are in a hurry, head home. I know the way."

"Very well," Àtíòro responded, "so I will. You are like the person who sits by the partridge's nest watching and waiting to steal its eggs; your eyes may yet find what they seek."

Àtíòro flew off across the sea with the one yam he had dug up. Àjàpá dug and dug until he was satisfied that he had enough. Then he tried carrying them all, but not only were his limbs too short, but the shapes of the yams made them an awkward pile to carry together. What's more, he also needed his forelimbs for flight.

In the end, regretfully, he was forced to leave most of what he had dug and take off with only a few that he could hold with his hind limbs, or hold on to with his teeth, or wedge in available spaces between his shell and his body.

With some difficulty he was able to get airborne, but he had not flown far when he began to wonder if he had not reached out for disaster. The sun was now much hotter than when they set out earlier in the day, and he could feel the wax on his fore limbs softening. He looked ahead and saw Àtíòro as a small speck in the distance. Still, he thought he would call and ask him to slow down a bit. But as he opened his mouth the yam he held there fell into the sea. In his vain attempt to catch it he lost the ones between his hind limbs. Those wedged in nooks and crannies on his body were soon gone, also, but by then Àjàpá had something far more serious than lost yams to worry about.

He looked below him at the heaving sea. It would not be long, he knew, before he would plunge into it, for the wax holding his wings was now quite soft, and the feathers were flying off in ones, twos, and bunches. In dismay he felt the air disappear from under him and watched the water rush up at him. This time, he thought, he was surely on his way to join the spirit of his dead father.

The water closed on him and tossed him about; it pressed against his ears and forced his eyes closed. The light above him receded and his chest felt like exploding. But soon he could feel the pressure around him lessening and his discomfort decreasing. Death, he knew, was on its way. He knew that he was dead when he found himself in a habitable place before a royally attended sea creature who said she was Ìyá-Olódò, ruler of the undersea world.

"You are a land creature, are you not?" she demanded sternly.

Àjàpá said indeed he was.

"I am Ìyá-Olódò," she announced, "you have heard of me, have you not?"

He hadn't, but somehow he knew that the correct answer in the circumstance was yes.

"So I have."

"I alone rule the undersea world. Around me you see my attendants and my seven children."

She let her eyes rest lovingly on the seven little creatures before continuing.

"You and your fellow land-living creatures, not content with what you have on land, invade my realm to prey on my charges. And now you invade even my home!"

"Not so," Àjàpá hastily assured her. "In fact, I have no taste for sea creatures."

"Liar!" she exclaimed. "Why then are you here? An accident, perhaps?"

His ever-alert brain told him that an accident would be the worst explanation to give, even though it was the honest answer. That brain had already taken in the situation and suggested a most beneficial course of action to Àjàpá.

"Ìyá-Olódò," he said, "good fortune has sought you out as you deserve, as your fame deserves."

"Where is this good fortune?" she asked.

"Behold before you," Àjàpá told her, "the greatest beautifier that ever inhabited the land. Some may scorn, some may scoff, and yet others may praise me, but none of it matters. The truth is, no creature knows as I do the secrets of beautification."

"How does that explain your being here?" Ìyá-Olódò wanted to know.

"The explanation is simple," he responded. "Indeed your fame covers the land like the breeze that blows over it, and the regard land dwellers have for you is boundless. Their only wonder is, why a venerable and illustrious ruler like you would deprive your children of that ultimate mark of beauty, facial scarification."

"What is that?" she asked, puzzled.

"The supreme marks of beauty. The indispensable sign of royalty. Royal children should not go about without carrying the sign of royalty on them."

Ìyá-Olódò looked at her children and saw the reproach of their unadorned faces. She imagined patterns of scarification breaking up the bare smoothness and saw the truth in Àjàpá's words.

"You say you adorn faces?" she asked.

"Ask about me anywhere and you will be told none does it better than I."

"If I gave you the task, what fee would you ask?"

"Fee?" Àjàpá asked. "Fee? Who speaks of fees? I offer my service to you free, in homage to you."

"In that case," his elated hostess said, "set about it, and you will earn my gratitude."

Àjàpá undertook to begin the job as soon as the necessary preparations were completed. These were that a building large enough to accommodate himself and the seven children be constructed well away from any other dwelling. It was to have only one entryway that could be sealed from the inside, and also one small opening near the roof. All necessary ingredients and utensils to provide meals for himself and the children were to be stocked in the building. He was then to be left with the children for seven days. He would beautify one child each day, but they would all be released together after he had performed a necessary ritual for all of them on the final day.

None of this seemed unreasonable to Ìyá-Olódò, but she wanted to be able to follow Àjàpá's progress somehow. He stressed that the delicate task demanded undisturbed seclusion, but if Ìyá-Olódò would come in the evening each day and call from a reasonable distance, he would lift the children he had scarified thus far so she could see them through the small opening.

Ìyá-Olódò gave the order to make the preparations Àjàpá called for, and by the end of the following day he was ensconced in the building with the seven children and all he would need to feed all of them for seven days.

Towards evening on the following day Ìyá-Olódò went towards the building, and from a distance called to ask Àjàpá how the scarification was coming. In response he lifted one of the children to the opening where Ìyá-Olódò could see it, and from that distance what she saw made her congratulate herself for her astuteness in deciding to take Àjàpá up on his offer.

The following day, in answer to her inquiry about the progress of his work Àjàpá lifted the same child to the opening twice, and Ìyá-Olódò went away elated, and gratified at the progressive enhancement of her brood's appeal. The third day Àjàpá presented the same child for viewing the third time to the mother's growing pleasure.

The wise ones say one should not negotiate how much one would pay for cloth one has only seen as a bundle, for who knows what flaws and blemishes the bundling hides? Without knowing anything about Àjàpá beyond what he said of himself Ìyá-Olódò entrusted her children to him, and under conditions that presumed complete trust. She was soon to find out why the wise ones warned as they did. Àjàpá's work on the one child he beautified confirmed the ability he boasted of, but his real intention was not beautification. After working on the one child he killed the rest one by one, and with the provisions stewed and ate them.

On the seventh day he stewed and ate the last child, the only child he had scarified, and before it was time for Ìyá-Olódò's arrival to reclaim her children he slipped out and made good speed to the ferry docks.

Several ferry owners were there assembled. Àjàpá approached them in turn to engage them in conversation, but as soon as the one he addressed responded he quickly moved to another one. Those toward whom he so behaved shrugged off his rudeness; what is normal behavior in one land, they thought, was taboo in another land. Eventually Àjàpá found a ferry-plier who neither showed any sign of hearing him nor responded to what he said. After repeating himself a few times only to be rewarded with a blank stare, he concluded he had found what he wanted—a deaf-mute. By urgent gesticulation he communicated to the ferry-plier that he wanted to be ferried to the bank, and very urgently. He got his point across, and very soon he was in the ferry and making speedily for the bank.

In the meantime Ìyá-Olódò had discovered the reward for her trusting a stranger with her most precious possessions. When after repeated hails no response came from the beautification building she had panicked and ordered the door forced open. The sight that greeted her on entering was the sort that would make a grown person go insane. What was left of the children was their bare skeletons, and, keeping them company, the left-overs of the culinary ingredients Ìyá-Olódò had provided. For Ìyá-Olódò it was as though an enemy had doused her with oil and set her afire. Despite her agitation, though, she knew what she wanted most—the apprehension of the culprit. She accordingly gave the order that he be found and returned to her. Ònì the Crocodile being the swiftest and strongest swimmer around, he received the assignment to go after Àjàpá.

Àjàpá was fortunate in his choice of transporter; in addition to being a deaf-mute he was also exceptionally strong. With powerful strokes he sped his vehicle toward the shore, and before long Àjàpá's apprehension that he might be discovered and apprehended before he was out of Ìyá-Olódò's realm subsided. The shore loomed ahead and approached fast.

But as he was about to offer his usual gratitude to the spirit of his dead father for watching out for him, he heard some commotion some distance behind them and turned to look. To his alarm he saw a long wake fast approaching, and as he looked he saw Ònì's snout momentarily rise above the water, holler to them to stop, and submerge again. The next time he surfaced to order them again to stop he had reduced the distance between them considerably. Àjàpá was truly alarmed, and he wildly gesticulated to his rower, who was oblivious to any pursuit, to redouble his effort. He complied.

The ferry shot ahead, but just as its nose touched land and Àjàpá hopped ashore, his pursuer also made landfall. He hurried around to confront Àjàpá so that Àjàpá stood between him and the sea.

"Ask the earth to open so you can disappear into it, or take to the air, for otherwise there is no escape for you."

"Be gentle with me," Àjàpá pleaded, "and tell me what you want with me."

"I want nothing with you. Ìyá-Olódò has a matter to discuss with you, and I will take you to her," Ònì informed him.

"But I left her only a short while ago!" Àjàpá pleaded. "Urgent matters await me at home. Some other time, perhaps? Tomorrow, perhaps? I have no time right now."

"No time?" Ònì's laughter was sinister but so hearty that tears streamed from his eyes. "When Ìyá-Olódò summons you, all you have is time. Ha, ha! Your ugly eyes are time. Your repulsive head is time. Your ridiculous shell is time. Why, all of you is time! No time, indeed. Make ready!"

Àjàpá could see that this messenger meant to do as he was bid, but he knew his life depended on delaying Ònì until he could think of a way to save himself. The spirit of his dead father must have been alert, for an idea struck him.

"Very well," he said, "I will come with you. But the strenuous trip back has quite exhausted me. Let me rest awhile."

He saw that Òni was rather doubtful in considering the request, and he hastily added.

"You also look as though you could use some rest. That was a fast trip you made across the water, and you would need all your strength to take me back. Stay awhile, rest, and enjoy the sun, and then we will depart."

"And why not?" Òni agreed. "A short rest." With that he lay in the sun with his eyes trained on Àjàpá.

Some time passed, and suddenly Òni's repose was replaced by full alertness, for Àjàpá was gathering and assembling dry twigs.

"What now?" Òni demanded.

"I have just enough time for the daily routine that ensures my good health. It will be over in a very short while, and then we can be on our way."

Òni did not object, but he remained alert. He watched as Àjàpá built a sizable mound of dry twigs, he watched as he provided himself with a forked long stake, and he watched as he struck flints to start the mound of twigs smoldering. Then he looked somewhat despondently at Òni.

"What?" Òni asked shortly.

"I quite forgot," Àjàpá responded. "The routine takes two. I cannot do it by myself. I need someone else to help. You see, the routine is that I lie for a few moments on the smoldering twigs while someone presses me down with this forked stick. All it takes is a few moments. Perhaps you could help."

Òni thought about the request. It was strange—the whole routine was strange—but strange people have strange customs. He was about to agree to help when Àjàpá offered him some inducement.

"Help me," he said, "and you too can have the benefit of the routine. After all, who would refuse the gift of good health?"

The arrangement sounded appealing to Òni, and he told Àjàpá to take his turn. With considerable alacrity he was on the twigs.

"Press me down with the forked stake and release me when I say 'enough.'"

"Very well," Ònì agreed and did as he was asked.

Àjàpá stayed atop the smoldering mound for only a short while.

"Enough!" he called, and Ònì released him.

He clambered down and told Ònì it was now his turn. The mound was smoking less now, as the fire was catching, but Ònì paid no attention to that development. He climbed atop the mound and Àjàpá positioned the fork in the stake on Ònì's neck, pressing him into the now glowing embers with all his force. An obliging stiff breeze just then fanned the embers into flame, and Ònì screamed:

"Enough!"

"What?" Àjàpá responded.

"Enough!"

"I can't hear you!"

"Enough! Enough!" Ònì screamed, struggling mightily free himself.

Àjàpá held fast to the stake and pressed his victim to the fire with all his strength; it was his life or Ònì's, he told himself, and he would rather it was not his own. That preference gave him the determination he needed to keep his adversary pinned until he was dead. He left the carcass in the flame a while longer until the aroma coming from it told him it was done just well enough to eat. He removed it from the fire, cut it in small pieces, and wrapped it into a bundle. He would transport it home, where it would feed him and his family for some time.

He lifted the bundle and headed for home. Resolved to share his good fortune with no stranger, whenever he saw or heard anyone approaching he fell into loud lamentations about his mother, with whom he went in search for food, but who died of hunger during the search, and whose corpse he was now carrying home. The wayfarers, characteristically sympathetic, offered him condolences: the time after the mother's death will bring prosperity to those she left behind . . . the gods will place the dead mother in a good and gentle breeze . . . the time of the survivors will be long removed from that of the dead mother. Àjàpá tearfully thanked them all as he continued on his way.

Close to home he saw Kìnìún the Lion approaching and he went into his now well-practiced lamentation. Kìnìún offered his condolences and walked past. But as he did his keen nose caught the aroma of roasted meat.

"Àjàpá," he roared, "stop there and let me see that corpse!"

"What!" Àjàpá exclaimed. "Surely you will not insult the dead!"

"Surely *you* would rather not be dead!" Kìnìún retorted. "And you surely will be, if you do not quickly show me what it is you have in your bundle."

Àjàpá knew when he was trapped, and he quickly thought of minimizing the trouble he was in.

"I knew you would not be fooled, but I thought I would tease you," he said with an unconvincing grin. "I know of course that you know that my mother a while ago went where all the aged eventually go. The gods will pamper her in heaven."

"What, then, is in your bundle?" Kìnìún wanted to know.

"Something to gladden the mouth. Not long ago the spirit of my dead . . ."

"I did not ask you about spirits," Kìnìún cut him short.

"Forgive me," Àjàpá said. "No you did not. What is in my bundle is food that came my way today. The kind of food an insignificant being like me dares not eat alone, the kind of food in fact from which the first share belongs to you."

"Set it down," Kìnìún commanded.

Àjàpá did so, and without waiting to be asked undid the bundle. At the sight of the abundant meat Kìnìún made no further sound but immediately sat and attacked it. His appetite was ravenous, and the speed at which the food was disappearing alarmed Àjàpá. To his relief, Kìnìún stopped after eating only about half of the meat and ran his tongue over his mouth, grunting with satisfaction. Àjàpá assumed the king of beasts had taken what he thought was his share and had left the rest for the owner. But Kìnìún's words prostrated him with dismay.

"Bundle up the rest and bring it to my lair. I have a small yam there; I have not had *èbe* with meat this good for a while." With that he led the way.

Àjàpá had no choice but to do as he was ordered, but his eyes smarted with tears that he had to keep back with all the self-control he could muster. Only a being mightier than you can slap you in the face with your own hand, he reminded himself, and if you resist abuse when you lack the means to make your resistance meaningful or effective, you invite even greater abuse. He resigned himself to the misuse he was suffering at Kìnìún's hands. All the while, though, he was plotting his revenge.

Kìnìún was relentless in his mistreatment of Àjàpá. On arrival at his lair he brought out a fair-sized yam and handed it to Àjàpá, ordering him to set about making the *èbe*. He complied, still pondering his revenge, and by the time he had put all the ingredients on the fire to simmer, his plan was formed.

"The gods certainly did not make all creatures equally beautiful," he remarked for Kìnìún's benefit.

Kìnìún was resting after his earlier meal and in anticipation of the meal then simmering, and his response to the statement lacked real interest.

"What?"

"Your mane," Àjàpá said

"What about my mane?"

"I was looking at it and thinking what wonders other animals would do with such hair if the gods blessed them with it."

"What wonders?"

"Braiding, for example. Such hair should not be left to blow in every breeze and get tangled in every brush. It deserves to be braided."

"Hmm," Kìnìún grunted and prepared to ignore the speaker. But Àjàpá persisted.

"And in the forest there is no braider of manes whose skill matches mine."

Kìnìún's only response was to open one eye to look at Àjàpá briefly and to close it again.

"I will braid the hair while the *èbe* simmers if you will let me," he said. "See if you like it. If you do, leave it braided, and any time you wish I will rebraid it. If you do not like it, I will unbraid it."

Kìnìún considered the proposition and found it reasonable.

"How long will it take?" he asked.

"No time at all," Àjàpá assured him.

"The *èbe*?"

"Long before the *èbe* is ready."

So Kìnìún consented to have his mane braided. To do the job properly, said Àjàpá, Kìnìún would have to be on an elevated platform in the shade. He suggested placing a mortar in the shade of a tree for Kìnìún to sit on. Fortunately, a large tree with branches hanging low was close by, and Àjàpá said its shade made the location ideal. He found a mortar in Kìnìún's lair and placed it under a low-hanging branch and asked if Kìnìún would climb on it. He did, and Àjàpá perched on the branch right above Kìnìún to commence the braiding. When he had completed a fine, long, and immaculately woven braid he held it before Kìnìún's eyes.

"Does this please you?" he asked.

Kìnìún eyed it critically and liked it.

"It is good!" he said.

"Good," Àjàpá told him. "Now rest, shut your eyes and take a nap. I will wake you when your mane is all braided.

Kìnìún complied, and Àjàpá's fingers busied themselves braiding his mane into thick cords around the tree branch. Kìnìún slept through it all, not stirring until he felt Àjàpá moving on the branch. He roused himself then and asked if the job was done.

"Only one thing remains," Àjàpá replied. "I will step down to the ground and walk back a short distance to see the whole effect from there."

With that he clambered down the tree, and as soon as he was on firm ground he gave the mortar that supported Kìnìún a powerful shove. It slipped out from under the hapless king of the animals, and he was left dangling by his braided mane from the branch.

"What is this, you rascal?" he roared. "Let me down!"

Instead of responding, Àjàpá quickly went to where the pot of èbe was simmering and removed it from the fire.

"Let me down, I say! Let me down or you will find yourself on your way to heaven in the heat of the sun. Let me down!"

Àjàpá ignored him, concentrating on testing the èbe for coolness. As soon as it was cool enough he ate it all, with Kìnìún watching, struggling angrily and roaring threats at him.

When the èbe had disappeared completely, Àjàpá sauntered away, but not before addressing a lesson to his victim:

"The pepper seed may be small," he said, "but the fight in it is mighty."

Kìnìún stayed dangling from the branch and calling to all passers-by to set him free, but no animal would risk doing him such a favor. Who wants to do a favor and wind up inside Kìnìún's stomach? they asked themselves as they hurried away. In the end it was Ìgbín the Snail who took pity on him.

"If I help you down, will you not make a meal of me?" he asked.

"What kind of meal could you possibly make for me?" Kìnìún asked with an indignant tone that ill suited his circumstances.

"Did I hear you promise not to eat me?" Ìgbín insisted.

"What meal?" Kìnìún retorted again. "What sort of meat does the toad think he is that he scurries for cover when one comes upon him? Let me loose and go on your way, you and your shell!"

Ìgbín did not much care for his words or tone, but he decided to base his action not on what he thought of Kìnìún, but on the ancestors' promise that whoever does good can be sure that his home will never collapse.

He climbed on the branch and walked up and down Kìnìún's mane, lathering it generously with his slimy saliva. When it had quite saturated the mane the braids loosened and Kìnìún crashed to the earth with a thud that left him dazed. Ìgbín did not wait to find out if he could take Kìnìún at his word; he quickly found himself a good cover before the other regained his senses.

After looking perfunctorily around him and seeing no sign of his bene-factor, Kìnìún set off in search of Àjàpá, fully intending to send him on his way to join his ancestors.

Whether he found Àjàpá or not, no one knows to this day, but the two have remained enemies ever since.

ÀJÀPÁ AND ÌNÀKÍ THE BABOON

The elders say that "I was sitting quietly in my own home" is a plea that will not fail to absolve anyone accused of disturbing the public peace. But they also constantly urge the gods to keep them out of the path of mischief vendors who, with their sacks of catastrophe, seek unwitting customers.

This tale involves none other than Àjàpá and his close friend Ìnàkí the baboon—a trouble vendor and his unwitting victim. The two were good friends, much to the unending amazement of all who knew them and who also knew the age-old saying that compatibility of character is the best prescription for a lasting friendship. Àjàpá and Ìnàkí could in fact not be more different in habits and, especially, in nature; everyone knew Àjàpá to be lazy, wily, and utterly unreliable; by contrast Ìnàkí enjoyed the reputation of being industrious, honest, and completely dependable. Also, as will eventually become clear, the two harbored very different conceptions of the obligations of friendship.

What brought them together was no more than the proximity of their habitations and their consequent practice of whiling away long stretches of their leisure time together, trading observations on what face the particular day wore, or simply watching time pass. Those who wondered at the inexplicable friendship could not have known how right they were to be astonished, for they did not know how much Àjàpá bedeviled his long-suffering friend with pranks in his perverse hankering for excitement, excitement that often took strange forms. On this day the prank began with

Àjàpá sighing gravely and saying to Ìnàkí, "Of all the dangers on earth, none worries me more than falling afoul of a tormentor for no reason at all." He paused briefly, then pointedly added, "The spirits of our fathers will keep opportunistic troublemakers from our paths."

The statement and the prayer, coming after a long period of contemplative silence, left Ìnàkí wondering what brought them about. It was some time, therefore, before he responded.

"Better worry about disasters you might bring about your head with your own hands."

That sort of response was precisely what Àjàpá had hoped for, a response that opened the way for argumentation, and who knew what else.

"My friend," he began to lecture Ìnàkí, "knowing that the world is full of creatures on the lookout for opportunities to add to your burden instead of helping you with it, when you hear the sort of prayer that has just passed through my mouth you should say 'Amen' rather than argue."

Ìnàkí was for once in a mood for contestation; it was one of those rare occasions when he would not concede superior insight to his friend.

"I know all about prayers, all sorts of prayers," he responded impatiently, "and I know that a great many prayers add up to not much more than stammering. The elders whose words of wisdom you never tire of citing also say that one's fortune, and misfortune also, are of one's own making. I would worry about your actions and what they bring your way before I became paranoid about unprovoked troubles."

Judging by the wide-eyed delight with which Àjàpá received his friend's unusually long statement, an observer who had not heard it would have concluded that it was an unqualified approbation of Àjàpá's position. He was in fact delighted because his ever-busy brain was even then at work on an appropriate practical strategy to enlighten Ìnàkí.

"My friend," Àjàpá conceded cheerfully, "your words are fine. You will never hear me say that the elders lie. Besides, I admire self-assurance, and I see in you an abundance of it. If any creature can stay clear of undeserved trouble, that creature is you."

He accompanied his speech with preparations to depart, and soon he was ambling away from Ìnàkí, tossing in his direction the customary parting greeting, "Our next meeting will be sweeter than honey."

Ìnàkí doubted that it would be, but he did not bother to respond. Àjàpá ignored his friend's petulance; he had a delicious scheme to hatch, and he hastened home to bring it to life.

Once there he soaked black-eyed peas in cool water until the skins were soft and loose enough to rub off. After thus skinning them he ground them into a paste, adding not only the usual bits of fresh onion, tomatoes, and red peppers, but also a generous splash of honey. He had a particular client in mind whose weakness for honey was common gossip in the forest. He deep-fried the paste in melon-seed oil—the special occasion called for better than the usual palm-oil—and the aroma of the àkàrà wafted deliciously all over the forest. Using broad leaves, he wrapped them in a bundle and made his way with them to the lair of one of his most reliable dupes.

Ekùn the Leopard was snoozing in the cool shade of a fallen tree branch when Àjàpá greeted him with "Elder, you will always be there for us!"

Ekùn slowly roused himself from sleep and looked warily at his visitor. He managed a grunt, yawned extravagantly, and tried shaking the sleep from his eyes.

"Who sent for you?" he mumbled to his visitor, but even as the question formed on his mouth his nose busily sniffed the air and his neck craned animatedly around in his effort to determine the direction from which came the sudden aroma his nose registered.

Àjàpá casually held his bundle forward while pretending to be put off by the unenthusiastic reception.

"If it is now taboo to do a favor for the patriarchs who keep the forest safe for us little ones," Àjàpá responded with feigned injury, "then I will redirect my feet toward my home."

The gambit had the desired effect on his host whose eyes were now riveted on the bundle.

184

"What favor? What have you got there?"

He could never resist offers of free gifts, especially if these were in the form of edibles, as they most often were.

"A favor I cannot disclose if my presence is a burden to you."

"You *are* touchy," Ekùn remonstrated, still ogling what Àjàpá carried in his hands. "What sort of welcome do you expect when you rouse someone out of a restful snooze? Make yourself comfortable and show me . . . er . . . tell me about this favor."

Àjàpá made sure that Ekùn saw how difficult it was for him to master his hurt, taking his time to settle down. The more time he took, he knew, the more Ekùn's mouth would drool, and the more he could be counted upon to act the part expected of him. Finally, Ekùn's impatience got the best of him.

"You do not plan to sit there until nightfall before disclosing this favor, do you?" he demanded.

"As you elders say," Àjàpá said, "much hurrying will not snare a crown; the one who bides his time is more likely to earn it. Patience is the chief of virtues; an elder blessed with patience lacks nothing else in this world."

Ekùn was irritated by what sounded to him like a lecture from Àjàpá, of all creatures, but apart from the baleful look he gave his visitor he permitted himself no other reaction that might deprive him of the favor he was dying to get into his already salivating mouth.

"I have no wish to provoke you," Àjàpá said after a pause. "I only thought of letting you in on a secret as sweet as honey."

"What secret is it?" Ekùn asked.

"Have a taste of these," Àjàpá said as he finally proffered the *àkàrà*.

Ekùn was halfway through the food before he remembered that an elder does not eat using all his digits. The rest he consumed in a more decorous fashion. Not until he had licked his paws clean did he ask what the uncommonly delicious thing he had just eaten was.

"It comes from Ìnàkí the Baboon."

"Ìnàkí?"

"None other."

"Ìnàkí makes such good food?"

"Hmm, hmm," Àjàpá chuckled, "you would not think that the belly of such a scruffy creature is a reservoir of the sweetest food you could ever wish to taste."

Few animals in the forest had avoided the fate of falling prey to Ekùn; he was thus no stranger to the taste of their innards. True, he had never tasted a baboon, but he could not imagine that what its stomach enfolded could be any more delicious than, say, that of Ìgalà the antelope, or indeed that what he had just eaten was any animal's organs.

"You are thinking of branding me a fool, are you?" he asked in disbelief, rousing himself and letting out a threatening grunt that caused Àjàpá to fear momentarily for his life.

"Hear me through," he pleaded quickly. "Where is your gratitude, or the patience that distinguishes you as an elder?"

"Then, talk some sense, fast," Ekùn roared, "or I will forget your gift. Where does it come from?"

Àjàpá, who saw the danger of dawdling with his scheme, immediately laid it out.

"What you do not know," he told Ekùn, "and what no other creature knows but which I found out because of our friendship, is that what comes out when Ìnàkí empties his bowel is what you have just tasted."

Ekùn looked at his visitor very closely but detected no indication of mischief on his face. Àjàpá's already long career as a dissembler proved a reliable asset. Yet Ekùn could not lightly discountenance the lessons of his own past experience with Àjàpá.

"Àjàpá," he said sternly, "you are never happier than when you make others seem like imbeciles; but surely even you know the perils of trifling with me."

Now Àjàpá's indignation seemed uncontainable.

"This, I see, is the new way the powerful repay service from the powerless," he fumed. "I offer you a secret that will mean some relief from your exertions to find food and that would delight your palate, besides—a secret no one else knows but which came my way, as I said, because I am close friends with Ìnàkí—and what is my reward? A threat of disaster! You will make me into a benefactor whose reward is a cudgel blow! No matter; you will not catch me in a similar role tomorrow."

With that he made to leave, but Ekùn restrained him.

"Now," he conciliated, "you need not take offense. I meant you no harm. You must admit, though, that your story is somewhat . . ."

"Strange?" Àjàpá interjected. "Of course it is! Ìnàkí is nothing if not a secretive creature. He is also concerned for his own well-being, as I would be! If the other animals knew the bounty he carries around with him, what rest or peace of mind would he have?"

Ekùn saw the wisdom of Àjàpá's argument and, having thanked him, asked how one coaxed Ìnàkí into parting with such bounty.

"Simple," Àjàpá said. "The easiest way would be to ask him to bring forth some of the stuff, but as you can imagine he will pretend not to know what you're talking about. His way of protecting himself, you see. What you must do is apply some practical persuasion, like a few smart blows to his stomach."

"Hit him in the stomach?" Ekùn asked.

"In the stomach," Àjàpá confirmed. "Smack him smartly in the stomach, enough to set his bowels working, but not enough to cause him any injury."

"Just a gentle pat," Ekùn suggested.

"No, not that," Àjàpá objected. "Remember, no one teases the nut out of a kernel by being gentle."

"True," Ekùn agreed. "Or the coconut meat out of the shell, for that matter."

"Precisely," Àjàpá said. "A few emphatic smacks on the tummy, and the sweetness should come gushing out."

"Good, emphatic smacks."

"Be sure to do it right," Àjàpá warned. "Too gentle a pat and nothing comes out. Too rough a blow and you get nothing but bloody, steaming waste."

"Not too gentle, and not too rough," Ekùn repeated to himself.

He was already on all fours as he expressed his gratitude to his benefactor, telling him he meant to put the information to use without delay. Àjàpá agreed that no time was better than the present, but only warned him in parting not to reveal the source of his information.

Ekùn had no difficulty finding Ìnàkí, who was enjoying the cool of the day in the shade of a tree. He exchanged greetings with Ekùn, who he thought was foraging, expecting him to continue his search for unwary prey, but he was somewhat surprised and worried to see him loitering and throwing furtive glances in his direction. Uneasily, he asked what the other was about. At that Ekùn went closer and squatted by Ìnàkí.

"I know your secret," he said.

"My secret?" Ìnàkí was somewhat baffled.

"The secret of your belly."

"My belly has a secret?"

"Come now," Ekùn coaxed, "no other animal will find out from me."

Of course Ìnàkí had no inkling of what Ekùn was talking about and he said so, but the more he displayed his puzzlement the more impatient Ekùn became with what he thought was Ìnàkí's prevarication. Finally his patience left him.

"Look," he snapped, "many are the seasons I have seen come and go since I began roaming this forest. For that reason alone I deserve your respect. I am not one you want to trifle with. You should behave toward me as I deserve, given our stations; bring forth some sweetness."

"What sweetness?"

"Sweetness from your stomach!" Ekùn snapped. "The sweet stuff you keep hidden in your stomach."

Ìnàkí was tempted to laugh at the silliness he was hearing, but Ekùn's mien dissuaded him.

"Believe me," he whined, "I do *not* understand what you want."

"Will you do it without urging," Ekùn asked, "or do you need some persuasion?"

"I tell you I don't know what you mean!" Ìnàkí pleaded.

Without further ado Ekùn grabbed and lifted Ìnàkí's fore legs to render his stomach more accessible, and commenced to administer blows to it with his open palm.

"Drop the sweet stuff!" he commanded with each smack, and with each Ìnàkí yelped and protested his ignorance of what his assailant wanted.

Too long a story sinks into lies. Soon enough Ekùn's blows produced an effect on Ìnàkí, from whose rear some steaming stuff came spurting out. Ekùn released him and quickly bent to the matter Ìnàkí had involuntarily dropped. The latter took instant advantage of his freedom and scrambled as fast as he could atop the nearest tree.

If any other animal had been around to see Ekùn's face when he tasted Ìnàkí's droppings, he or she would have seen the true complexion of disgust. Ekùn's was quickly overtaken by embarrassment, which caused him to look anxiously around to see if he had an audience. Satisfied that he did not, he trotted away from the site as fast as he could, blaming himself for not getting the smack to Ìnàkí's stomach just right.

The Ìnàkí Àjàpá saw shortly after the ordeal seemed to hover between life and death.

"Whatever could be the matter with you?" he asked his friend.

Haltingly, Ìnàkí related the story of his unexpected encounter with Ekùn, Àjàpá all the while expressing disbelief and commiserating like a true friend.

"Never doubt the wisdom of the elders," Àjàpá admonished Ìnàkí when he had finished his report.

"What wisdom?"

"The one saying that whenever you hear the prayer, 'The spirits of our fathers will keep unprovoked troublemakers from your path,'" Àjàpá quoted, "you should respond lustily with 'Amen!' So, now I offer you the prayer once again: 'the spirits of our fathers will keep opportunistic troublemakers from your path.'"

The words were barely out of Àjàpá's mouth before Ìnàkí's response came: "Amen! Amen! Amen!" he repeated over and over.

And to this day no one has been able to keep him from repeatedly stammering "Amen!"

Vanity

Àjàpá, Ajá the Dog, and the Princess

This tale sways, creaks, and snaps, and, predictably, lands squarely atop Àjàpá, a creature who has arms but does not lift them to engage in labor.

Àjàpá and Ajá the Dog were close friends, so close that they owned adjoining farms a short distance from their town. But, as the whole world knows, being in the same company is no indication of similarity of character; in one important regard the two friends differed markedly: Ajá was industrious, far-sighted, and thrifty, but Àjàpá was lazy and carefree, living opportunistically only for the moment. The saying that when the cock crows in the morning the lazy person hisses in disgust might well refer to him. Thus, while the rising sun daily found his friend already hard at work tending his farm, Àjàpá hardly even bothered to go to his farm to see what condition it was in; much of the time, therefore, passers-by could not distinguish it from the surrounding forest.

Ajá planted his farm with corn, and when in due time it was ready to harvest he had a steady supply of food. As for Àjàpá, because he had neglected his farm, while his friend enjoyed the fruits of his labor, he had nothing to feed himself and his family, and everyone knows that opening one's mouth in the direction of the wind is no way to fill the stomach, and no way to relieve the pangs of hunger, either. Moreover, what Àjàpá lacked in industry he made up for in appetite. Soon he could feel his stomach collapsing onto his backbone, and he resolved to renew his friendship with

193

Ajá. But when he made his plea to his friend the response he received was far from comforting.

"When the thorns tore at my skin as I cleared my farm, did you join me?" he asked Àjàpá.

"But you did not ask me to," Àjàpá responded.

"When you saw the sun melting all the fat on my back as I planted the farm, did you offer to help?" Ajá asked further.

"You did not ask for help!" Àjàpá pleaded.

"When the early morning dew on the leaves washed my legs on my way to the farm, did you venture out of your home?" Ajá persisted.

"But," Àjàpá whined, "when did you ever call to me that I ignored you?"

"Well," Ajá's said, "now is not the time to change the habit of a lifetime. Wait for my call to share my harvest before you come forward."

Àjàpá pleaded until his lips blistered, but Ajá was unyielding. In the end, a despondent and furious Àjàpá went his way, vowing to make his false friend pay somehow for his hard-heartedness.

For several days he thought of ways to get at Ajá, but no punishment he considered harsh enough suggested itself. Ajá had denied him the very essence of life, he thought; what he deserved was a revenge that was equally dramatic.

The farms of the two friends lay along the path the *oba*'s only daughter, a most attractive young maiden, took daily on her way to bathe in the stream. Seeing her walk by one day gave Àjàpá the idea he had been waiting for. She would be the means by which he would extract his payment from his friend.

On the day Àjàpá would put his scheme into action he rose early and went to his farm. There he busied himself fabricating a snare of the kind which when sprung catches and suspends its victim in the air. When it was ready, he carefully set it where the princess was sure to trip it, and then he hid in the nearby bush. In due course the unsuspecting princess came by, alone as usual, and fell prey to Àjàpá's snare. She screamed in alarm and struggled frantically to free herself, but no one besides Àjàpá heard her, and no one came to her rescue. Àjàpá's desire for revenge on Ajá was so strong that he thought nothing of hastening the princess' end. He found himself a club, and with that he quickly dispatched his victim. Without delay he cut the body down and dragged it to Ajá's farm, and there hid it so carelessly that the most cursory search would reveal it. He went home then to await developments.

When far more time had passed than the princess usually took to return from the stream, the palace residents became concerned. The anxious *oba* summoned a bevy of servants and sent them in search of his favorite off-spring. One can only imagine his reaction when they returned with her lifeless body. Rage vied with anguish for control of him.

"Who dares thus to run his finger along the edge of my sword?" In mounting fury he spat on the ground and ordered his guards to appre-hend the criminal and bring him to the palace before the sun dried the spit on the ground.

The guards' task was simple; they had found the body on Ajá's farm, so surely he had committed the crime. Accordingly he was duly delivered, bound and trussed, before the *oba*.

By now the entire town had assembled in the palace; some came to com-miserate with their *oba*, some to see the daring Ajá who had done what nobody else had ever done or even contemplated, and some merely to be part of the excitement. Àjàpá was there, also, but he came to exult in his former friend's destruction.

The *oba* as a matter of form asked what Ajá had to say for himself, but despite his protestations of innocence no one was really interested in his story. The princess's body was on his farm; that was strong enough evi-dence of his guilt. The *oba* predictably ordered that he pay with his life for that of the murdered royal maiden.

After the verdict Ajá pleaded to be granted one last wish. It was to be granted a private audience with the *oba* and his chiefs. It was not a difficult wish to grant, and the *oba* obliged. He gave the necessary order, and after the orderlies and hangers-on had removed to some distance Ajá made his case to the *oba* and his chiefs.

"Your Majesty," he began, "live long on the throne of your fathers. The crown will sit long on your head, and the shoes under your feet. You have condemned me to die for killing your daughter; that is well. The body was on my farm, and you must hold me accountable. But," he continued, "what you want is justice, not just any life, even an innocent life, in return for the princess's. What will you have accomplished if you take my life and spare the real criminal? You will have confirmed his belief that he can poke his finger even into the *oba*'s eyes and escape the consequences. If that is the result of your judgment, may the emboldened killer not come after the *oba*'s own head tomorrow?"

The *oba* and his chiefs considered his words and were obliged to concede some sense in the prisoner's words. Who then was the real killer, they asked, and how did Ajá intend to expose him? He replied that although he could tell them who committed the crime, he would rather not, his reason being that words could lie. He asked instead that he be allowed to try a scheme that would reveal the criminal in a way that would leave no doubt in any mind. If his suspicion about the identity of the murderer was correct, he said, the criminal would surely expose himself; if the scheme failed, he would gladly submit to the fate the *oba* had already pronounced for him. In the end, in the interests of justice and public safety, the *oba* consented to the plan.

Hard though the townspeople thought, they could find no explanation for the inexplicable events of the days following Ajá's condemnation to death. No one had doubted that the *oba* would swiftly put an end to the miserable life of his daughter's murderer, but to everybody's astonishment not only did the execution not happen, but instead the court embarked on elaborate preparations for a feast. It was not unusual, of course, for funerals to entail lavish feasting, but that was only if the deceased person had lived a long and fruitful life and the death was both peaceful and timely. For the *oba*'s daughter, however, death had been violent and untimely. The people were greatly puzzled, wondering if grief had deranged their ruler; but, as the saying goes, each mouth wisely resolved not to be the one that would proclaim the Queen Mother a witch.

The hustle and bustle went on for several days; the *oba* filled the house with wine and the doorway with food. Finally the town-crier made the rounds of the town and nearby communities, proclaiming that in three days the *oba* would honor Ajá with a rich feast. He announced that the oracle had declared the princess's death most fortunate for town, *oba,* and court. It had averted a terrible pestilence that was about to descend on them. Ajá had thus been the gods' agent in offering the sacrifice that proved their salvation. The *oba* was rejoicing that his daughter's death had proved a boon to the entire community.

The late developments had puzzled Àjàpá as much as they did others, and although the proclamation offered an explanation, he nevertheless thought it prudent to sit back a while longer and watch events. The feast day duly arrived, and just as the town-crier had said, the whole town resounded with the noise of celebration. The cock had hardly crowed when music filled the air—bugles sounded, guns discharged, the talking drum ensemble, the *bàtá* ensemble, and a host of other percussion groups shook the earth with their music. The town square quickly filled with people kicking up a cloud of dust and straining not to miss the arrival of the guest of honor. Àjàpá was there, too, his skepticism quickly departing.

A sudden roar from the crowd, accompanied by an increase in the volume of the music, heralded the entry of Ajá, dressed in the most resplendent garments Àjàpá or any being at the gathering had ever seen, and mounted on a tall horse. The *oba* was himself dressed as befitted his station, and was attended by his chiefs, all well mounted. The women of the court followed behind, richly dressed, and gyrating to the music.

Àjàpá's nature overrode his caution. The sight before him was more than he could abide. He had thought to make Ajá pay with his life for his ungenerous behavior, but what had he accomplished? He had made his adversary the equal of an *oba*! The time called for action!

He fought his way to the path of the procession and fell prostrate before the *oba*'s horse. The procession came to a halt and Àjàpá rose to say that he had important news for the *oba*. The latter bade him speak.

The sages long ago said that even if Lie has a three-day head start, Truth will catch up with it the day Truth gets underway.

"Your royal Majesty," Àjàpá began, "your illustrious breath will last long. No impostor will usurp whatever is yours to accomplish."

The *oba* and the chiefs responded with "So it will be!" and asked him to state his business. Pointing to Ajá, Àjàpá announced that the creature they had dressed and mounted so royally was an impostor; he did not deserve the honor the *oba* was doing him.

"How so?" the *oba* asked.

"The lying rascal had nothing to do with the death of the princess," Àjàpá declared. "It is just like him to want everything for himself, even if that means stealing what belongs to others."

"That is a weighty accusation, Àjàpá," the *oba* observed. If Ajá did not kill the princess, and therefore did not deserve the honor, he asked, who did? Àjàpá drew himself up to his full height and looked proudly around the now silent crowd.

"If you seek your daughter's real killer," he boasted, "you have found him."

"But, did you not say that he is an impostor?" the *oba* queried, gesturing in Ajá's direction.

"Oh, yes, he is an impostor," Àjàpá repeated, pointing disdainfully to Ajá. Striking his breast he declared triumphantly, "Here, standing right before you, is the one who killed your daughter."

"You killed the *oba*'s daughter?" a chief asked, and Àjàpá became impatient.

"Why," Àjàpá asked impatiently, "is my speech garbled, or do I not speak the language of these parts? I said that the creature you have dressed up and set on a horse had no hand in the death of the *oba*'s daughter; I, Àjàpá, killed her!"

If it is possible for the mood of an assembly to change more swiftly than it did on that occasion, no one has yet or since seen it happen. As if on cue the *oba*'s guards descended on Àjàpá and bound him. What was one moment a festive celebration became in the next moment a mass of confusion. The revelry stopped, the *oba*'s demeanor resumed its woeful aspect, and the court women who had been swaying to music gave way anew to crying and wailing. From one moment to the next, the pall of sorrow, bereavement, and outrage enveloped the town again, reinforced this time by a sense of the strangeness of recent events.

The *oba* pronounced the expected verdict on Àjàpá, and without delay his guards conducted the criminal to a high cliff, far below which a forest of jagged rocks reared their menacing spikes skyward. From there they hurled him unto the waiting rocks that would send him reeling from one heaven to another. They watched him land and spatter, and, satisfied that his life of mischief was over, they went home to report the accomplishment of their mission.

If the owner and giver of breath has not called it back, nothing can remove a creature from among the living. Àjàpá's time was apparently not ripe, for although he was spread over the rock like overripe paw-paw his breath did not desert him. Many animals passing by heard his groans and weak pleas for help, but because of his well-known reputation as a mischief-maker and an ungrateful wretch, none would even pause long enough to commiserate with him, let alone offer him help. But, as the elders say, one's lot is never so bad that one would not find at least one benefactor; what we never know beforehand is who or where that benefactor might be. Fortunately for Àjàpá, his happened to be Ìkamùdùn the Stink Ant, who just then came sauntering by.

"Ìkamùdùn," Àjàpá called in pain, "prince of all ants, I implore you on your mother's head: do not pass by without listening to me."

Ìkamùdùn paused and moved closer to him.

"What terrible fate befell you to spread you so?" he asked.

"Your ancestors will keep you from harm you do not deserve," he responded. "What you see of me is what results when a small and helpless creature tangles with a bigger, more powerful adversary. Being small yourself, you undoubtedly know the dangers of stumbling into the path of the mighty. My legs led me astray, and here I am, as you see, paying the price. Out of sympathy for a small and innocent creature like yourself, do not go by without helping me."

Àjàpá's plaintive words filled Ìkamùdùn with compassion, although he doubted the truth of the words he heard, the speaker's nature being alien to truth.

"I know you well," Ìkamùdùn said after some consideration. "I know well that your own actions brought you where you now find yourself and that you will not learn from this experience. I know, most of all, that anyone who offers you help might as well walk into the river to drown. Nevertheless, I will think not of your nature but of what will please the gods, and I will help put you back together. And do not think that I expect gratitude from you, for I know that whoever does is like a fool who sits and watches for a crab to blink; such a person will be long at the riverbank."

With that, Ìkamùdùn settled down to the slow and painstaking task of matching the pieces of Àjàpá's shattered shell and gluing them back together with his saliva. His plan was to proceed in two stages: first to set the pieces in place, and then to smoothen out the joints. As he restored more and more of the pieces his patient's pains decreased, and with his lessening pain his spirits progressively brightened and his nature began to strain for expression.

Ìkamùdùn was working to place the last few pieces when he heard some sniffing from Àjàpá.

"Did you say something?" he asked.

"Yes, I did," Àjàpá replied. "I said there are few friends truer than you."

Ìkamùdùn felt gratified and resumed his work. Perhaps he had been too harsh in his judgment of Àjàpá?

He had only one more piece to place when he heard Àjàpá sniffing again. "What did you say?" he asked. "I can't make out your words."

Again Àjàpá replied, "I said, had the spirit of my dead father not brought you my way today, I might have died."

Ìkamùdùn thought it just might be possible that Àjàpá's latest experience, this close call with death, had wrought some change in him. He continued working.

"There now," he announced cheerfully after setting the last piece in place, "all the pieces of your shell are now back in place."

When Àjàpá wriggled in his shell, nothing creaked or rattled. He walked back and forth, but nothing came loose. His happiness brought forward his familiar personality, so that when Ìkamùdùn approached him to prepare him for the next stage of the task, that of smoothing the joints, he backed away, sniffing more loudly than before, grimacing, and wrinkling his nose.

"Whatever is the matter with you now?" Ìkamùdùn asked. "Did something fly into your nose?"

Not realizing that his shell was not yet back in its original shape, Àjàpá looked his benefactor squarely in the eyes and said:

"Yes, Ìkamùdùn, something has got into my nose."

"What is it?" Ìkamùdùn asked uncertainly.

"What you were hearing," he said, "was my sniffing, and what is in my nose is a bad stink. I was sniffing because I could hardly breathe for the stink that filled my nose. In truth I still can hardly breathe on account of it. And I think it comes from your direction!"

Even though Ìkamùdùn at no time really harbored illusions about Àjàpá, and even though he expected no gratitude for his help, he was nevertheless stung by the insult from a creature he had spent so much time and skill to restore to wholeness. There was nothing to do but bear the pain and go his way.

"You deserve no blame," he told Àjàpá. "The animals who walked by you without coming to your aid did not hear any insult from you. The sages say this year's wisdom is another year's madness. If my arms ever again stretch themselves to render you help, you may feel free to cut them off."

With that, he left Àjàpá.

Not until Àjàpá encountered other animals who asked why his shell was such a mosaic did he realize that insulting Ìkamùdùn had been premature. By then the glue had set, and, in any case, he could find no other creature to finish the job.

Thus did Àjàpá condemn himself to go through life in a rough shell.

Àjàpá and the Bounteous Ladle

Days pile upon days and seasons pile upon seasons as time goes its relentless way. Some days are as sweet as honey, and some are as bitter as the sap of the brimstone tree. As with days, so with seasons; some bring bounty, but others are laden with torments. One especially harsh season came with the scourge of famine so severe that corpses were the only crops the world produced in abundance. People and animals known for the strength of their arms and the sturdiness of their will strove in vain to secure the means to keep themselves and those who depended on them alive and in health; one can imagine, therefore, the plight of Àjàpá and his family, famous as he was for his shiftlessness. His children wasted away and died, and his wife Yánníbo became so emaciated that she was no more than a sack of bones rattling in an oversized shell. She had hardly enough strength left to lift her arms and legs. The death that kills one's age-mate, they say, is sending one a message, as well. Àjàpá, though the laziest of creatures, knew from watching those around him dying or making overtures toward death the fate that awaited him unless he acted to save himself.

Arriving at that resolution was by no means easy for him, but even more difficult was deciding on what, exactly, to do. In the end he embarked on the easiest and most obvious course; he would go foraging in the forest and trust the spirit of his dead father to bring some good fortune his way. He was soon intimately acquainted with every shrub in the forest, but nowhere could he find anything that could pass for food. By and by it dawned on him that he was not the first creature to think of scouring the forest for anything edible. His search took him across the breadth of the forest, but it proved fruitless. Beyond it he came to a stand of palm-trees bordering the ocean. So dispirited was he at the failure of his search that he silently berated the spirit of his dead father for slacking in its watchfulness. He did not know it, but the spirit was not lost in sleep, for when Àjàpá chanced to glance upward to the top of one of the palm-trees, what he saw made him blink in disbelief and rub his eyes to clear them. But when he looked again he knew his eyes had played him no tricks. Up at the neck of the palm-tree was tucked a bunch of unripe palm-fruits.

The succulent, oil-filled flesh of ripe palm-fruits was a great delicacy, especially when slightly heated, and the nut in the shell no less delicious, particularly in the company of steamed black-eyed peas. But in the midst of a killing famine, no food seemed nearly as appetizing as even unripe palm-fruits. Àjàpá crawled to the base of the palm-tree and, marshaling the strength left in his limbs, began to inch his way toward its neck. It was an arduous and dangerous climb, for long near-starvation had left his muscles weak and his grip uncertain. But he finally gained his objective, and after gnawing awhile at the stem attaching the bunch of fruits to the tree, he saw it detach itself and crash to the ground.

His descent from the palm-tree was speeded by the anticipation of at last filling his stomach and taking food home to restore his wife to life, but a terrible shock awaited him. He was still sliding down the trunk of the palm-tree when he saw the precious bunch of fruits roll inexorably towards the water's edge. He hastened his descent, almost breaking his limbs, and scrambled with as much speed as he was capable of after the fugitive fruits. He was still some distance from the bunch when he saw it roll into the water to be borne out to sea on the waves.

Àjàpá stood at the water's edge watching his treasure bob up and down as though taunting him as it went farther and farther away from land. When faced with situations that call for crying, adults steel themselves and laugh instead, but Àjàpá was incapable of that feat. What the ocean had taken from him was perhaps his last chance at survival and saving his wife. In desperation he cried out to the ocean:

You thieving ocean!
You stole my palm-fruits,
You thieving ocean!
I'll shout it to the hills,
You thieving ocean!
I'll shout it to the forests,
You thieving ocean!
Give me back my fruits,
You thieving ocean!

But the ocean was dead to his pleas and threats; it went its indifferent way with the fruits.

"A chicken cares not what manner of death claims it when its time comes," he told himself, "and death comes only once to all beings." Having fortified himself with such thoughts, he plunged into the water determined to retrieve his palm-fruits or give himself also to the ocean.

The waves and the currents bore the fruits ever farther to sea, and Àjàpá swam determinedly after them, until all he could see in all directions was the infinite expanse of water. Time passed, and soon whatever doubts he might have had that he was soon to be reunited with the spirit of his dead father diminished. As though to confirm his expectations, a sudden heave of the ocean lifted him skyward, and from its heights he saw the palm-fruits pulled into the center of a swirling eddy and disappear from view. His inclination was to follow in their wake, and in fact he had no choice in the matter, anyway. When the wave that had borne him aloft carried him down again he was at the edge of the eddy, and in another moment he was drawn into its center and sucked into the belly of the ocean.

When Àjàpá regained his senses he found himself in the middle of a large, well-furnished hall in the middle of which an old woman reclined on a velvet-covered dais. She was clothed in the richest hand-woven *aso-òkè* he had ever seen, and because she was also attended by several maidens in rich attire, he concluded that he was in the presence of a ruler. He uttered the first greeting that came to his head.

"Your noble life will be long," he said respectfully.

"So it will be!" the attendants responded in unison.

The woman sat up and studied him awhile before she spoke.

"Your place is on land," she addressed him. "What drew you from the safety of your home to the perils of the ocean?"

"Your noble life will be long," he repeated, and the attendants repeated their affirmation. "Our fathers say when a parent gives his newly born daughter a name that says death has just claimed a stalwart, he must have a very good reason. Pardon my forwardness in using a proverb in your presence."

"You have my leave," the woman excused him, "and you will live to speak more proverbs."

"You see me here before you," he continued, "apparently somewhere in the depths of the ocean, because the ocean has done me wrong."

Murmurs of disbelief rippled through the ranks of the attendants, but the noble woman stopped them with a gesture.

"Àjàpá," the woman said, "—for I know that is who you are—you surely know that the ocean, like the wind and the rain, bears no being any malice, but performs its task only as it must."

"Yet," Àjàpá insisted, "it stole my bunch of palm-fruits, the fruits the spirit of my dead father brought my way after a long day in which my head parted the forest to make a path, the fruits I hoped would save me and my wife from certain starvation. I risked death when I climbed the palm-tree to get the palm-fruits, and the ocean claimed them when they fell to the ground. I called in vain for their return, and in the end, since death seemed my fate whether I remained on land or followed the fruits, I chose to do as I did. And thus you find me here before you."

The woman regarded Àjàpá pensively for some moments, and when she finally spoke her voice was soft with compassion.

"The great difficulties of you land creatures I have known for a long while," she said. "Many have perished in the ocean in their thoughtless and sometimes careless pursuit of fish and other sea creatures. I know also that the waves robbed you of your bunch of palm-fruits, which lies even at this moment in my great stores. For your desperate trouble I will spare your life and give you a gift that will ensure that you and your household never again suffer for lack of food."

She sent one of her attendants to bring a special ladle from her stores. When the attendant returned, the woman took the ladle from her and she presented it to Àjàpá.

"Take this ladle," she said. "Whenever you are hungry, command it to produce food and it will do so in abundance."

The eyes Àjàpá fixed on the ladle were wide with amazement that robbed him of speech.

"It is bounteous," the woman continued, "but it is also fragile. Take care you do not break it."

She then directed Àjàpá to open a door to the side of the great hall and step through it.

Àjàpá was beside himself with both gratitude and anticipation. He stammered his thanks and stepped through the door, expecting to find himself in another room beneath the ocean. But to his surprise the scene before his eyes was most familiar, for it was in fact his own room that he had left in search of food. His surprise delayed him very little before he decided to put the ladle to the test.

"Ladle, ladle, do your duty and give me food!" he commanded.

The words were hardly out of his mouth when he saw before him foods of all sorts: steaming pounded-yams and vegetable stew, boiled rice and stewed chickens, cooked and well-seasoned black-eyed peas, *àkàrà, dòdò,* and a rich abundance of fruits. The ladle had not neglected to provide several gourds of palm-wine from whose mouths froth welled up and spilled down the sides. Àjàpá ate as he had not eaten in years, and when he was sated, he took some of the food to his wife and coaxed her to eat. He then turned his attention to the palm-wine.

The sages say when one has stuffed one's belly to its capacity, one must surrender oneself to sleep. Àjàpá's sleep was long and deep, and this time he didn't dream of starving creatures, as he had lately. When he woke up his wife suggested that since there was no limit to the amount of food the ladle could produce, perhaps they should extend their good fortune to the entire town. Àjàpá's first instinct was to reprimand Yánníbo for speaking like a being besotted. His ungenerous nature was such that those who knew him well had invented a proverb stating that not even his children could ever hope for a taste of his food. But he was also as vain as he was selfish, and it was his vanity that finally goaded him to agree to do as his wife suggested.

He spruced himself up as best he could and set his face in the direction of the *oba*'s palace. There he asked to see the ruler on a matter that would change his town's fortune for the better. The *oba* was skeptical, but the dire straits his town was in made him receptive to all offers of help. He granted the audience and asked how Àjàpá proposed to improve the fortune of his benighted town.

"I have the means to feed the whole town," he said, "and, what's more, the means to keep them from ever going hungry again."

The immediate response from the *oba* and his chiefs was to roar with laughter, weak though they, too, were from hunger. The laughter soon subsided, and in its place was anger.

"You dare to come before me with such a frivolous joke," the *oba* fumed, "to make fun of the plight of my dying people. Surely you deserve to die for your impudence."

"*Kábíyèsí*, your Majesty," Àjàpá said in a long-suffering voice. "Long life to you. Who does not know how the whole town has suffered because of this great famine that has been our lot all these years? Have I not lost all my children, as have many others? If I make fun of the dying people, do I not make fun of myself, also? What I propose to do is not a thing about which there can be any doubt, as to whether I have done it or not. Would it not be better to wait until I fail before you put me to death?"

The *oba* and his chiefs discountenanced the testiness in Àjàpá's speech because they saw the wisdom in it, and they saw also that their initial reaction lacked wisdom. The *oba* therefore ordered Àjàpá to do as he promised.

"Assemble the entire town in the palace compound tomorrow at the height of the sun," Àjàpá told the *oba*, "and when I am done there will not be one hungry stomach left in town."

The *oba* ordered his crier to walk the length and breadth of the town to make the proclamation, and Àjàpá returned to his home.

The next dawn found the entire town already assembled in the palace compound, and what a pitiful sight they were! So weak were they that in the place of the usual hubbub of so large a crowd only a ghostly silence reigned. All too slowly the sun made its way into the sky while all eyes strained to see if Àjàpá was anywhere in sight. But it was not until the sun stood directly overhead, when the growing heat had intensified the lassitude of the pitiful gathering, that he walked importantly into the middle of the compound, his extraordinary ladle in his hand. He paused while the *oba* and his chiefs took their seat under an awning provided for them, then he looked all around the crowd, savoring the satisfaction that he was the cause of the great assembly. Finally, he set the ladle down and stood back.

"Ladle, ladle, do your duty and feed this crowd!" he commanded.

As before, it responded with a feast that was extravagant in abundance and variety. As one would expect of starving people suddenly exposed to food and drink, they climbed and tripped over one another in their feeble rush to get at the bounty. Even the *oba* and his chiefs forgot to be the epitome of decorum their positions required of them. The people fed and fed, and drank and drank, and eventually realized that their stampede was unnecessary; the supply of food and drink was exhaustible. Unfortunately, the initial pandemonium had been costly: the ladle had been smashed to pieces under many feet.

It was a most disconsolate Àjàpá that railed against his wife for her foolish suggestion and that bemoaned his own folly in acceding to it and revealing his secret to the *oba*. They had caused him to lose the precious gift he had received at great risk to his life. What was he to do? The ladle was broken beyond the possibility of repair, and he had been warned to ensure that it was never broken. In the end he reasoned that there must be more ladles where the first one came from, and he resolved to go back after it.

When the next day dawned he hurried to the beach in search of unripe palm-fruits, but no matter how hard he looked he saw only barren palm-trees. Finally, just as he began to think of abandoning the search, he saw a palm-tree bearing a bunch of fruits. But even from the base of the tree Àjàpá could see that far from being unripe the fruits had in fact dried. His mind was so set on finding another ladle, though, that he told himself any bunch would do. Soon he was at the top of the tree, and shortly thereafter he had gnawed the bunch free of the tree. It crashed to the ground, becoming half-embedded in the sand. Àjàpá hurried down from the tree, picked up the bunch of fruits, and carried it to the water's edge. There he flung it as far as he could into the ocean. To his dismay an incoming wave caught it and brought it right back, leaving the fruits high on the beach when it receded. Àjàpá would not defeated. He picked up the bunch again and this time waded some distance into the water before flinging it out to sea. Once again a wave brought it back and beached it. But when he angrily threw the bunch into the ocean a third time, he was relieved to see it bob away from land. Determined to do everything that he had done on his previous trip, he paused to make his call to the thieving ocean:

> *You thieving ocean!*
> *You stole my palm-fruits,*
> *You thieving ocean!*

I'll shout it to the hills,
You thieving ocean!
I'll shout it to the forests,
You thieving ocean!
Give me back my fruits,
You thieving ocean!

His call concluded, he plunged after the fruits, helping them along whenever they seemed hesitant in their progress.

Long-windedness often leads to lying. In short, Àjàpá eventually arrived in the same hall as before, and in the presence of the venerable woman. She asked what he wanted this time. He explained that he had broken the ladle she gave him and was thus reduced again to foraging for food. When he was fortunate enough to find another bunch of palm-fruits—and now he lied—the ocean once again beat him to it, and he found himself repeating the trip he had made once before.

The woman studied him silently for some time

"I see that a ladle is too fragile for you to keep whole," she finally said. "I have something else that will serve you well and that will not break."

She ordered an attendant to bring a special whip from her store. This she gave to Àjàpá, telling him to use it just as he used the ladle. Gratefully, he stepped through the door indicated to him, and he was instantly in his own room, anxious to test the efficacy of his new boon.

"Whip, whip," he commanded, "perform your task to my satisfaction."

Even as he spoke the whip jumped out of his hand as though pulled by a powerful arm, and before he could wonder what was happening he felt himself being laid into by what seemed to him like a hundred whips instead of one. He screamed involuntarily and thrashed around in pain, but the whip would not let up. It must have been the spirit of his dead father that eventually brought him to the door as he thrashed about blindly. He crashed through it to safety outside.

It took some time before he recovered his breath and before the intense pain of his weals and welts subsided. It took even longer before he dared venture into his room. But when he did, he saw the whip lying innocently on the floor. He approached it cautiously, ready to spring for the door if it made the slightest movement, but it remained inert. He picked up and hid it safely away. The next day, he promised himself, he would perform another feat in the town such that no one would soon forget.

The sun had barely risen the next morning when Àjàpá stepped on the path that led to the palace. This time he had little difficulty persuading the *oba* to reassemble the town, for, he said, he had been to the bottom of the ocean from where he brought the ladle, and he had returned with an object even more wonderful than the ladle. He promised to share his boon again with the entire town on the morrow.

Once again the proclamation bade the townspeople assemble, and everybody responded with great eagerness to the invitation. Satisfied that the whole town was present in the compound, including the *oba* and his chiefs, Àjàpá set the whip down and backed toward the exit.

"Whip, whip, perform your task and offer this assembly satisfaction!" he called when he was just at the gate.

The whip flew into action, and he flew out of the compound. His feet bore him swiftly away from the scene, while the screaming and wailing of an entire town lashed by a single whip reassured him that it worked like a thousand whips.

As the distance increased between him and the screaming town, Àjàpá said to himself, "Whoever eats of your delights should stand ready to partake of your distress, also."

Àjàpá and the Gourd of Wisdom

An astute observer of Àjàpá and his ways is the subject of an eloquent proverb. Àjàpá sets out on a journey, it says, and is asked when he will return. He replies that he will not return until he has earned disgrace. The observer restates the well-known adage that whoever does not heed the limits of permissible behavior, any form of behavior, will wind up disgraced.

In addition to his other qualities, Àjàpá was afflicted by extreme vanity. He reveled in his reputation among all and sundry as a crafty and wily creature, but he was not content to rest on his laurels; he devoted considerable thought to seeking some means of enhancing his reputation. When the dried-mud idol craves humiliation, the elders say, it announces that it will dance in the downpour. He did not know it, but Àjàpá was about to emulate the folly of the idol.

Characteristically, his brainstorming yielded a scheme that even he concluded was worthy of a genius. His cleverness was already legendary, but the result of the scheme he hatched would be, he was certain, that the whole world would acknowledge him as the sole possessor of wisdom on earth. He would walk the length and breadth of the world, he resolved, and gather all the wisdom in existence, and thereafter hide it where only he would have access to it.

He put his plan into action by providing himself with a gourd capacious enough for his purpose and equipped with a tight stopper. He then crisscrossed the world gathering every bit of wisdom and stuffing it into his gourd, being careful to permit none to escape once trapped in the container. After he was satisfied that he had missed not even the tiniest bit of wisdom, he returned home with his gourd of wisdom.

Behind his dwelling there stood an *àràbà* tree so tall that its branches scraped the sky. Àjàpá reasoned that there could be no better hiding place for his treasured gourd than in the lofty branches of the tree. Accordingly, he tied a rope around the neck of the gourd and made a loop in it to slip around his own neck so that the gourd dangled on his belly. Thus prepared, he made his way to the bottom of the *àràbà* tree.

Àjàpá might be possessed of the largest brain in the world, but his limbs are far from being the longest in the world. Once at the foot of the tree he began to realize what a handicap short limbs could be: no matter how hard he toiled, no matter what approach he tried, he could not get his limbs to the tree, past the obstacle of the gourd dangling on his belly. For hours on end he struggled, sweating and panting, and becoming ever more angry with the tree and the gourd, both of which he held responsible for his plight.

Frustration was on the verge of turning to dementia when, at the close of the day, a farmer returning home saw him clawing at the air beneath the *àràbà* tree.

"Hello there, Àjàpá," he hailed. "Whatever are you up to?"

Àjàpá was happy for the rest the diversion offered, and he returned the farmer's greetings.

"Your head will steer you clear of problems that defy solution," he prayed. "All day I have been here where you now find me, at the foot of this tree, trying to climb it, but it has stubbornly stayed out of my reach."

"And why must you climb the tree?" the farmer asked.

"Do you see this gourd I have around my neck?" he asked, and the latter admitted he did.

"I mean to take it to the branches of the tree and hang it up there."

"Really," the farmer said. "Why would you want to do that?"

"This is no ordinary gourd," Àjàpá responded. "No other place is safe enough to keep it than the top of this tree."

"In that case," said the farmer without so much as a pause to think, "why not swing the gourd around to your back and try climbing the tree that way?"

Àjàpá considered this advice for a moment and decided there was no harm trying it. He did, and to his relief he was soon inching his way up the tree as fast as his tiredness and his heavy burden would allow. In his preoccupation he gave the farmer only off-handed gratitude as the latter continued on his way.

Halfway up the tree Àjàpá suddenly froze. A terrible thought had just hit him. The farmer had considered his situation and offered him an advice that solved the problem he had unsuccessfully wrestled with all day. Was there any other name for what the farmer displayed than wisdom? Did that not mean that he had failed to collect all the wisdom in the world, as he had hoped?

Angered that his attempt to be the sole possessor of all wisdom had been thwarted, he slipped the noose off his neck and let the gourd of wisdom crash to the ground. It shattered and all the wisdom he had so diligently collected was released to be scattered again all over the world.

Thus it has come about that the sages say "No one is, or can be, all-wise."

GLOSSARY

Àgbámùréré	audience refrain response to the lead singer (not translatable)
Àgó	a nimble type of rat
àkàrà	fried, seasoned bean fritters, a Yoruba staple
apàlópadídùn	teller of sweet tales
àràbà	white silk cotton tree, the largest tree native to Africa
àsáró	yam pottage; also *èbe*
aso-òkè	rich, locally woven cloth
babaláwo	diviner priest of Ifá
Basòrun	the highest-ranking chief and the *oba*'s closest adviser
dòdò	fried plantain slices
èbe	yam pottage, also *àsáró*
ègúsí	dried melon seeds, ground and used in stews
Ifá	oracle god
iwin	fairy
Kábíyèsí	title of address for a king, comparable to "Majesty"

Glossary

Kumolu	proper name meaning "Death has taken a hero"
oba	king
olósè	a sluggish type of mouse
Olú Awo	chief of diviners
Olúóde	chief of hunters
Òsanyìn	a god versed in charms